Pin-up Fireman

Book Three in the *Wild Heat* Series

VONNIE DAVIS

Harper*Impulse* an imprint of
HarperCollins*Publishers* Ltd
1 London Bridge Street
London SE1 9GF

www.harpercollins.co.uk

A Paperback Original 2016

First published in Great Britain in ebook format by Harper*Impulse* 2015

Copyright © Vonnie Davis 2015

Cover images © Shutterstock.com

Vonnie Davis asserts the moral right
to be identified as the author of this work

A catalogue record for this book is
available from the British Library

ISBN: 9780008120252

Automatically produced by Atomik ePublisher from Easypress

Printed and bound in Great Britain

I have a Street Team that helps with my promotion. I call them "Vonnie's Vixens." Each one is supportive, a total joy and priceless. I love them all.

CHAPTER ONE

"I want *him*."

A pink fingernail pointed at Boyd Calloway, and he stopped mid-stride. He scowled at the tall, curvaceous brunette at the front of the meeting room, her sapphire blue eyes focused on him.

"Oh, yeah. I *really* want him."

An unexpected and unwelcomed zing of sexual awareness fried a few of his brain cells, the timing of which did not make him happy.

Late for the mandatory meeting the station captain called first thing this morning, Boyd had tried to sneak in without being noticed. The strange woman certainly shot his efforts all to hell with her sexy remarks.

Dammit, his tardiness couldn't be helped. He'd been on the phone with his aunt Jinny, who took care of his son while Boyd worked. Matt was headed for another asthma attack; the familiar signs were there.

Boyd grabbed the last empty chair and rubbed fingers across his forehead where a headache brewed. Hopefully, Aunt Jinny could get Matt a pediatrician's appointment today or tomorrow, which would mean another day of missed school. This wasn't the best way to start first grade.

The very last thing Boyd wanted to go through right now was some kind of fluff meeting. No matter how attractive the person holding the gathering was—and she was a stunning beauty.

Pink stilettos clicked a staccato beat on the tile floor of Fire and Marine Rescue Unit Thirty-two as the woman with the silky voice and slim pink skirt strutted to the table where she tapped a notepad with a pen, making a few notations. She swiveled and pointed at Boyd with her pen. "I'll want him twice."

"Hey, Tiny hit the jackpot!" Wolf slouched farther in his chair, hands clasped at his crotch, and grinned like a fool, which seemed his normal state these days. He'd just found out last week his wife Becca was pregnant. They'd evidently been trying for over two years. Dan Wolford, known as Wolf at the station, was over-the-moon happy.

"Tiny, which part of you is she gonna work on first? 'Cause she can have all of this anytime she wants." Darryl Weir, their newest man, chimed in, moving the edges of his open hands down his torso. "Believe me, I'm the best here in the station," he declared, making inappropriate kissing noises.

Still trying to find his place within the top-notch crew, the young fellow was too mouthy for Boyd's liking. Darryl hadn't been baptized with a nickname yet and since the kid had Boyd's hackles up, he figured he'd do the honors.

"Well, now, Kissy Boy, whatever part she wants."

The rest of the team hooted and hollered the new fireman's nickname before Captain Steele barked a stern command to "mind their manners and shut the hell up."

She aimed her cornflower blue eyes at Boyd. "So, your co-workers call you Tiny? Why? Because you're so tall and muscular? What are you, six-seven?"

"Close enough. Six-eight. The muscles come from working out stress on the weight machines. That, and the demands of the job." He thought of asking her how tall she was, but that would only stir the guys up more. Even without those killer heels, she was about six feet. Dark brunette hair to the middle of her back. All-in-all, a cute package, but then, he'd once thought that of Chantel, and look where that had gotten him.

The attractive stranger sashayed closer, the smell of expensive perfume aroused his senses. A powerful jolt of sexual need Boyd hadn't felt in over a year traveled down his spine and singed all his ignored parts. "And what kind of stress could a good looking man like you have?" She extended her hand. "I'm Graci-Ella, by the way. I'm a photographer and I'd really, really like to use you twice."

This time the raucous remarks from the squad were aimed at him. Bastards that they were, they knew of his monk-like existence.

"Twice for what?" Heat flamed up his neck and made a U-turn to prickle the other parts of his body he ignored except in the shower.

"The cover and a monthly picture in the calendar I'm doing on the heroic firefighters of this station. All proceeds will go to the local food bank here in Clearwater, Florida. The firm I work for does a few charitable acts per year. A fourteen month calendar that goes on the market on or before October first will help give some needy food to those who could really use it over the holidays."

Boyd crossed his arms. "I'll write a check for the food bank, but no way in hell are you getting me in any beefcake calendar." Hell, that's all his ex-wife and her expensive lawyer would need to prove he wasn't a positive influence for Matt. His forty-eight hour shifts on and off, at the station, was one strike against him. He didn't need anymore.

"How many of you firefighters—men and women—are seriously interested in posing for this calendar? They would make some wild Christmas gifts." Most everyone raised his or her hand as Graci-Ella took a count and wrote the number on her notepad.

Ivy Jo leaned forward in her chair. "How revealing are you getting in these pictures?"

"No nudity from the waist down. For the women firefighters, tank tops or sports bras. Their choice."

Ivy Jo and Emily glanced at each other, nodded their approval and raised their hands.

Graci-Ella wrote something on the paper and looked at her

watch. "Cripes. I have a meeting in half an hour so I need to head off. Captain, may I meet with your team a few more times after they've had a chance to think about it? And talk to their significant others, of course. I'll bring by some calendars tonight I've done for various groups as fund raisers. Give them a chance to look over my work."

"Sure, as long as we're here and not out on some kind of emergency. Call first to save yourself a trip. Tiny, give her your cell number." The corners of the chief's mouth quirked—match-making bastard.

She sat next to Boyd and swiveled in her chair so her knees touched his thigh. Between her perfume and those long legs so close he could touch them, he was six heat beats away from doing something stupid. Just how would it feel to trail a finger up her firm thigh? The desire was so strong, he could sense beads of sweet popping out on his forehead.

Her blue eyes focused on his as she held her cell. "Your number, please? I really would like to talk to you some more about being in the calendar. Maybe tonight we can have a few moments of privacy?"

"Why me? Look around, there are plenty of muscular men in this unit. A little powder and lip gloss and whoever you pick will grab anyone's attention."

She smiled and looked away as if she didn't want him to see it. So, her reply surprised him. "You have a sense of humor, kind of sharp-witted. I like that." She rested her soft hand on his. "Please, give me a chance."

Oh, he'd like to give her more than a chance, but this custody business had put a hold on his sex life. Boyd couldn't allow any rumors to detract from the judge's opinion of his ability to take better care of Matt than Chantel.

Two hours, four cups of coffee later and Graci-Ella was wired. She'd worked for Baker, Brannock, and Hughes law firm for two years, putting in extra hours just to keep her head above the heavy load. Too bad no one seemed to notice. Of course, how could anyone even see her behind the stacks of files on her desk? The new cases seemed to multiply at a faster rate than those she had ready for their court dates.

Her square office, with a small window, was claustrophobic. What she needed to do this weekend was rearrange the mismatched furniture, find a better way to store her files and add some plants. She glanced at the metal strips holding up the ceiling tile. If she got the right kind of hooks, she could add hanging plants without using any of her small floor space. How could her clients have any faith in her when they walked into this pitiful looking postage stamp?

Then there were her parents, who were chomping at the bit to fly south from Maryland to see her. They'd been aghast at her office on their first visit, but she'd told a small fib that she'd been working out of this tiny space until an office opened up. Her mother nearly turned herself inside out with outrage—*her* daughter deserved better. Yeah, well, the newest lawyer got the leftovers.

She glanced around her space. It was wall to wall, mismatched odds and ends. If her parents came down again, they'd insist on coming by to see her office. How could she face them with any pride when they saw she was still in the same spot, with zero career progression? Her dad would storm to one of the bosses' office and demand to know why. For a classic car mechanic, her dad had a lot of nerve.

Co-worker Elizabeth Stone popped her head in Graci-Ella's open door. "Hey, are you playing in the basketball game at the Y tomorrow? Lots of cute guys usually show. Of course you'll have to let them make a basket now and then, so you don't wound their male egos."

"Ugh! I get so tired of the fragile male ego." Graci-Ella forked her fingers through her long hair and chuckled. "No, I have a breakfast meeting with a client and then I'm thinking of coming in here to better organize this miniscule office the firm so kindly gave me. I feel like I'm working out of an old closet. Gives me the willies sometimes."

Elizabeth looked around. "Come to think of it, paper, ink cartridges and toner used to be stored in here." Both women laughed. "I need a favor. A *huge* favor." Elizabeth extended three files.

"Beware of lawyers bearing files. What are they?" Why was she even asking? Obviously it was more work for her. Her gaze shifted to her two "in" piles and sighed.

"Cases I'm representing that I can't handle right now. Baker assigned me the Middleton case this morning and it's the most important one I've ever had. I need to do a top notch job in negotiating a huge payout. It could mean a big jump forward in my career."

Ignoring the pang of jealousy, Graci-Ella congratulated her friend on the coup. "Look, hon, anytime one of the senior partners hands you something this important, it's a colossal compliment. Take it and run with it. So, you want me to take over some of your cases?" Maybe she'd get some recognition for this extra effort.

Elizabeth leaned against the doorjamb. "Yes, Patrick's taking over four. I gave three to Joe, but I figured you were the only one strong enough to handle these." She shook the thick folders at her.

"Beware of sneaky lawyers bearing cases *and* compliments." Graci-Ella laughed and extended her hand. Elizabeth had been the first lawyer to make her feel welcome at the firm. How could Graci-Ella forget her co-worker's kindness by refusing to help her?

"Warning," Elizabeth said before passing her the files. The one client is a whiny bitch. Name's Chantel Calloway—a custody hearing. Woman needs a reality check and a bottle of Ritalin. I declare, she'll be bitching one minute about how her ex ignored her and turned cold. Then suddenly ask you if you like the color of her fingernail polish. Don't let her air-headed façade fool you, though. She'll be bossing you around in no time. The woman's obviously used to getting her way.

Graci-Ella leafed through them. "The custody case shouldn't be so bad." She smiled at Elizabeth. "Don't worry. I don't take shit from anyone. When's the court date?" She found the page she was looking for. "November third. Looks like you've gotten most of the work done. Background check on the ex-husband completed?"

"Yeah, he seems clean to me. Still, I can understand a mother wanting custody of her kid. The second case is what should be a simple land dispute. We've got two senior citizens who want to argue over a foot of property, fifty feet long. Martha O'Shaye, the party we represent, and Nancy Beech, can't be in the same room without World War Three breaking out. Martha claims the foot of land is hers and she wants to widen her driveway by twelve inches. Nancy wants to plant flower beds in that strip. I call it the case of the divas." Linda shook her head. "One old woman claims the other's dog craps on her yard in revenge, as if the damn dog would know the difference."

Graci-Ella glared at the lawyer whose short, blonde hair was frizzier than usual. The humidity must be high today. "Oh, you're going to owe me big time for this one. A whinny bitch and elderly divas?"

"Hold on. It gets better. The third is a DUI and disorderly, second offense."

"Am I supposed to thank you for these cases?" Graci-Ella fought back a grin and lost. "Don't expect me to buy you any coffee today…or tomorrow." She glanced at the third file. What's the deal with this one?"

Elizabeth folded her arms. "Paul Steinway is a horny bastard who chases any woman who breathes. The man even had the gall to proposition me. I fried his ears, but good. He has an alcohol problem and can't say a sentence without two cuss words in it. Has temper issues—big time. Drove his truck into a convenience store when he found out they no longer handled his favorite brand of snuff." She tipped her head toward the folder. "Thus the offense. A real class act. And he expects us to perform miracles so he doesn't lose his job." She glanced at her cell. "Look, gotta go. If you need me, I'll be in the legal library. Thanks a lot." She whizzed out of the doorway and, like last month's paycheck, was gone.

Graci-Ella attached a court date label onto the edge of each file and placed them in chronological order to the stacks of files she needed to work on. She swiveled her chair to her computer and continued typing on the brief for a car theft ring she represented. Why did she always get the guilty jerks? She'd much rather represent some good people and see justice shine on their side.

To please her parents, Graci-Ella entered the legal profession, just as Eli had planned, when she'd sooner have gone into photography. All the years of law school, internship and cramming for the bar exams just to satisfy her folks, while they enjoyed their dreams of her future—especially after they'd lost Eli. Thank God her parents didn't know she often had to represent the armpit of society.

Anytime she called home, the first words out of her dad's mouth were, "Did you make junior partner yet?" From his jovial tone, she figured he was kidding—at least she hoped. He didn't seem to understand she had several years of hard work ahead of her before she made that feat, no matter how many times she explained it to him. "Had you stayed here in Maryland, you'd have a junior partnership already."

Of course when she was courted by the senior partners to join the firm, no one told her she'd get the worst cases until she proved herself. And just how was she to do that from a former closet? Her mother's words came back to disturb her. "Bloom wherever you're planted. Just make sure the soil is rich." Graci-Ella growled deep in her throat. *Achieve, triumph, surpass, I've had those words shoved down my throat since Eli was broadsided by another car. I am his substitute, which I understand because I miss him as much as my parents do.*

Eli was the oldest and the brightest. He was also her hero.

Without a word of complaint, he put up with her following him around, even to the community basketball courts. He taught her all he knew. So did his buddies. She held the old photo of the two of them under the basket over their garage door. Eli held the basketball in one hand and his other arm around her shoulders. His smile illuminated the picture while she stared up at him—her best bud.

Too bad she couldn't have played basketball forever. The wooden court was where she felt at home throughout her high school and college years—running, dribbling, shoving, shooting. That was her first love. She glanced around her storage room turned legal office. This was her current cramped reality.

She groaned as she wrote her brief; wondered how her acquittal rate would be if she delivered her opening and closing arguments while dribbling a basketball. Her weird sense of humor fanaticized a hoop over the judge's head and Graci-Ella shooting a three-pointer whenever the judge disagreed with something she said. Her laughter bubbled forth as she imagined beaning the opposing counsel on his ass whenever he made her client look bad.

By far, the basketball court outshone the legal court. At least for her, which was a sad admission when she'd worked so hard to pass the bar and get in with a firm. Maybe she needed to open her own office. Or perhaps she needed to make photography more of a vocation than a hobby. Especially if she could meet men like Tiny. Sweet chocolate cheesecake, but he was delicious looking. She'd like to bite his bicep and then kiss him all over just to make up for it.

Even so, the keep-your-distance vibe he emanated like a light-house beacon practically shouted he wasn't interested in her, or any female. Just her luck. She'd like to go a little one on one with him and not just on the basketball court, either. Something about him stirred her hormones, which was quite peculiar for her—the focused, determined lawyer with goals a mile long.

CHAPTER TWO

After lunch, Graci-Ella hurried to the law library for a book on quasi-torts and opened the glass door to find the lawyer at the top of the firm's food chain. After a polite exchange of greetings, she took a deep breath and asked if she could spend some money to make her ex-storage room, now office more workable. To her relief, he gave her permission and also told her to have the building manager show her the office furniture the firm no longer used. Maybe she could find some things there, especially since some of the junior partners had just ordered new office cabinets and desks.

Mental fist pump. Score!

So, when she normally took her afternoon break, she knocked on the building manager's door. With her room's layout sketched on paper, she'd asked him if he had anything that matched and was usable. "Oh, and comfortable would be nice too."

He scratched his head for a minute. "Didn't this used to be the old supply room before they made a bigger one?"

"You got it, Jo-Jo. In there sits a huge metal desk—brown. Two metal file cabinets—gray. One metal folding client chair—red. A black office chair that leans and has upended with me in it—five times."

"How long you been here? A couple years?" He shook his tanned bald head, trimmed with a fringe of white hair. "Ain't that a damn shame. Bet you're still getting the shit cases no one else wants. And I lay you dollars to donuts, you're putting in more hours than anyone else, trying to prove yourself." He ambled away from her and motioned over his shoulder. "Follow me. Ol' Jo-Jo gonna treat you right." He glanced at the paper again. "These measurements correct?"

"Yes, sir." She glanced around and saw two dark-green leather, club chairs that matched. She rubbed her hands over the soft leather. "Oh, wish I had room for these. I love the color."

Jo-Jo shoved a matching wheeled office chair her way. "Try that on for size. I can adjust the height for you, lumbar support too." He pulled out a unit with two horizontal filing drawers and book shelves on top of those. A corner unit was next, along with a desk. He measured the corner unit and desk together and looked at his paper. He found two other matching units. One had filing drawers, but was deeper. A skinnier one had shelves with lockable sliding doors. "Which one do you want?" He pointed to the thinner one. "This will give you eight more inches of room."

"I'll take it. One question. The aluminum strips that hold the ceiling tiles, are they strong enough to hang a plant?"

"If the pot's plastic and you don't drench the plant with water, yes. No more than two, though."

She opened her arms. "So, I can have all this? And it'll still leave me room to move around in my tiny office?" After Jo-Jo showed her how to place everything on her drawing, she hugged him and squealed with joy. She didn't think she'd stopped smiling the rest of the afternoon.

Once her day at the office was over, she grabbed a salad at her favorite take-out spot and went home to eat and unwind. High heels in hand, she went into her bedroom to change into something cool and comfortable. She called Tiny to make sure the firefighters were there before she drove to the station.

"Boyd here."

"So, I finally learn your real name." She smiled as she pulled a tank top from her drawer.

"All you needed to do was ask me. I have no secrets." His deep voice raised goosebumps on her skin.

"Are we in a grumpy mood this evening?"

"No." He sighed. "Maybe. Was my night to cook and I burned the lasagna. We had a marine rescue earlier this afternoon, so I thought if turned the oven up to five hundred, supper would get done quicker."

She laughed. "Oh no. Who puts the oven up that high?"

"A man who's hungry, that's who. All it did was set off the smoke alarms and cause me to get my ass chewed out. I'm trying to figure how to get the scorched cheese and meat out of the pans. Hey, you don't do dishes do you?" A tinge of his humor was in his voice. "Have you ever eaten lasagna with a fork in one hand and a chainsaw in another?"

Once she stopped laughing, she made a suggestion. "Run a knife along the edge to get out what you can and then soak them in hot, soapy water for a while. I'm just calling to make sure the team will be there if I come by."

"As of now, we're just cleaning equipment. Routine stuff. Come on over."

When she pulled into the parking lot of Fire and Marine Rescue Station Thirty-two, Wolf and a curvy redhead were sitting at a picnic table under a palm tree. A German shepherd sat on Wolf's lap as if he hadn't seen his master for weeks. Wolf waved her over as she pulled out a canvas bag of calendars and a portfolio of pictures.

"Graci-Ella, come meet my wife, Becca. Don't you think she glows with her pregnancy?" The man's smile nearly split his face in two. He reached for his wife's hand and kissed her knuckles.

Becca pursed her lips and blushed. "I'm surprised you don't make me wear a sandwich sign that reads, 'This woman is pregnant!'" She stood and shook Graci-Ella's hand. "Never mind him. He's just happy we finally got it right. So, you're the photographer everyone's teasing Tiny about?"

Something in the woman's kind demeanor made Graci-Ella smile. "Yes, I'm the photographer, but why are folks ragging Tiny about me?"

Becca leaned in. "Because he hasn't dated since he was served with custody papers for his little boy. He's trying so hard to be Mr. Perfect. You evidently rattled his celibacy cage when you showed up this morning."

Was that why he was so adamant about not being in the calendar? Did he think avoiding women would look favorable to the court? Was he divorced or still married? That would be the deciding factor, that and how often he left his son with a sitter overnight.

The dog looked at Wolf as if he were insulted and whined. He licked Wolf's chin, no doubt to remind him he was there.

Wolf rubbed the canine's head. "Sorry, buddy. Graci-Ella, this is Einstein. If you call him over, he'll offer you his paw to shake. He's the best dog in the world."

Einstein barked and jumped down. Graci-Ella called him over and he pranced around the end of the picnic table, his tongue lolling crooked from his mouth. He sat in front of her and held out his paw. She shook it gently. "My, aren't you handsome? Do you have a leash along? I'll walk you around the building."

Einstein romped to Becca and gently took a leash from her hand before giving it to Graci-Ella. "Does he enjoy running?" She petted Einstein as she clipped the leash onto his collar.

"He loves a good run. Wolf won't let me take him on runs anymore, just slow jogs."

Graci-Ella stood and rubbed the dog's neck. "Einstein, sounds like we could both use some fast exercise. Two times around the building."

Wolf laughed. "If you sense twenty pair of male eyes on you, it's not a phantom feeling."

Right, as if I haven't had men watch me run before. She and Einstein took off.

13

CHAPTER THREE

Feet pounded past the opened kitchen windows while Boyd and Quinn were rinsing dishes and loading dishwashers. Boyd's neck snapped a fast second glance, and he nearly got whiplash. He kept holding a plate under the water spray as he leaned toward the screen to watch Graci-Ella—her come-to-Jesus legs in navy shorts, full breasts in an apricot tank top and a long ponytail that swished back and forth with each stride. His heart pounded with every pace she made.

Quinn jerked the plate from Boyd's hand. "Man, I don't know who's breathing faster right now. Her running or you watching."

"Bite me." Boyd leaned farther toward the window so he could keep his eyes on her after she passed by with Einstein. Quinn shifted behind him and shouldered Boyd's ass until his knees were on the counter. "What the fuckin' hell, Quinn?" A giggling shove and Boyd's knees slipped into the double sink—one side full of hot soapy water soaking lasagna pans and the other with the faucet running cold water.

Quinn, the bastard, was laughing and grabbing for the sprayer.

"Oh no! Oh, hell no!" Boyd struggled for the sprayer, too, in an effort to avoid the shower he was about to get. In the scuffle, he slipped forward and banged his chin on the window sill, which gave Quinn enough time to gain control of the sprayer and douse him good with cold water.

Boyd elbowed his co-worker, who lost his balance, slipped on the wet floor and ripped the sprayer's hose from the faucet assembly. Water flew. Guys came running to see what all the commotion was about. Boyd didn't doubt for a minute he made a fine sight with his ass in the air and his knees in the sink. He pushed off the window sill and flipped backwards, his sneakers skidding in two different directions until his back hit the floor.

Quinn, bless his demented ass, laughed so loud it evidently drew the captain out of his office.

"What in the God damn hell is going on? Someone turn off the water and fix the hose. One of you *little boys* better mop up the floor." Captain Steele was known for having spic and span station and that included the kitchen.

Quinn was known for his big mouth. "Hell, captain, I was only helping Tiny watch the photographer run by the building with Einstein."

Feet stampeded to the windows on the other side of the building. Whistles and crude remarks exploded from the gang at the other windows. Damn the rest of the guys for watching her run. They had no right to drool over her.

Boyd was so pissed, he spun to head for the mop and bucket, shooting Quinn a glare as he stormed to where the cleaning supplies were stored. Never one to back down, Quinn grabbed Boyd's bicep and leaned in. "If you want her, you better make it known."

"Oh, like you did with Cassie? You damn near drove her away. Besides, I've got that custody hearing…"

Quinn's voice softened. "Don't pound the hell out of me for this, but I think you've got a worthless lawyer. He's got you scared to do anything but work and take care of Matt. What do you do the weekends the kid's with his mother? Do you party, date, bay at the moon? No."

"I get together with you guys when you have picnics or

15

basketball games."

"You need to live, brother. An occasional date would not make you a bad parent. The *hell* with what that lawyer told you. Cassie's afraid you've turned off your sex drive. She wants to line you up with some of her friends. You know how she gets once she snags onto an idea."

Boyd, who was still dealing with half a woody, chuffed a laugh. "Tell her my sex drive is working fine. I'm just keeping it in neutral until after the hearing." He shook his index finger at Quinn. "Tell that sweet wife of yours I would not appreciate her matchmaking help." He made a snap decision to get out of his wet clothes and headed for the sleeping quarters to change before he mopped the kitchen floor.

He'd just swabbed the area in front of the sink when the horny herd charged toward the open back door where Graci-Ella was evidently passing. He spun to snatch another look at her after she rounded the building, but thought better of it. Surely she deserved more than to be ogled like some sex object.

When he stepped outside to empty his bucket, Einstein barked a greeting as he cleared the end of the fire station. Boyd stepped inside to grab a bowl to fill with water for the dog and snatched a bottle of water out of the refrigerator for Graci-Ella. He carried both outside for the runners. He set Einstein's bowl on the grass next to the sidewalk. Both the dog and the beauty stopped running.

"Oh, a life-saver." Graci-Ella accepted the bottle and unscrewed the top. "Thanks for being so considerate." She gulped a few swigs, watching Einstein put his muzzle into the bowl, take several laps and then lick Boyd's calf in gratitude. The corners of her mouth quirked. "Just don't expect me to do that."

"What? Lick my calf?" Hell, his voice cracked like an adolescent. He had to get a grip where she was concerned.

She nodded, guzzling more water.

His cock nodded, too. Thank God he'd changed into a pair of baggy cargo shorts. His instant erection wasn't so obvious, but

16

since he couldn't stop thinking of her tongue on any part of his body, the damn thing lengthened and thickened some more. He stooped and petted Einstein in an effort to hide it until his mind got off her tongue. Of course, the damn dog licked Boyd's crotch, then lifted his hind leg and licked his doggie privates.

"Do you have some free time to talk to me? We could sit on the bench in front of the palms and those pretty orchids." She motioned with her bottle to the bench she meant.

"Sure. Let me go in and grab a soda. Do you want one or maybe some more water?"

She flashed him a heart-melting smile. "No, I'm great. I need to get Einstein back to his owners and then I'll be over."

Boyd was sipping his Coke when Graci-Ella carried a canvas bag over to the bench. "How long have Wolf and Becca been married? They seem so much in love."

"A shade over three years. He bought a townhouse next to hers and couldn't keep his eyes off her as she took her daily jog with the dog. He put out a lot of effort to get her to date him and, thank goodness for the guys at the station, she finally gave in. There's nothing worse than a man who has his heart set on a woman and can't make any progress with her."

Her blue eyes fixated on his. "Women are no different when they want to know a man better. In fact, sometimes we can be kinda sneaky about getting his attention." She shoulder bumped his and he choked on his Coke, rasping to breathe.

She straddled his lap and leaned over to pound his back. He got an up close and personal glimpse down her tank top. Now he knew where she stored a pencil, a *thin* pencil because there was very little room between her firm breasts. Struggling with the urge to cross the line and touch them with his fingers or tongue or face, he squeezed the bottle of Coke in a fit of stress. Soda shot upwards. Graci-Ella laughed as she wiped it off her face and he soon found himself joining in. Hell, it was either laugh or slither away in humiliation.

A narrow finger ran over his chin. "You've got a scrape here. Want me to kiss it and make it better?"

His mouth had gone dry, too dry to talk; so he just nodded. Her lips gently covered where he'd bumped his chin on the windowsill. His hands covered her back and he inhaled whatever get-your-sex-here perfume she wore.

She moved off his lap to sit on the bench again, and his heart began beating once more. "I think I sat on your spilled soda. My ass is wet."

God help me. I can't think of her ass—dry or wet.

"What did you want to talk about, Graci-Ella?" He bent and set his crunched can on the ground.

"I'd like for you to be honest about why you won't even consider posing for the calendar I'm doing. You're the best looking guy on the squad. You should be plastered across the front of the cover."

Years had gone by since he'd been complimented with such enthusiasm. He wasn't so sure he believed her or felt comfortable with her praise. "My reasons are legal and pertain to the person I love most in this world—my son."

"How so?" Graci-Ella took off her sneakers and slid her naked soles back and forth in the grass. "These were not the best sneakers to run in."

"Says the woman who wears stilettoes to work." He patted his thighs. "Put your feet up here and I'll rub them while we talk." She pulled her canvas bag onto the bench and lay her head on it as she stretched out on the seat of the bench. He tried not to focus on her hot pink toenail polish as he explained his legal circumstances as well as Matt's health.

Every so often, she'd ask a question or moan if his thumbs rotated over a tender spot. "Yes, but since you'll be wearing jeans, no one—not even a judge—would label it as obscene. Especially for something to help the local foodbank."

"I can't take that chance, Graci-Ella. Matt depends on me to keep him safe. Everyone wants to give me legal advice today. First the captain, then Quinn and now you. My lawyer told me to lead an exemplary life, and I've tried my damndest."

"Is your divorce final?"

"Yes. Thank God. She's someone else's problem now. She lives with a guy who gives off bad vibes. I think he may be dealing. I don't want Matt around that danger."

"Then you're free to date." She shifted the bag she rested her head on. "I wouldn't suggest having a parade of different women in and out of your house, but a date now and then does not make you less of a parent. Not in the eyes of the law."

"Oh yeah? How would you know?"

"Because I'm a lawyer."

His hands stilled. *I will be damned.* "Would you mind repeating that?"

She straightened and slipped her feet off his thighs. "I said I'm a lawyer. Don't you narrow your eyes at me like that. I wouldn't be crazy about dating a man who works a dangerous profession, but I'd alter my way of thinking to date you." A blush slapped both her cheeks, and she glanced away, exhaling through pursed lips. "Wow, that was bold. I shouldn't have said that. I apologize."

He wrapped her ponytail around his wrist, brought her face to his and locked his eyes on hers. "Are you being honest here? I'll be damned if I'll be played again."

"I'd enjoy getting to know you better. There are some things I like about you, especially your dedication to your son."

"I'd enjoy spending more time with you, too, and I never expected to say that again." He lowered his face to hers and inhaled her intoxicating essence, becoming dizzy with each breath.

The fire alarm went off and the dispatcher's voice traveled over the outside speakers giving the location and type of fire.

Boyd rubbed his cheek against Graci-Ella's. "Duty calls. Gotta run, dammit." His lips barely dragged across hers before he took off on a run, cursing whoever or whatever started that blaze.

CHAPTER FOUR

Saturday, after a breakfast meeting with a client, Graci-Ella hurried into the big-chain hardware store, a list of items the building manager had recommended for her little office redecoration jotted on a sticky note.

In fact, she nearly danced through the large chain hardware store as she picked out a rug for under her client chairs, a lamp for her desk and paint. She chose a cheery shade of yellow for the wall with the window and a paler tint of yellow for the other three walls. Jo-Jo said he'd do the painting if she bought the paint, and also install a ceiling fan if she purchased a new one.

And, of course, the palm leaf shaped fan she fell in love with was stacked on the top shelf of boxed fans. She tried reaching. Tried jumping to slide a corner out far enough she could grab it on her next jump, but that didn't work either. The darn box was just too heavy, even though the fan was small.

"Need some help?" A pair of hands encircled her waist and she spun—in shock and ready to knee some guy in the balls—only to glare into Boyd's grey eyes. "Need me to lift you a few inches?" Wrinkles creased the corners of his eyes as a slow, sexy grin spread. My God, what a smile could do to his severe expression.

He had one of those faces of angles and planes that made a man look hard-edged, especially with that perpetual whiskered scruff he had going on. Her fingers itched to sift through his wavy, dark hair that barely rubbed the neckline of his t-shirt. And he smelled of woodsy soap.

Beat, heart, beat!

"I'm betting you could reach it for me." *Shut up, are you stupid?* her hormones hissed. *Let him keep his hands on you and lift you. Don't you want to feel his strength?* Good Lord, her female bits hadn't been this bossy in ages.

"True." His thumbs rubbed slow circles at her waist, sending "come to me" signals to her hormones in Morse code. "But I think Confucius said, 'a job worth doing is worth doing in twos.'"

She laughed. "He did not. You just made that up."

"Turn around and I'll lift you. Think you can handle the weight of the box once you get it in your hands?"

"Oh, I can handle the weight. I could even handle you, once I got you in my hands." *That's telling him, her female bits squealed. Look at his shocked expression.*

He leaned and pressed his lips to her ear and repeated his command in a sensual whisper. "Think you can handle the weight once you get it in your hands?"

Oh, sweet climax. It was a good thing he was there to lift her because her legs had just turned to mush. Plus, she was going to have to go through check-out wearing wet panties. Better to go through the self-serve aisle—and damn quickly. She needed her vibrator.

By the time her feet hit the floor again, her back had rubbed against every delectable hard inch of his pecs and abs and, if she wasn't mistaken, one rock-solid erection. Maybe she needed two or three fans for her office.

He took the box from her arms and set it in her cart. "Gee, you're getting a lot of stuff here. Doing some redecorating at home?"

"No. In my tiny office at the law firm where I work."

A groan tumbled from his throat. "*Please* I'm trying to forget you're a lawyer. I'm pretending you're one sexy photographer and

21

nothing more."

"But I *am* an attorney." She planted a fist on her hip and hiked her chin at his scowl. "It's an honorable profession." Why did she feel the need to defend herself? "We're not all bad. Just at certain times." *Now why the hell did I say that?*

"Yes, I suppose there are some good lawyers. I know there are a few who smell like sin." He leaned in and inhaled her fragrance and she trembled in response. The corners of his lips twitched and one of his dark eyebrows rose. "What do you need next?"

"Wh…what?" The man had just boosted her as if she weighed no more than a basketball and then slid her over his erection—one that resembled a fire hose full to bursting…set her hormones in a line dance to do the bump and grind to, "Can't Get Enough of Your Love Baby."

He backed her against the shelves, his fingertips lightly skimming the skin of her arms. "What else do you need, Ms. Good and Bad Attorney? Can I help you with it?"

For the life of her, she couldn't recall why she'd come in this hardware store. A new pair of high heels? Shampoo? Ice Cream? Her mind was all befuddled. All she could see were intense steel-gray eyes, darkened and hooded with desire. His head tilted as if he were studying her. Her mental focus floated away on an internal heated breeze.

I need to date more.

Those man-hungry hormones of hers were pushing her closer to him and making her lips pucker in the most embarrassing way. Could anything be more humiliating? Like he would ever kiss her. And could she survive if he did? For this guy oozed an excess of testosterone. She cleared her throat. "Plant hooks for those aluminum strips that hold up ceiling tiles."

He placed one hand on the small of her back and pushed her cart with his other. "Hey, that's what I'm here for. We can find them together. Suddenly, the captain's on a plant kick, so he sent me for hooks and some hanging plants. He'll need to keep Emily away from them though. The woman has a black thumb."

"You seem in a happier mood today."

"Talking to you yesterday helped. Plus, I called my lawyer this morning and pressed him for some answers. Old Henry wasn't too pleased. He prefers safety, but I got him to admit I could date—occasionally."

"Henry? Not George Henry, mister conservative from the fifties." Geesh, no wonder he had Boyd afraid to lead a normal life.

Boyd chuckled. "Yeah, he is in a bit of a time warp. He's good, though, right?"

"Yes. Very thorough." They turned into another aisle, his hand still on the small of her back.

"You know, I recognized your high heel clattering and knew you were in the store somewhere. You have a distinctive walk, as if you're almost running. Few women can manage that in heels as high as you wear."

"You must have good ears." Being near him had her in a happy Zen place.

He laughed. "I'm a dad. I can hear a six-year old doing something he shouldn't be doing at twenty paces. I call it daddy hearing. Gotta admit, I dig your blue toenail polish to match your dark blue stilettoes."

"Most men don't notice things like that."

"I'm a fireman. I'm taught to be super observant."

They talked while they shopped and picked out plants. She was surprised to learn he was a gentle giant. Quick to help her choose things. He also seemed to be leaning close to her neck as if he were smelling her perfume. Normally, she'd confront a guy about invading her personal space, but he invaded in such a sweet way.

"I need to pick up a case of chrome cleaner for the station. If you'll walk along with me, I can help you load the fan and paint and stuff into your car, after we check out. Besides, my male plants are hanging from your cart watching your female plants."

She rested her hands on her hips. "Oh? And how do you know

23

yours are males?"

He slapped his chest with his palm and feigned astonishment. "Do you think a macho man like me would…" he leaned in to whisper in her ear, "choose feminine *plants*?"

The way he'd uttered the word plants as if it were something utterly obscene made her laugh out loud. "Okay, I'll walk along with you. Only because I think you need a keeper." Well, there was also the thought of his leaning into the back of her RAV-4, loading her things.

Normally, she wasn't one to play the weak woman role, but he wore worn jeans that hugged every curve and showcased every bunch and stretch of his thigh muscles as he moved. Was she a perverted woman for wanting to see him bend over in those jeans? It was a simple question and, frankly, Charlotte, she didn't give a damn.

She walked him to her car and unlocked the hatch. He grabbed two cans of paint and bent over to place them inside.

Mental fist pump. Score!

Next, he grabbed the boxed fan and bent over to put it in.

Sweet Lawd, I'm going to hyperventilate in a second. What an ass he's got!

He picked up a brass pot and a bag of soil she was going to use to repot a palm for one corner of her office.

Would he notice if I bit his ass? Just once?

With gentle movements, he set her plants inside.

God, if my panties get any wetter, I'll have to swim to my door. Just look at how his jeans fit. Like lover's hands.

Boyd turned to her. "Are you feeling okay? You're flushed and breathing rapid." He pressed the back of his hand to her forehead. "Are you a diabetic? Do you need to eat?"

Now, there was a loaded question if ever she'd heard one.

She waved an open hand. "Oh, I'm fine. Really. You can put the rolled carpet on my ass…er…seat." She laughed weakly. *I am such an idiot!*

24

He stood there and stared at her as if he'd heard the last marble roll out of her head. "Graci-Ella, were you watching me a little too closely as I was bending over to load your car?"

Humiliation hopped in. "Of…of course not!"

He leaned next to her ear. "I hoped you hadn't noticed I'm going commando."

A couple seagulls cawed overhead. Graci-Ella gasped and back-handed his abs. "That was TMI, buster."

"Now don't get angry with me. If I offended you, I apologize. Other than the women at the station, I haven't talked to many since my divorce. Obviously, I'm rusty as hell." He glanced away for a few seconds. "For all I know, you're already involved with someone. Although I'd like to think you'd tell me not to touch you if you were."

"I'm not seeing anyone. And, yes, I'd have told you to back off if I was."

"I've got my beeper on in case there's an emergency somewhere. Would you like to go to Ryder's Health Bar for a fruit smoothie?"

"I've heard of that place, but I've never been there. Sounds great."

"Ryder dates Ivy Jo. He'll enjoy meeting you since you'll be taking pictures of his Sugar Doll, as he calls her. I guess we should both drive our cars in case I have to leave in a hurry."

"Okay. I'll follow you then."

He leaned and rubbed his cheek against hers the way he'd done last night. For some reason, she found it the most sensual action. Her hands slipped up his t-shirt over hardened muscles. "Sweetness, you need to think long and hard about dating a man with a child. Especially with a little boy, who has a physical condition that can ruin date plans at the last minute. There will also be times when we'll have little privacy. Matt loves to be included. I can't say he's spoiled, but he is excitable. There's no use in our starting a relationship if that kind of life doesn't appeal to you. Take your time and think it through. My work hours are a hindrance, as

25

well. I work forty-eight hour shifts and then have forty-eight off."

He retreated and pushed the cart with his case of chrome cleaner and male plants to his gray Mustang.

She got in her car and closed the door, watching him in her rearview mirror as her female parts cooled down. There was something appealing about the man—his honesty, his sexuality and his devotion to his son.

Could she become involved with a man and his child? The kind of relationship she had with the man was more important. How he treated her. She'd always gotten along well with children and was the most popular babysitter in her hometown neighborhood when she was a teenager.

She followed him a few blocks to street with touristy shops. Boyd helped her out of her car, took her hand and opened the door to the cool interior of Ryder's. Jamaican music whispered from the speakers. Ryder's bald head rose from the plate of fruit he was fixing for a customer. A wide smile greeted them both. "Tiny, my man! Who's the doll you've got your fingers locked with?" He jerked his chin to two empty stools in front of him. "Sit and introduce me."

"Ryder, this is Graci-Ella, the photographer who's doing the calendar for the fire department."

Ryder wiped his hands on a paper towel and passed the fruit tray to a waitress. Then he crossed his muscled arms and leaned back against the counter where he stored the glasses and flavorings. "Oh, I know one little Sugar Doll who's going to get her pretty ass smacked. She told me the photographer was an ex-Ranger and kind of cute." He snatched a bar rag and wiped circles in front of them both. "She had me worked up into quite a jealous lather, me being an ex-SEAL and her main squeeze." He grinned. "Oh, she will so pay." He winked at Graci-Ella. "God, I do love my Ivy Jo. How come you women have to get us all worked up? Hell, it took three times to get me to calm down enough to agree to it. Had she told me someone like you was the person taking the pictures,

I'd have agreed right away."

"Maybe that's why she fibbed a little. Look at what she got out of it." Graci-Ella winked back. Boyd's knee leaned against her thigh and her sex started pulsing.

Ryder laughed. "Yeah, you got me there. So, what are you two having?"

She knew a man's blood could drop from his brain to his gonads, but she'd never experienced it herself, didn't know it could happen to a women. So she stared at the menu, trying to calm herself. Boyd ordered and she finally chose, too.

While Ryder made their icy drinks from fresh fruit, she asked Boyd questions about Matt. Boyd's face brightened; the man dearly loved his son. "Sometimes he acts like an old man. It's the strangest thing, the wisdom this kid's got." He waved an open hand. "And I'm not just saying it because I'm his dad and I'm prejudiced or anything." His gaze turned to her and he gave her a sheepish grin.

"My grandma used to say a child who behaved or thought like that had an old soul and was destined for good things." Graci-Ella suddenly missed the grandma who was always in her corner while her parents focused on Eli's many activities.

Sadness swept across Boyd's face like a hand smoothing sand. "If I can keep him alive between the asthma and pneumonia. Which is why I have to win the custody battle. His health issues really bother me."

"Is Matt's doctor going to be a witness at your hearing?" She sipped her lemon-lime drink.

"Yes. His pediatrician has agreed. Matt is in a pattern. Two, maybe three, days after spending the weekend with his mother, he's in the hospital with a severe asthma attack that's progressed to pneumonia. It's too hard on him." He took a long drag of his blueberry pomegranate smoothie.

This was a man who cared deeply. She wondered what it would be like to be loved by a man like him to such a deeply protective degree.

"You asked me to consider if I'd date a man with a child. The answer is yes, if he's like you."

He brought her hand to his lips and an arrow of need shot to all her female parts. "Dammit," he muttered and looked at his beeper. "Gotta go. Fire." He tossed some bills on the counter. Then cupped her face and kissed her forehead. "Call me at bedtime, Sweetness." He ran out the door to his Mustang parked next to her SUV.

Ryder handed drinks to another waitress and then propped his forearms on the counter in front of Graci-Ella. "Seeing Boyd with you did my heart good. I've been worried about him for a long time. Lord, how he needs a good woman." He winked again. "Someone like you. I'm good at picking up vibes. That's how I knew Ivy Jo was it for me as soon as I laid eyes on her. Boyd's been through a lot. Scuttlebutt has it he caught his ex-wife in bed with two men. Nearly did him in. Now this custody hearing." Ryder shook his head. "That boy of his is one of a kind. I love him to death. The only customer I have who marches up to me, shakes my hand and thanks me for making him such a good drink. I'm betting the Mattster, as I call him, would love you to pieces."

"Well, it's a little early to be thinking on those terms."

Ryder laughed. "You just keep telling yourself that, you and your blue fingernail polish."

She leaned toward him. "Yeah, and your momma wears combat boots."

His smile widened. "Well now, we got us a girl who knows how to play the dozens. I'm liking you more and more. What position did you play?"

She stood and smoothed her skirt. "Point guard. All American."

A low whistle followed her. "Boyd's gonna have his hands full with you, ain't he?"

She glanced over her shoulder. "Poor man has no idea."

28

CHAPTER FIVE

Boyd inserted his Bluetooth as soon as he started the 'stang and called the head of the marine rescue team. Wolf told him some kids had set fire to a dock. Two teenagers had fallen into the water while the blaze was moving from the dock to the board walk along the causeway.

He asked Wolf to grab his equipment, so he could jump on the boat as soon as he got there. Then his mind drifted back to the hardware store. He had to admit after flirting and talking with Graci-Ella, he felt like a new man. He'd avoided the opposite sex like lima beans since the legal papers suing him for custody had arrived. Christ, the whole lawsuit had him tied up in knots for so long.

Until her.

Something about her stirred him up and soothed him at the same time. Thank God he'd called his lawyer this morning and pushed him for answers because staying away from Graci-Ella was going to be hard. The attraction was just too strong. Now, maybe he wouldn't have to.

As soon as he'd heard her heels clicking through the hardware store like a "come-get-me" tune, he'd been on the hunt like a wild, horny beast. When he'd set eyes on her jumping for that boxed fan, he had to put his hands on her—had to, as if laying claim to her was some invisible driving force.

He bolted from his car as soon as he hit the dock. Quinn gave him the "you're fuckin' late glare" and Boyd shot him the finger. He jumped onboard and started putting on his uniform and boots.

The captain sent Wolf's team out to rescue the teens and assigned Ivy Jo to drive the fire truck Quinn always drove. Quinn grumbled about someone else operating what he considered his personal apparatus. "I told Ivy I didn't want a scratch or a dent on my truck when she brought it back."

"Bet she liked that." Boyd yanked on his gear and stored his street clothes in a cabinet under his seat.

"Told me to kiss her lily white ass." Quinn jerked the boat into gear and Boyd rode shotgun. Once they were on their way, Boyd lugged the fire hoses out of storage. Wolf and Barclay were in their scuba gear in the stern, hanging on while Quinn skimmed the boat across the gentle waves of the water; the stern end of the boat bouncing. In a matter of minutes, the smoke was visible.

Evidently Wolf's keen eyes saw something, and he ordered Quinn to take the boat dockside beside the fire hydrant. Then Wolf and Barclay flipped backward into the water and swam toward two teens thrashing around.

Boyd hopped out of the boat and tied it to one of the piers away from the fire. He dragged the coupler end of the hose to the fire hydrant Jace had just opened and attached his hose to one of the openings. Once Jace turned on the hydrant, both he, Ivy Jo and Boyd aimed the force of water at the fire. Out of the corner of his eye, he saw Wolf and Barclay unceremoniously throw two kids into the boat.

The police on the scene arrested the underage drunken party-goers who had destroyed some property, in addition to setting the fire. Wolf, who was never one to mince words, claimed the kids all needed their asses kicked before *and* after they repaired what they had ruined.

Then Wolf and Barclay went underwater again to investigate

the pylons and see how far down the damage had gone. Boyd focused on the plants and palm trees to contain the width of the flames, in an effort to keep the condominiums safe. Ivy Jo and other firefighters took care of the wooden deck and walkways. Most of the furniture was ruined.

A couple hours later, the crew returned to the station. Then the work began of cleaning gear and trucks, as well as themselves. By the time the firefighters were done, the captain had asked for Boyd's car keys so he could retrieve the items he'd bought. The captain hung plants in front of every window, issuing strict orders they were to be taken care of and not knocked about.

Boyd went into the sleeping quarters and called home to see if Matt was still up. He could tell his son was fighting sleep just to hear his dad's voice.

"Daddy, you're late. Was there a fire?" Matt's impatience over waiting sounded like whining.

Boyd lay across his bunk bed, tired now that he was coming off the adrenalin rush. "Yeah, buddy. Some teenagers were partying and they started a fire on a dock. Two kids fell in the water. The fire spread to the condominiums' picnic area. But we put it out."

"That's good. I...I been waiting for you to call." Matt yawned.

"How did you feel in school today?"

"Aunt Jinny wrote a note asking I not go outside for recess. I stayed in and helped the teacher with stuff. Guess what? You'll never guess in a million years!"

"What." Boyd grinned, wondering how many times his son would ask him the same question and how, just once, he wished he could shock him with the correct answer.

"I got two stars on my math paper, cause...'cause I got all the answers right and the teacher could read them. Sometimes I get in a hurry and get sloppy."

Boyd gave a low whistle. "Wow, two stars!! That's totally awesome. Did you hang your paper on the refrigerator?"

"Aunt Jinny did." Matt coughed a deep, rattily cough. One that

31

was too familiar to Boyd.

"Good, because I'll want to see it. I'm real proud of your hard work, Matt. Now go to sleep."

The typical sound of Matt curling up on his side and the blanket rustling came through the phone line. He coughed again. "I love you, Daddy."

"I love you more." He ended the call and rolled over for a little nap before he would scrounge the refrigerator for something to eat. Before his eyes closed, he sent Graci-Ella a text. *Call me.*

His phone chimed. *R U safe?*

He stared at the text. It had been a long time since a woman cared enough to ask him that. Needing to hear her voice, he called her. "Hi Sweetness."

"Are you okay?" Water sloshed.

He pinched his eyes shut. "Don't tell me you're taking a bath."

There was no reply. Just water splashing. And his dick hardening. "Well?"

"You told me not to tell you. Besides, I'm shaving."

"Don't cut your leg."

"That's not what I'm shaving. Sleep well, big guy." She hung up.

Daybreak and a case of yawns brought Graci-Ella to the fire station—well, that and a chance to see Boyd. She lugged in two big boxes of four dozen glazed donuts in one arm and an equal number of mixed donuts in the other. She set them on the dining room table, along with her bag of calendars she'd done last year of the Buccaneers football team, a collegiate female swimming team and a wrestling team from a Florida University. Visuals for the firefighters to look at to get an idea of her style of work she meant to show them the other night, but her run with Einstein and talk with Boyd had taken priority.

She noted the petite plant hanging above the small window at the sink and complimented the captain on it, which seemed to please him. He showed her around to see the other plants she and

Boyd had picked out yesterday. Since the captain didn't mention Boyd's running into her at the hardware store, he'd evidently kept their shopping together a secret.

Ivy Jo was making several pots of coffee. "Grab a cup and a couple donuts before the vultures start circling to snatch a donut in each grubby hand."

"Don't mind if I do." She sat at the large table as the firefighters stumbled in in various stages of dress. Emily, like Ivy Jo, was already dressed. As for the men, some wore jeans and t-shits and others were still in their sleep pants or shorts. Her mouth opened and froze, so did her hand with a donut partway to her mouth. Boyd wore nothing but jeans, the first two buttons open, showcasing his obliques. Thank God, he wasn't into waxing his chest for he had just the right amount of nipple teasing chest hair, and her nipples were cresting for a looksee.

His son's name in script was tattooed near his heart. Tribal tats ran across one wide shoulder and continued down to his elbow.

He smiled at her before bending over to kiss her forehead. "Do we have you to thank for the donut treats this morning?" His voice was still thick with sleep. "I know I have you and your shaving routine to thank for a restless night."

She smiled as she took a bite of donut. Good to know. "Yes, I brought the donuts. Take as much as you want."

His gaze shot to her for a minute and swept over her attire—a short-sleeved, purple dress with a cowl neckline and slim skirt and purple heels—in a hungry caress. "I'll have just one, thank you."

She smiled and placed a second one on his napkin. "Confucius said only a weak man can live on one puny donut."

He snorted before strutting into the kitchen to get a cup of coffee. He sat next to her when he returned. "Please tell me you didn't cut yourself shaving." His voice lowered. "Although I do have lots of experience at kissing boo-boos, you know." He bit into a donut and chewed.

She sipped her coffee and glanced at him through her lashes.

"No, I'm fine."

He leaned his knee against her thigh. "That's good to hear since I dreamed about it. The kissing, I mean. Lots of kissing. Listen, Sweetness, I need to call Matt to see how he's doing this morning. He was coughing last night."

He gulped his coffee as he thumbed a number. "Matt?" His forehead wrinkled in concern as his son's raspy voice sounded over the cell. "Is your throat sore, buddy?"

"Yeah and my chest hurts." There was a slight wheeze to the child's breathing.

"You better hand the phone to Aunt Jinny." Graci-Ella hated to keep eavesdropping in on Boyd's conversation but his little boy sounded terrible. "Jinny, did you take his temperature?" There was a reply. Boyd repeated it. "One-hundred-and-two point six? Call the pediatrician as soon as his office opens. Keep Matt home from school. Call me with any news."

He sat back in his chair and sighed. "Fuck! We go through this same list of medical complaints so often, it wears on my nerves. When it's his weekend with his mother, I know he spends a large part of that time with my ex-wife's housekeeper, I suspect he is still exposed to a lot of smoke—and not all of it legal, either."

"Which is one of the reasons you're seeking permanent custody." Her remark was more statement than a question.

"Almost every asthma attack morphs into pneumonia. The worry for him tears me apart. I love that little fella is if he were the whole light in my world. He depends on me to take care of him." He stood and went for another cup of coffee, his pace slower this time as if he had the weight of the world on his shoulders.

Darryl, or Kissy Lips, picked up a glazed donut, caught Graci-Ella's eye and then wiggled his tongue in and out of the hole.

If he thinks this is turning me on, his brain has dropped into one of his balls with room left over for a dozen hot wings.

Wolf told Darryl to act his age, while Graci-Ella made a mental note to remove him from her list. This was one asshole she didn't want to work with.

"Oh, come on, Wolf, chicks dig this stuff."

"What stuff?" Boyd turned his chair around and straddled it, his head swiveling from Darryl to Wolf to Graci-Ella. Like a gentleman, he picked up his donut and started eating it and watched Darryl select a strawberry iced pastry from another box and do his tongue waggling.

Boyd jumped out of his chair and fisted his hand in Darryl's t-shirt, yanking him nose to nose. "You'll damn well show my lady some respect and stop flirting with her. Know what, Kissy Lips? Women appreciate a more subtle, flattering approach."

Darryl sneered. "Listen to this, guys. Some expert advice from a looser who couldn't hang onto his wife. What the hell would he know about turning on a woman?"

Graci-Ella took Boyd's hand and shot a glance at Darryl. "You'd be surprised at how completely he can turn on a woman and barely touch her."

Boyd's arm slipped around her waist. "Would you like to walk to our apparatus garage? You could look at some of the equipment to see if there's any you want to include in your pictures as a backdrop?"

"Sounds like a great idea." She stood, snatched her camera and followed him down the hallway. "I'll snap some photos of your equipment."

Boyd stopped on a dime and she rammed into his back. His hand swung out like a stop sign on a bus. "Don't say stuff like that to me unless we're alone."

"You're the one who loaded up my backend yesterday. After you picked me up." She smirked at her double entendre.

His back straight, he charged ahead. "Careful. I'll sue you for sexual harassment. I see how you are. All tease." He grabbed the door handle and yanked it open. "And stop wearing that damn perfume! You drive me freaking insane."

"Okay, no perfume." His arm was around her waist, holding her close, but he wouldn't look at her. "Look at me. Is that so hard?"

"Oh, Sweetness, you don't even want to mention the word *hard* right about now. You have a way of teasing…and you speaking up in my defense back there threw me for a loop. I want to make love to you so badly right now. Slowly. Sweetly."

This man was a rare combination of tenderness, strength and blatant sexuality that drew her near him so strongly she wanted to burrow into his warmth and spend a couple hours there, in his arms, skin to skin, lips to lips, and fingertips exploring.

"Yeah, me too," she breathed.

"So, what is this we're doing here? Teasing? Having a good time? Or dancing toward something more serious?" He looked at her then, his gaze hot. "Because I have to be damn honest and tell you I don't want any man touching you but me. Is that clear? I know I have no right to lay down demands, but…" He backed her against the wall, heat rolling off him. "I want to get to know you better, not just sexually," his voice lowered to an intimate whisper. "Though that craving is eating at me from the inside out right about now, but I also want to know you better as a friend, a woman, someone I can talk to when I have a need to. You make me feel like a man again, and damn if I don't need that." His hand reached out to touch her hair. "Need you."

Her palms itched to forge a trail up his bare chest. "I need you too, which is so unlike me." Firemen were passing by and crisscrossing the wide hallway. And the two of them were voicing their personal desires for a relationship neither was probably ready for; still, the man was her captivation. He had been since she laid eyes on him. "If you think for a minute that you're not sexy as hell, then your ex-wife is still controlling you. Now, show me your equipment."

Boyd leaned his head back and laughed. "God, woman. Come on, I'll show you my bright red fire truck."

36

CHAPTER SIX

On their return from the large garage area full of huge fire trucks and ambulances, Graci-Ella told Boyd she'd already decided not to use Kissy Lips in the calendar. "From what I've seen of the rest of the squad, he doesn't measure up to their standards, physically or heroically. I don't want any trouble out of him. He reminds me of some of the whack jobs I have to represent. Could you sit near him?" Her blue eyes implored him; how could he possibly resist.

Boyd squeezed her hand. "Whatever I can do to help, all you have to do is ask." They entered the dining area where the fire-fighters and EMT's, as they ate, were glancing over the calendars she had bought with her.

Graci-Ella smiled when she opened her briefcase, removing her tablet, pencil and tape measure. "I'll need all of you men to take off your shirts, and that includes you, Captain Steele. I love the highlights of grey you've got going on in your hair."

Quinn leaned as he walked behind the captain. "What she's trying to say in a nice way is old farts can be sexy too."

The captain raised his coffee mug. "Well, thanks, Quinn. I didn't think you noticed." The rest of the men laughed, including Ivy Jo and Emily.

Boyd slid his chair behind Darryl's, so he'd be nearby in case the jackass got rowdy or mouthy over Graci-Ella's decision.

She waved some papers. "I also have a spousal agreement form for your wife, husband or significant other to sign, giving their approval for you to be in the calendar. Please turn them into the captain as soon as you can, so I can move ahead on this project." She waved the yellow forms. "These puppies are important. I don't want a jealous mate chasing me down. I could probably outrun him or her, but not if they're pointing a gun at me and I'm in high heels."

Everyone laughed and teased her. Before long, one of the guys nicknamed her Stilettoes, which she graciously accepted on a giggle. "I think I like it." She wiggled back and forth which got Boyd's sex meter revving, as if it hadn't been on full charge since he first laid eyes on her this morning.

"I'm going to need about six of those forms. Maybe even ten." Darryl leaned on the back legs of his chair as he boasted. Other firefighters groaned.

Other than flicking Darryl's ear with his thumb and index finger, Boyd didn't move. The rest of the squad wasted no time in shucking their shirts and posing for her as she looked at each one, asking them questions in a sexy voice, taking their bicep and chest measurements, for God's sake, and noting it all down. Boyd kept his jealousy on a slow burn, mainly because she was all business about everything.

The nickname angle evidently fascinated her, for she asked every fireperson what the rest of the squad called him or her. When she reached Kissy Lips, she cocked her head to the side and frowned. "I don't know. You're pretty beefy."

His head reared back as if she'd slapped him. "What are you saying, bitch? That I'm too fat?"

Boyd had him on the floor, his knee across his neck before the chair he sat in had a chance to clatter onto the tile floor. "We don't call our feminine co-workers that name and certainly not our guests. Apologize."

"Like hell!" Darryl Weir's face was crimson with anger.

"Graci-Ella did you measure the captain yet? Why don't you do that while Kissy Lips thinks of a suitable apology?"

"I'll kill you, you big bastard," Darryl spat.

Boyd spared him a glare. "Yeah, you work on that."

The captain, dressed again after being measured, stroked and purred over by Graci-Ella, stalked toward Boyd and raised his eyebrows. "Did this mouthy kid think of a request for forgiveness yet? Oh, did I overhear you talking to your babysitter about Matt's temperature earlier?"

"Yeah," He ran a hand across the back of his neck, squeezing the tight muscles. His knee was still on Darryl's neck as he struggled to get away from Boyd. "We'll know after the doctor visit. Aunt Jinny's going to call as soon as his office opens. Same old asthmatic symptoms."

The captain leaned over. "I'll take care of numb nuts here. Thanks for keeping him under control." Boyd pivoted his knee off the young man's neck and the captain jerked Darryl onto his feet.

Graci-Ella sat on an empty chair next to Boyd. "Thanks for staying."

The captain had Darryl by the scruff of the neck. "State your apology, Weir."

His glance shot daggers at Boyd before he glanced at Graci-Ella. "I'm sorry for calling you a bitch. Can I still be in the calendar?"

"It is my choice who does and who doesn't go into the calendar. I'm focusing on the heroes of this unit. Neither your behavior nor your remarks strike me as especially heroic." She exhaled a sigh. "Look, I'm doing this project on my time, for free." She stared him down. "What hours I spend here, I have to make up for on my regular job. I'm a lawyer. Believe me, I have no problem with saying no to someone with anger management issues."

His face reddened with rage before he turned and ran his fist into the side of the refrigerator, cursing and throwing a tantrum. The captain ordered Wolf and Quinn to take Darryl to the equipment room to scrub down the fire trucks until he worked off some steam. They each grabbed an arm and dragged Darryl down the steps to the garage area.

"This is what happens when you get stuck with the Fire Chief's nephew. I'm going to have to walk through burning coals to fire his ass. But it looks like I'm going to have to call the boss this morning and explain how unsuitable the kid is. He's plain spoiled. Zero self-control Graci-Ella, I apologize for his behavior. I really do." The captain strode into his office.

She smiled at Boyd, and his mind damn near went blank for a minute. Her pen tapped against her paper. "I've decided to use everyone's nickname instead of their real names. I think it'll add a bit of humor and charm to the calendar. Plus, it'll help keep all the men more anonymous." She placed her warm hand on his wrist. "That should also help alleviate any remaining concerns you might be harboring about the project."

She leaned toward him and he got a stronger whiff of her perfume. *Holy hell, I want to run my nose all over her body.*

Boyd shook his head a couple times to clear out the sensual fog. "I thought I made it plain. Guess I didn't. You've got my mind all mixed up. I'm in on the calendar project. I gotta admit it was a hard decision to make. As I've told you, by their lifestyle, I think my ex-wife's new love is selling or running some kind of a drug operation. I've got a private investigator on that aspect of her life. She can live it any way she wants. My main concern is how it could affect Matty." He winced. "Sorry, he doesn't like for me to call him that anymore. He says it's 'babyfied.'"

She laughed, low and sultry. *God, can this woman get any sexier?* "Sounds like he's growing up, Dad."

"I still slip and fall back into old habits."

His cell phone rang a loud beat. "Sorry, that's Aunt Jinny's ring." He slipped his cell from his pocket. "Yeah. Okay, I'm on my way." He disconnected the call. "It's my son." Boyd charged out of the dining room and the tap-tap of high heels followed him as he knocked on Captain Steele's door.

40

"Yeah? Come in."

Boyd pushed open the door. "Captain. Aunt Jinny just called. Matt's having such a hard time breathing, his lips are turning blue. I'm taking him to the emergency room."

"Kid needs oxygen now, Tiny." The captain spied Ivy Jo, part of one of the EMT teams, walking by and yelled for her and Jace to take an ambulance to pick-up Matt. Tiny jogged behind them to the apparatus storage area. Since the required equipment was always kept in the vehicles, all they had to do was open the garage door, hop in and haul ass.

Graci-Ella was impressed with how quickly an ambulance could hit the streets, siren blaring. Captain Steele walked her to the coffee pot and poured them both a cup. "He's got his hands full with his little boy, doesn't he? He's been telling me bits and pieces as we talk and grow closer."

The station chief poured some creamer into his coffee. "Yeah, the kid's a charmer. Well behaved thanks to Tiny teaching him manners and telling him bad behavior is unacceptable." The captain grinned and elbowed her. "But don't let that fool you. That child has six-feet-eight of macho male wrapped around his little finger."

She took another sip of her coffee, surprised at how good it was. "Lucky kid." She glanced at the captain, and they both laughed.

"I'm glad to see he's taken an interest in you. His first wife burned him pretty bad. The weekends he doesn't have Matt, Tiny usually hangs out with some of the guys here at the squad. Basketball, beach volleyball or riding Harleys. Be nice for him to have someone special to join in the fun."

"I've never ridden a Harley or any type of motorcycle for that matter."

"I bet if you'd ask, he'd take you for a ride." The captain smiled as he raised his cup to his lips.

She shook her open hand in an erasing manner. "No. No. If he wants me to have it, he'll give it to me." *Oh God, tell me the heat*

41

I'm feeling on my face is not something he can see because I wouldn't mind Tiny giving me a good ride—motorcycle not mandatory. I'm awful. Just awful!

The captain chuckled and shook his head. "Sorry to leave you, but I have to fill out paperwork on the use of the ambulance since we didn't get a nine-one-one request for it. Call me when you want to start taking pictures of the men. I'm quite pleased with the idea. I'm proud of my group of firemen and firewomen." He glanced at the dent in the refrigerator. "Well, except for one, who I've been ordered to give one more chance. I'm not in the best of moods over the Fire Chief's orders."

"A decision like that could prove dangerous. I think the guy's unstable." She glanced at the large clock on the wall. "I better head into the office. Thank you for agreeing to all this."

"No problem. I've seen too many people lose everything in a fire or hurricane. The local food bank helps a lot of families."

Hurrying down the hallway to her office, the rolled carpet draped over one arm and her new desk lamp under her other, she was surprised to see the furniture she'd picked out yesterday setting outside her door. She placed the lamp and rug on top of the desk before walking into her cheery yellow office.

"Wow, what a difference over that dreary beige!" She glanced at Jo-Jo, standing on a rung of a short ladder and installing her fan. The window was open to allow fresh air in to dispel the paint vapors. "I had no clue you could get all this done so quickly. It looks fabulous so far."

"You picking out a darker shade for the end wall with the window gives the optical illusion of a longer room. Good choice. We'll clean the floor and move in your furniture. Then you can start organizing stuff the way you want it. By the end of the day, no one will recognize this ole closet."

Jo-Jo was right. While he mopped the tile floor, she hurried out to her car to bring in the pictures she wanted hung and her plants. She helped him carry in the desk furniture and place the rug before bringing in the leather club chairs.

Jo-Jo slipped the hammer from his tool belt. "Now, show Ol' Jo-Jo where you want these pictures. On the section of wall at either end of the long, narrow window, she wanted framed prints of two of her favorite Monet paintings—Irises and Wooded Scene. On the wall beside the clients' chairs she wanted framed copies of her diplomas from University of Connecticut, Harvard School of Law, her basketball team at UConn after winning a National Championship, and one of her jumping, making a basket.

"Think you can place them in a large square?"

"Is this you, child?" Jo-Jo stared at the one of her shooting the basket.

"I made All-American with that shot." She elbowed him. "String music. What a night!"

He smiled wide when he looked at her. "Well, I will be! As tall as you is, I shoulda figured you for an athlete and All-American too! Well, bless my stars." He got his tape measure out to start marking where he'd hang them.

Meanwhile, she lugged in her palm tree, remembering Boyd's leaning over to place both the plant and the large pot in her car. She set it in the empty corner so she could look at it whenever she wanted. Dear God, he was a sexy man. Nice too. She unboxed her coat tree and screwed the sections together.

Jo-Jo hung her two plants from the ceiling strips and declared his work done. "The rest is for you to do. Set up your computer, put away your books and files and set out the doo-dads you women like to have in your offices."

"Thank you. I really didn't think it would all fit in here with room to move. You proved me wrong."

"Oh, yee of little faith…" he laughed and ambled up the hallway, pushing his cart holding a ladder, painting supplies and empty paint cans.

By the time Graci-Ella left work that day, her office was up and running. Her files were neatly stored. Files for trials not yet held were stacked on the narrow unit. Shelves were filled with legal books, family pictures and basketball trophies. Everything was organized at last, just the way she liked it. In fact, she was so thrilled with the transformation of her little office, she almost hated to leave it.

CHAPTER SEVEN

Boyd's aunt dropped him at the station about five hours later. He collapsed onto a chair at the large wooden dining room table, the heels of his hands over his eyes as he mentally shifted from scared dad to macho fireman. He took a deep shuddering breath and straightened. The crew had stopped their various chores to circle around him to ask about Matt. Someone set a cup of coffee in front of him. He gave a mock salute with it. "Thanks."

After a couple sips, he sat the cup down and laced his fingers at the back of his head. "Matt has pneumonia. They've got him on oxygen and an IV of meds. He was sleeping when I left. My aunt's going home for something to eat, to grab his favorite books and her crocheting. Do you know all the nurses in the ER know him by name? Isn't that a damn sad state of affairs?"

Jace sat a sandwich in front of Boyd. "Thanks, Jace."

"Sure. You gotta be emotionally beat. I go nuts when little Andy gets the sniffles and cries all night. My wife stays calm, thank God, because I fall apart. It's gotta be doubly hard on you, playing both roles."

This group of co-workers—sometimes pains in the asses, sometimes understanding siblings—were Boyd's family. They understood the emotional stress he was under. "Did the EMT's tell you how bad he looked when we got there?"

Ivy Jo rubbed her hands over his shoulders, massaging his tense muscles. "I told them, Tiny. He was weak as a puff of air. As soon as he saw you, his arms rose toward you. He adores his daddy. That much is clear." She leaned over his shoulder to look into his eyes. "Tiny, we need to get him seen by a specialist in asthma and lung diseases. Want me to look online for some?" She spoke as if this little white boy was her son or nephew. Her genuine concern had Boyd dangling by an emotional thread.

He patted her brown hand and brought it to his lips for a kiss. "If you have the time, I'd really appreciate it. You sure Ryder won't mind?"

"Ryder? You still dating that ugly, old, reprobate?" Quinn winked at her. "He's not getting too frisky, is he?"

She planted a fist on her hip. "Do I ask you questions about your sex life? Don't be prying into mine, which is just fine and double-dandy, by the way."

Captain Steele exited his office and asked about Matt. The siren went off and the location of the fire announced. Half-eaten sandwiches in hand, fire personnel raced to the uniform rooms. How Quinn was able to get in his uniform and gear before anyone else, no one knew. As driver of the largest and newest fire truck, Quinn expected the men assigned to his apparatus to be onboard seconds after he was settled in the seat and revving the diesel engine. Heaven help you if he had to blow the horn and holler your name, because he would ride your ass until the next slow-moving fireman rose to the top of his shit list. His truck *always* had to be the first one out of the station.

Smoke rolled skyward as they turned onto an older residential street. The houses were so close together, the blaze had spread to the homes on either side of the building of the fire's origin.

Boyd dragged the main hose to the fire hydrant farther up the street and, using a large wrench with a pentagon-shaped socket, opened the hydrant and made the connection. He opened the valve and ran to attach the hose to the fire engine, which used a powerful pump to boost the water presser and split it into multiple streams for numerous hoses.

Ivy Jo handed one off to Wolf who slung the hose over his shoulder and practically ran up the rungs of the ladder to reach the roof of the middle house. Boyd co-joined other hoses so more firemen could try their best to extinguish the fires on the nearby homes. Jace took a section and followed his brother Wolf up the ladder, too, in an effort to contain the blaze from the top down.

More fire trucks rolled in and hoses hooked up to distinguish the flames. Captain Steele ordered all the occupants of the houses and onlookers to stand across the street. He inquired until he found out who lived in each house. Had they gotten out safely? Did they have their kids and pets? One mother suddenly went ballistic and could be heard screaming above the din of machinery. Her son was missing. He was with her just a few minutes ago.

The captain spoke into his mouthpiece. "Boyd, got a missing boy. Ten years old. Lives in the middle house, his bedroom is upstairs, middle door on left. His mother thinks he went back inside for a ball glove."

"On it. What's his name?" Boyd grabbed a hose.

"Dustin. It's his dad's glove. He gave it to the boy to keep until he got back from Afghanistan."

"Oh hell, of course he'd risk his life to retrieve it." His Matt would do the same. Boyd flipped down his mask, turned on his oxygen and charged inside to the smoky pandemonium. The blast of heat hit him like a motherfucker. What was it doing to Dustin? Would he know enough to stay close to the floor?

Boyd raced up the steps, going as light on his feet as a giant like him could. He rounded the corner and there lay the boy on the floor. Boyd ran water over the walls and carpet surrounding the kid, not wanting to hit him full force with the hose, lest it take off any of his skin. This way it would soak into him. He reached into the bathroom and hosed down some towels and laid them over Dustin's back before he scooped him off the floor. Sure enough, the boy clutched his dad's baseball glove.

Speaking into his mouthpiece, he told the Captain he had the boy and he was still breathing, although unconscious. "On our way out. Have a stretcher and oxygen ready."

About three steps down, Boyd's boot broke through a step. On a twist and a roll, he maneuvered the kid on top of him when he landed. He jerked his boot out of the hole, but most of the old wood of the step came with it. Holding the kid and the hose took some finesse as he turned around so he could stand. Trouble was he was facing going up instead of going down and the soul of his foot hurt. His mood was going to hell in a hurry.

He backed down a few steps until he passed the solid wall and reached the banisters. At the next step, the board broke, forcing him onto the step he'd just vacated. The stairway was weakening. He kicked the banister free with his good foot and jumped to the floor with the kid, hoping like hell the fire hadn't deteriorated the floor. The last thing he needed was for them to end up in the basement.

The floorboards cracked when his boots hit, splintered, broke and through the dust of a century or more of life. Boyd and the child he held close to his chest fell to the top of the washer and dryer in the basement. The jagged edges of the old lumber tore off part of his face gear. Pain shot through Boyd's head, back and that damn step still clung to his boot. *Fuck!*

He rolled off the dented appliances and, limping, searched for an outside door. On the other side of the basement, concrete steps lead to locked double doors. Laying the kid aside, he checked his pulse and respiratory rate. Both were fair. Boyd snatched his ax from his utility belt and hacked his way out of the wooden portal. Once he had a hole big enough to pass Dustin through, he gave his position and handed the boy off to another firefighter. He made the hole bigger and pushed himself and his step buddy nailed to the bottom of his boot through the ragged hole he'd made.

Once he'd hobbled his way to the ambulance, he could hear

Dustin's mother giving the kid holy hell. Boyd stood beside her. "Ma'am, I know you're upset because your son risked his life and is lucky to have survived. But your husband put him in charge of something." He tipped his head toward the glove Dustin clutched to his chest. "He took the lessons of being responsible you've probably been drilling into him and knew he had to get that glove for his dad. Kids think differently than adults. They haven't mentally matured the capacity to reason things through, they just react."

She nodded and started to cry. "Yes, I know."

"You've got a fine son, ma'am. He's one to be proud of. He truly is."

He hobbled away to the other ambulance and asked someone to remove the board from his boot. It was all he could do to keep from yelling a string of cuss words when the EMT pulled out the nail for it had gone through his boot into his foot.

"Take your boot off. Let me look at that hole. You up to date on your tetanus shots?" The older, barrel chested man gave him the stink eye which galled him even more.

"Aren't we all? It's a company requirement." He removed his boot and blood ran out. "Put some antiseptic on it, a patch and wrap it up. Looks like we've got hours of work left here today."

"If you think I'm letting you…"

Boyd grasped the old man's shirt. "You have no freaking idea the day I've had already. Don't give me a bunch of bullshit. Fix my foot so I can do my damn job."

The old man yelled for the captain who took one look at Boyd's foot and pointed to the ambulance where the boy was being cared for. They rode to the hospital together, an ice pack on Boyd's face where the wood had ripped away part of his protective mask.

A shower, a salad and a glass of wine and Graci-Ella had unwound enough from her day at work to watch the news she always recorded on the TV. Tonight, local news topped national. A fire destroyed one house and did serious damage to two others. One fireman rescued a boy from a burning building, falling through the steps and floor to the basement in the process. The boy sustained minor injuries and was released. The fireman was hospitalized.

The camera panned on the kid who talked in a hoarse voice about this giant of a man who kept him safe as they fell through floors and then carried him out of the building. "He was like Superman, but with bigger muscles, and he kept telling me I was going to be okay. Sometimes he called me by my real name and sometimes he'd call me Matty. I think maybe he got hit on the head and was confused."

She sat straight in her comfy chair. Matty? The man the kid boasted about had to be Boyd. How badly was he hurt? She thumbed through her cell phone numbers until she found Noah Steele, Station thirty-two. A press of her thumb to call, and he answered on the second ring.

"Captain Steele here."

"This is Graci-Ella. I just heard about the fire today on the news. I record it every day so I don't miss it." *Stop rambling. I sound moronic.*

His smile almost filtered across the phone lines like a handful of glitter. "And you want to know if it was Tiny who was hurt and how bad his injuries were and what room he was assigned at Bay Care Health System?"

Lord have mercy. Is this man a mind reader?

She twirled a strand of damp hair around her finger. "Well… ah…I knew he had a rough day with his son. I was hoping it wasn't him. I do have his number, but I didn't know if he'd have his cell or be in any shape to talk."

A slow chuckle crackled over the line. "I'm an old army dawg, honey. I don't mince words, especially when I see an instant attraction between two people I like. He's in room three-ten. Take him some snicker doodles from Westside Bakery. Remember, room three-ten." He ended the call and she flew to her bedroom to put on some clothes.

She called the bakery to see if they were still open and did they have snicker doodles. Did they also have chocolate chip pecan cookies and coconut macaroons? She ordered a dozen of the kind Boyd liked and a dozen mixed for herself. A change from her pajamas to red shorts, a white tank top over a red bra and red sneakers, as well as a quick make-up job, a spritz of perfume and she was out the door.

The hospital elevator stopped on the third floor and she made a turn, following the corridor toward Boyd's room. Was she chasing after this guy like some needy female? He talked as if he was really into her, but was he? After all, they'd only met a few days ago. She glanced at the bag of boxed cookies. My God, she'd even gone out of her way to bring him his favorites. But, what if Captain Steele was teasing her, trying to make a fool of her? What if Boyd absolutely hated their cookies? She chewed her bottom lip; better to take them to work tomorrow and set the cookies out in the lunch room. Except, few of her co-workers would appreciate them. That was the thing.

She leaned against the edge of the open door to three-ten, working up the courage to peek in. If he was asleep, she'd just leave the cookies and run. Slowly she leaned around the doorjamb and peered in. His eyes were closed. His face was patched on one side. As quietly as she could, she set the bag on his nightstand and turned to leave. A wrist snaked out and grabbed her forearm.

Her head whipped around and gray eyes bore into hers. The heat of a blush traveled up her neck and across her cheeks. "I didn't mean to waken you."

"You didn't." His hand released hers and slid around her waist, pulling her closer to the edge of the bed. "Your perfume did. Why did you wait so long to come in?" His gray gaze slid over her face. "I didn't think women blushed anymore." His perusal continued downward until it landed on her red lace bra under her tank top. "Why is it everything about you turns me on in a heartbeat?" He cleared his throat and exhaled a deep sigh.

"Please don't tell me that pink and green bag is from Westside Bakery and has snicker doodles in it." He entwined his fingers with hers and drew her to the bed next to his chest and she sat.

Quietly.

"Well?" His other hand swept her long hair before he cupped the back of her head and brought her face close to his. Their breaths mingled. Her lips were an inch away from his, and temptation's fingers were pushing her closer.

"You asked me not to tell you." She offered him a sly smile.

"Woman, you could drive a man mad." He reached for the bag and shoved his hand in. His wide smile was a three-pointer from downtown. And she did love those three-pointers. What melted her heart even more, was he opened the box and offered her one first.

"The other box is for me. Chocolate chip pecan as well as coconut macaroons. The box you're holding is all yours."

He bite into one of his cookies and moaned.

She pulled her box out of the bag and opened it. "How's Matt?"

"A nurse was kind enough to wheel me down to see him. He's doing better. Poor kid got all upset when he saw my face. I told him a bedtime story. He'll be here until his pneumonia clears up."

"What did he say about your boo-boos?"

The corners of his lips lifted as did one dark eyebrow. "Boo-boos? Please tell me you've got experience at kissing boo-boos."

She bit into a macaroon and chewed. Hmm, the coconut was very moist, just the way she liked it. "Yes. As a matter of fact, I do. Even black eyes."

He stopped chewing for a couple beats. "I don't have a black eye."

"Oh, but you do. Right here above your patch." She poked it with her finger.

"Ow! You're mean! You're one of those *mean* lawyers." She started laughing. He reached for another cookie and waved it around as he told her about going into the inferno after Dustin and the kid's dad's ball glove. He listed everything that went wrong on their way down the stairway. He wiggled his eyebrows. "So, I've got a lot of boo-boos that need kissed."

Someone announced on the intercom that visiting hours were over. Boyd groaned.

"Don't worry, Boyd. I won't take your cookies away from you."

"There're two things I want from you before you leave. I want to hold you close so I can line my lungs with the smell of your perfume and I want a goodnight kiss." His gray eyes darkened to stormy gray.

"I'll hug you, but I never kiss a man on a first date." *Although, Lord knows I'd love a taste of your lips, cinnamon crumbs and all.*

"But this isn't a date. It's an appreciation kiss for a cookie run."

He wrapped his arms around her and pulled her over him. She allowed him to nuzzle the sensitive part of her neck beneath her ear. Being held within the strength of his muscles was probably the sexiest thrill she'd ever had. He inhaled her essence, and it was the most erotic thing she'd ever experienced because of the way he held her and groaned. Allowing him to kiss her would most definitely not be a good decision on her part.

She pulled back and cupped his one cheek. "Good night, Boyd. I'm glad Matt is doing better and I'm happy you're not seriously hurt."

He smiled wide and her heart turned over. "No kiss tonight?"

She patted his hard, muscled chest she'd just snuggled against. "Not on your life. I don't give them away freely."

He pouted. "But I've got boo-boo's." He pointed with his index finger. "See this big scratch over my forehead into my hairline?"

She pressed a gentle kiss to it.

"I tore part of my earlobe away from my head. They had to stitch it back on. See?" Again, he pointed.

Oh, she could see where this was going. She kissed it and his arm slid around her back. The warmth from his large hand sending wake-up calls to her sex-starved hormones as he slowly circled across her waist and hips.

"And I have a little black eye that didn't hurt at all until you

53

poked your finger into it."

"Oh, geesh, what a big baby." She chuckled and kissed his eye, checking his mouth for any damages, just in case he tried any shenanigans there.

"And…and I bit the inside of my bottom lip." Mr. Innocence pointed with his finger.

"Oh, you did not. Next thing you'll be telling me you scratched your cock." *Oh, crap! I did not say that.*

His face lit up. "Hey, I hadn't thought of that, but…"

She covered his lips with hers for a second just to shut him up. Only the second dragged on for minutes—heavenly minutes. His tongue ran across her lips as a signal for her to open them and she did. Her tongue touched his and fireworks went off in her sex. He tasted of cinnamon and sugar and sin. Oh, dear Lord, could she get enough? Much more and she'd be in the hospital bed on top of him. "That's it. I'm out of kisses. Finished. Kaput. Done."

His calloused hand slowly slid up her arm, sending both chills and waves of heat over her body at the same time. "That was a cure-what-ales-you kiss. Potent as hell. Safe travels home, Sweetness."

She looked at her clasped hands. "I think we're moving too fast. I want to get to know you better before this turns physical. I don't go into relationships lightly."

"However you want it. You want slow, we'll go slow. It's going to be hard for me to trust a woman again, but you have to know I'm very attracted to you. I enjoy your personality. It's both sweet and sassy."

She nodded and her gaze lifted to stare into his grey eyes. Her heart rolled over.

He smiled and winked. "Where do you get your coffee in the mornings?"

"Java Joes. Why?" If he thought she was going to bring him fresh coffee on her way to work, he was out of his freaking mind.

"I'd like hazelnut, tall, with half and half. A copy of *The Tampa Bay Times* and a pumpkin muffin."

She braced her hands on her hips and leaned down. "Mister, if you're looking for a Sugar Momma, you've missed your mark. A tall hazelnut and a pumpkin muffin…what do I look like? Boyd's private food delivery?"

He smirked as if he wanted to say something as he reached and opened the drawer to his nightstand. He pulled out a money clip with an emblem that read, "Clearwater's Fireman of the Year" and peeled off a twenty dollar bill. "Here. Let me treat you to your morning cup of coffee. And from here on out, don't ask me a question you don't want me to answer."

Somewhat chagrinned, she took the money. "What…what question did I ask?"

"You asked me what you looked like. I wanted to tell you that you looked vibrant as hell when you're pissed about something. That you're one gorgeous woman. And I can't wait until I have you under me, over me, up against the wall and bending over the kitchen table."

Holy Shit!

She glanced down and saw his erection tenting the sheet.

Too bad he didn't scratch his cock, because I wouldn't mind kissing all of that. Yeah, so much for my speech about taking things slow.

"I…I better say goodnight."

He'd obviously noticed where she'd been staring. "Goodnight, babe." His voice held a tender intimacy she'd not heard before. She leaned over him again and hugged him. "Get well, big guy."

CHAPTER EIGHT

Graci-Ella was like a burst of sunshine when she waltzed into his room the next morning, wearing a yellow ruffled top with a wide yellow belt and a black tight skirt. Her stilettoes were black. Everything about her stirred his libido, even the way she had her dark hair in one long braid.

It didn't escape Boyd that she looked tense. Their almost instant attraction probably had her spooked the way it did him. And her seeing his raging hard-on last night was a little embarrassing in the light of day, especially since he'd sported a woody as soon as she walked in this morning. Christ, he was worse than a teenager. He raised his one knee to try to hide it under the wrinkled sheets. "Good morning, Sweetness. You look beautiful."

"Thanks. I'm not used to compliments, but I'll take it just the same." She smiled and set his large coffee on his nightstand along with the pumpkin pastry. "Do you know how many calories are in one of those big top muffins?" Her eyebrow arched as she handed him the newspaper.

"I'll work the calories off." Fuck, how he wanted to tell her how he'd like to work them off making slow love to her. Then again, he'd pretty much told her that last night.

Her mind must have traveled down the same path for her cheeks blushed the prettiest color. "Well, ah…I need to get to the office. I'm in court today, defending clients I don't approve of and I know I shouldn't say that. But the law says we're all owed due process. These are a slimy bunch of car thieves who deserve a kick in the pants in my humble opinion. But my bosses take on these cases and then hand them off to flunkies like me." She brushed an errant strand of hair off her cheek. "I'm sorry. So often justice swings the wrong way."

"It's a little early in your career to be so jaded." He tugged the plastic lid off his coffee, the fragrant steam rolled out.

"There are times I wish I'd gone into photography, but I'd have hurt my parents. Besides, you have to be really good with a camera to make a career with it."

"Graci-Ella, I think you'd be damned good at anything you put your mind to." His gaze locked on her blue eyes and her plump lips. God, how he wanted to pull her to him and hold her for a while. Something in her career was making her unhappy. "Thank you for the coffee and calories. You have a good day, Sweetness."

She nodded, leaned over and, cupped his face, kissing him quickly, before hurrying off.

At lunchtime, hurried footfalls and bursts of gas headed for his room. "Which room is our boy in? Name's Boyd Calloway. He's our adopted son." Boyd knew who was coming. Two elderly men his squad had adopted—Milt, known as Gas Ass, and Sam, referred to as Hell's Bells. They lived in a world of their own but, damn, everyone at the station loved them to death. Milt was excitable, nosy and eager to help. Sam, whose daughter Molly was married to fellow fireman, Barclay, was under medication for the early stages of dementia. The two old men were thick as gray, wrinkled thieves.

Milt passed gas as he rounded the corner. "How come we had to hear on the news you were hurt and in the hospital?" His fists grabbed his belt and hiked up his pants. "We didn't even hear from Sam's son-in-law, Barclay, until this morning. I looked at Sam and said, 'Put your teeth in. We're going to the hospital to check on our boy and raise hell about why you didn't call us.' Are we family, or not?" The red-faced, skinny old man was puffing, no doubt from the exertion of getting there. He collapsed into a chair and put-putted some more.

"I don't have my phone, Gas Ass. We don't take them along to fires because the heat will melt them. I'm sorry no one thought to call you last night. I'm thinking the crew stayed on the scene until late in case timbers caught fire again. That's often standard procedure when the fire's bad—and that one was."

Milt huffed, somewhat mollified. "Well, okay then. You know how we worry, you guys being in dangerous work, and all."

Boyd turned his attention to Sam, who'd already slumped into a wooden chair and whose face was white. "Did Gas Ass drive here like a maniac?"

"Oh, Hell's Bells!" Sam removed his "Grandpa" ball cap and wiped sweat off his nearly baldhead with his handkerchief. "He honked his horn and cussed a policeman who didn't use a turn signal to make a turn. Ran an old woman in a new Cadillac off the road. Drove over the sidewalk twice, sparks flying from his undercarriage." Sam scowled at Milt. "And I ain't talkin' about his car, neither."

Boyd held his stomach as he laughed at those two old coots. Was it any wonder Milt and Sam had become the station's human mascots?

"We bought some little toys for Matt." Milt held up a bag. "Matchbox cars and fire trucks. How's he doin'? What room is he in?"

"Two-twenty-nine. I got to see him for a little while this morning. He seemed to breathe easier. Thanks, guys, for thinking of us."

Milt perked up. "Hey, you need a ride home? We'll come get you. Be right honored to do so. Be our pleasure to take care of one of our boys, won't it, Sam?"

Sam leaned toward Boyd. "You ain't got a bad heart, does ya?"

"I appreciate your offer, Milt, but my aunt Jinny's coming to get me. She lives a few doors up from where I do." Would be nice to have Graci-Ella take him home, but she'd be at work. He better fill in the guys. "Got some news for you. Something I haven't shared with the squad yet."

Both old codgers leaned forward, obviously pleased they were getting a scoop.

"You know I haven't dated because of the custody hearing coming up." Two bald heads nodded. "I met someone."

"You hear that, Sam? Our boy's found himself a woman. What's she like?"

"Gorgeous, tall, the bluest eyes you ever saw and a smile that's brighter than sunlight. She's a lawyer and does photography on the side. Her name's Graci-Ella."

"Pretty name, huh, Milt?" Sam settled his hat on his head and beamed a smile.

He might as well put the icing on the gossip cake for he knew the two would leave the hospital and drop by the station. "Don't say anything to the squad yet. They might have their suspicions, but we just decided to start dating. And we're both a little wary about it just yet. Dating at our age, with a child involved, can be a big step. Right?"

Milt passed gas and nodded. "I see your point. We won't tell a soul."

"Mums the word." Sam made a zipping motion across his lips.

Both men started making excuses to leave and Boyd could barely keep from laughing. He'd lay bet as soon as they gave Matt his present, they'd be headed for Station Thirty-two. "Our squad's off duty now." Both faces drooped. "Matt will be glad to see the both of you. I can't tell you how much you guys mean to him."

Milt's pigeon chest puffed out. "Ya hear that, Sam? Let's go down and entertain the little fella."

As soon as the senior citizens left, Boyd reached for the phone beside his bed and called Graci-Ella, hoping he'd memorized her cell number correctly. He got her voicemail.

"Sweetness, if you come by the hospital to see me, I'll share my gourmet hospital supper with you. There might be a kiss for dessert. Okay, there will most definitely be a kiss for dessert. Hope your trial case went well."

Shortly after six, a hand holding a bag from Crabby Joes waved up and down the edge of his open door.

"Do I get a kiss with that?" He slid up in his bed.

"Nope. Just fries."

"I damn well better get a kiss."

She strutted in and set the bag and drinks on the movable table. "How are you feeling, big guy?"

He pointed to his lips.

She rolled her eyes and leaned over him. He wrapped his arms around her and dragged her over him before he partially rolled on top of her. He slid his hand down her thighs and calves, tossing her black heels onto the floor. His fingertips trailed over her forehead and her eyes closed. He pressed a gentle kiss to each one. "You look tired, Sweetness." He rubbed his hand up and down her back as she snuggled closer and exhaled a huge sigh. "Tell me about your day."

"Our food will get cold." She kissed his neck.

"Give me the highlights first, then we'll eat and you can fill in the details." He rubbed his cheek against hers. "I hate seeing you so exhausted."

"Court plays me out mentally and emotionally when it's a difficult case to defend. Losing is never an option, not if I want to get ahead and make my parents proud."

Boyd pulled back and looked at her. "Isn't being the wonderful woman you are enough to make them proud?" What the hell kind of people were they?

Tears pooled and she rubbed her face against his neck, her arms tightened around his neck. Now was not the time to query her. She needed to get her mind off her rough day. After a few light kisses, they ate their soft crab sandwiches and Old Bay french fries. He told her about the visit with Milt and Sam. She smiled and asked questions about the two men. At last he could sense her relaxing.

He crumpled their trash and threw it in the wastepaper can. Trailing his fingertips over her face, he kissed her temple. "Sweetness, I want you to go to your place and get some rest. I'll be going home tomorrow. Would you like to go out to supper with me? Or, if you prefer, a picnic on the beach at sunset and a walk along the shoreline?"

"Oh, the picnic while we watch the sunset sounds great."

He kissed both of her hands. "We'll text about the time I should pick you up."

She was almost through the door when she stopped and looked back over her shoulder. "You never asked if I won or lost my case today."

"I figured if you wanted me to know, you'd tell me. Having you with me for an hour or so meant more to me than whether you won a case. You're a winner as a person. That's what matters."

She smiled and walked out as she said, "Thanks, big guy."

CHAPTER NINE

Matt had come home from the hospital with Boyd around noon. They'd played Wii games for two hours before Boyd put him to bed and read him book after book. Both napped. Aunt Jinny came over with two picnic dinners. One for her and Matt to eat on the patio, and one for him and Graci-Ella to enjoy on the beach.

Boyd rang her doorbell and could barely think of a coherent greeting when Graci-Ella opened the door in a one-piece, hot pink swimsuit with a sheer pink and lime green floral wrap tied at her waist and kissing her ankles. Her brunette hair was tied into a ponytail with a pink ribbon. The woman could be a model on a runway. She smiled and he forced out, "Hey."

"Did your aunt pack wine? I have a bottle and some plastic goblets, if she didn't."

"She stuck in a couple bottles of water, so some wine to sip as the sun sets would be great." The vision in pink grabbed a bottle in an insulated bag and some unbreakable glasses. She held her hand out for him to hold, but it was her whole body he wanted—needed.

He helped her into his Mustang and leaned in to buckle her seatbelt and kiss her forehead, lips and the curve of her neck before he closed her door. He pulled onto route 60 and sped toward Clearwater Beach. He hung a left onto South Gulfview Boulevard and pulled into a fairly deserted spot along the beach.

They spread a blanket at the base of a palm tree, and she kicked off their sandals. Boyd kept his sneakers on to protect his foot from sand. While they ate, they talked about their growing up years. How he ended up as a fireman and why she left Maryland to come to Florida. He opened the wine as the red ball of the sun rested for a few minutes on the watery horizon of the Gulf of Mexico. They sipped their wine and drank from each other's mouths.

"This is so romantic," she breathed as the sun sank below the horizon, turning the sky orange, pink and purple.

"Being alone with you is what's romantic, Sweetness." He lay flat on the blanket and she lay on top of him while they exchanged more kisses and caresses. Their passion grew and he pulled down the strap of her swimsuit and kissed her breast, drawing her nipple into his mouth. God, how he wanted her, but not out here where someone might see his woman or hear her scream as he brought her to climax. She was his; privately his. And he cherished her.

Boyd was positive he walked without a limp when he reported to work two days after he'd been discharged from the hospital. He'd been chomping at the bit to return to his job.

Jace glanced over his shoulder as he made a fresh pot of coffee. "Hey! Tiny's back!"

The squad chanted "Where's Tiny?" Then answered, "In the basement, doing laundry," referring to his falling through the floor and landing on the washer and dryer in the burning house.

He shook his head and grinned. Man, it was good to be back with this batch of misfits. They kept his mind off things, like his upcoming trial and the brunette he'd held in his arms to watch the sunset the other evening. He knocked on Captain Steele's office door.

"Enter. Unless you're Boyd Calloway trying to pretend you're okay and ready to come back to work. 'Cause I ain't believin' that shit."

Boyd opened the door and grinned. "Now, boss, you know

you missed me."

The captain sipped from his coffee mug and pointed to an empty chair in front of his desk. "Yeah. Like a hemorrhoid I had to have burned off with a blow torch." Boyd sat while the captain narrowed his eyes. "You still got a limp."

"The hell I do. Matt's back at school and I'm cleared for work."

"By who? Wanda, the Witchdoctor? Let me see the form declaring you fit for duty." He held out his hand.

Boyd gave him the paper and the captain scanned over it. "Says you're cleared for light labor for two weeks. That means you can help with general office work and cleaning equipment while sitting down. And…" the captain pointed a finger, "…if you don't whine your ass off, I'll allow you to help Graci-Ella with the calendar project."

Boyd knew when he was being railroaded. "Just what are you up to?"

The captain leaned back in his chair, his hands behind his neck. "Looks like you put on some weight while you were off. You haven't been eating a lot of snicker doodles, have you?" No doubt knowing he'd hit a soft spot, he sat forward and gulped his coffee.

"You!" Boyd exploded. "You were behind her coming to the hospital with my favorite cookies, looking sexy as hell in that red lace bra."

Captain spewed coffee over his desk and pristine shirt. "Hell! A red lace bra? Well, do tell." He held up three fingers. "And scout's honor, I won't repeat a word to a soul in the squad." He grabbed a rag to blot his shirt and wipe off his desk top.

Boyd stood, ashamed of his slip of the tongue. "You can kiss my ass. I'm not telling you a word about her. Where do you want me to start working?"

By his nonstop laughter, the captain was right proud of himself. "Use a stool and scrub down ambulance number three. Use a long-handled brush on the high sections and top. Shine all the chrome."

"You got it." He turned to exit the captain's office and noticed the door was cracked open about an inch. He passed by Darryl, who was filling the copier, that sat outside the door, with paper. Darryl glared at Boyd as he passed as if that was supposed to make him tremble with fear.

Time passed as a few of the crew stopped to inquire about Matt. It wasn't long until the guys didn't do much talking. They just stood there watching him, with ear to ear grins. Every once in a while, one would remark that they sure could eat a cookie.

Boyd stood, stretched his back and headed for the captain's office. He'd promised Boyd he wouldn't say a word about their previous conversation. As he passed the restrooms, a poster printed with a red, lace bra on a voluptuous, headless body along with the words, "No wonder Tiny healed so fast with his favorite cookies delivered by a certain brunette wearing a sexy red bra."

He jerked it down. Yanked an identical one off the shower room doors as well as the entrance to the captain's office. Boyd knocked on Noah's door and waited for the captain's typical "Enter" before he barged in, waving the papers. "Damn you! You told me you wouldn't say a word."

Captain Noah Steele had a way of puffing himself up when he was confronted about something. "What the hell are you ranting about?"

Boyd handed him one of the posters. "Are you going to tell me you didn't make these up? You're the only one I slipped up with and mentioned the red bra. It had to be you."

The captain scanned the page. "Hell, man. I didn't do this. I might verbally tease the hell out of somebody, but this is too far. Someone must have overheard our conversation. I don't agree with this shit. Are there any more?" He rounded his desk, and both men went on a scavenger hunt. Boyd spied one taped to the microwave and the refrigerator. The captain located another tacked to a piece of cardboard on top of the big screen television. "I'm gonna grind someone's ass when I find out who printed these up. That's the bad part of having free access to the computers in the lounge area. God knows what all gets done or seen."

A call came in for the marine rescue team; a boat was stuck on a sandbar. Wolf, commander of the rescue team, took Jace in Boyd's place. Wolf and Barclay did the diving. Quinn drove the rescue craft and Boyd normally handled any heavy equipment or bodies as they pulled them out of the water. Being left behind didn't help his mood any.

As soon as he had the ambulance shining, he went to the kitchen to see if he could help with supper. Emily, who was checking chickens in three crockpots, jerked her thumb toward the two bags of apples on the counter. "You can peel those apples to put in a pan along with butter, brown sugar and cinnamon. I'll scrub potatoes to bake. Might as well fill both ovens."

Emily glanced over her shoulder. "I plan on making a big casserole of baked beans. Gas Ass and Sam are coming for supper tonight."

"You're a demon. Doesn't the old man fart enough?"

She nodded, her mass of short red curls bobbing. "I've never heard anyone pass gas almost as continually as him. Honest to Pete, if he were a balloon, he'd be halfway across the Gulf Bay by now. If he'd only learn to leave those pork rinds alone. They're not good for him. Hey, how's your foot doing?"

"I don't see why everyone's making such a big fuss out of it. Hell, it's only a little nail hole." He yanked a big bowl from the cabinet and a large baking pan beside it. He was about halfway through the second bag when he heard the marine rescue team return downstairs, laughing and teasing each other. Evidently things had gone well.

The side door alarm buzzed and Emily jogged to let in whoever was there. "Hey! Wasn't expecting you tonight. Come on in."

"I thought I'd stop by to see who all turned in their significant others' signed agreement papers. Captain Steele called to say everyone who was going to participate had turned them in. Once I see who all's onboard, I'll know what months I'll want to assign

66

them and how I want to photograph each man."

Boyd pointed to his lips and Graci-Ella rolled her eyes before leaning to give him a peck on the lips. She slapped a permission form down in front of him with her signature signed in a bold purple marker. "There's yours, big guy."

He stared at it, absorbed the meaning of her signing one for him and warmed up inside. "I'll be sure to give it to the boss."

Her palm rested on his shoulder. "How's your first day back at work going?"

He wrapped his hands around her waist and set her on his lap. "I'm only half back. I'm on light duty. Cleaning equipment, cooking and office odds and ends for the chief." He stared into her pretty blue eyes. If he had to spend much time around her, he'd be a goner.

Yeah, as if I'm not already.

"Smells like chicken in the crockpots." She stood and sauntered toward them in a pair of pale blue, ankle strap stilettoes that matched the top she wore with her dark blue skirt, which was barely a swath of material. Lord, the woman had legs that went to her waist. Not those skinny peg legs either, but firm, fleshy thighs. The kind a man wanted to kiss until he reached paradise.

She stopped and stared at something hanging from the potted plant at the window.

Damn it to hell. Those red bra posters. I missed that one.

She ripped the paper off the plant and whirled toward him. Her blue eyes held pain before they flashed cobalt with anger as she tore the poster into pieces.

Why did he suddenly feel Graci-Ella was not a woman to mess with when she was pissed? By the time she got back to the table where he sat, her hands were fisted around scraps of paper. "Did you find my late night cookie run a joke? My attire something to boast to all the guys about? You and your *top notch* fire station can go to hell. I've worked too hard to be made fun of, *Tiny*." And there was something about the way she spat the name Tiny that sent his irritability up a notch or two. Hell, he'd never do such a thing to disrespect her.

"Look, Ms.-Temper-Tantrum, I didn't have anything to do with those posters. I did leave it slip to the captain about your bra, but it slipped out before I knew it. Someone must have overheard me."

Graci-Ella reared back like a boa-constrictor, ready to attack, spun and charged for Captain Steele's workplace. The sound of a feminine growl floated around the corner, as she tore another poster from his door before bursting in. Who the hell had put another one there?

"Most people knock before they barge into my space, young lady." The door slammed and raised voices filtered from the office.

Emily shoved Boyd's arm. "You better haul ass in there before those two come to blows. You need to state your side of things. Take her someplace private and smooth out the situation. Take it from me, women don't appreciate that kind of shit. And how I missed that paper while I was getting the chickens ready for the crockpot is beyond me." Emily eased the paring knife from Boyd's grip. "Her feelings are hurt, Tiny. You need to soothe them. Show her you'll take care of her, because that's what a man does."

When the voices emanating from the captain's office hit a higher octave, Boyd hurried to the point of origin and surged in. He didn't want Graci-Ella bellowed at like that.

Captain Steele threw up his hands in disgust as Boyd charged in. "Doesn't anyone knock on my door anymore? Hell, I might as well take it off the freaking hinges."

"I don't want her yelled at. I'm the one who wasn't in control of my mouth this morning and let it slip about the red lace bra. Hell, I haven't been able to get it out of my mind." He turned his gaze at Graci-Ella, who had her back to both of the men. "I'm sorry. I had no idea what would happen."

"And I didn't make them, but I'll find out who did." Noah jammed his hands in his pockets to jingle his change. "This is a high-stress job, Graci-Ella. We reduce those levels by teasing and harassing each other. That's why the nicknames. The games. But those signs went too far and I apologize for that."

Boyd saw tears hanging onto her eyelashes when she turned around. The urge to protect her raged through his system.

She wouldn't look at him, but spoke to Noah instead. "I still can't complete the job. How can I get the best photos out of the men when they don't respect me? When they'll be wondering or asking what color bra I'm wearing. I'll either go to a different station or pay for another photographer."

"Captain, would you mind going for a walk so Graci-Ella and I can iron this out in private?" Boyd hoped he could get her to listen and understand how his verbal blunder was just that—a slip of the tongue.

The door clicked shut, and Boyd ran his fingers through his hair, hoping like hell he'd find the right words. "I'm sorry, Graci-Ella. Surely by now, you know I think you're pretty special." He wiped her tears away with his thumbs. "I wouldn't have you hurt for the world." He kissed one eye and then the other. "Don't cry, Sweetness."

She narrowed her eyes and gave him a skeptical scowl. He'd better continue talking to keep her mind off how pissed she was. "When I returned to work, I was hoping the captain wouldn't ask for the forms from the doctor. I just wanted to dive back into my normal routine because I haven't been right since I first laid eyes on you. God, you're gorgeous." He glanced at his feet. "And nice. Very nice to bring me my favorite cookies from my favorite bakery. And at night too. I mean, you kissed all my boo-boos. Then you were doubly nice the next morning to bring me my favorite coffee, muffin and a paper so I had something to read. You sure looked beautiful in that yellow and black dress. And I don't know where you've been buying those sexy as hell shoes, but I want to buy stock in the company."

She laughed and his gaze rose to meet hers. "We've been growing closer. Please don't allow someone's idea of a sick joke pull us apart. I have a sneaky feeling Darryl was behind this, but I have no proof. I was sure I closed this door when I came in to turn in my medical forms. When I went to leave, it was cracked open, and Darryl was loading paper into the copier beside the door."

He shifted toward her and took her hands in his. "You know, I wondered how you knew about the kind of cookies I love until Noah, the captain, started teasing me this morning. Then I caught on that he'd talked you into doing it. I was embarrassed and hurt and pissed he'd stuck his nose in where it didn't belong, and my mouth just started running. Looks like I said some things I shouldn't have."

He circled her waist with his arms. "I want you to tell me if any of those sonsabitches says one thing out of line to you. And God help them if they touch you. We've talked about that already, you and I. A man would be taking his life in his hands to mess with you or hurt you in any way. You're a sweet person, Graci-Ella. You deserve respect and to be treated well."

She tilted her head. "Do I deserve a kiss?"

His eyebrows shot up. "From me?"

She looked around him. "I don't see anyone else in this office."

Oh hell, was she forgiving him this easily? He stepped her back against the wall, and her eyes widened.

He cupped the back of her head with one hand and tipped her face toward his with two fingers under her chin. His lips swept lightly across hers from one side to the other. "I've been starving for the taste of you since our goodnight kiss last night." There was more pressure in his lips as they brushed back to the other corner of her delectable mouth. "Between your eyes, your body and those legs that go on for a country mile, how could any man resist you?"

His lips covered hers gently until he needed more. He sucked her bottom lip, and she moaned. His tongue slipped in and caressed every part of the inside of her mouth.

Her hands fisted in his t-shirt and then slid over his shoulders and around his neck. His other hand left her chin and went to

70

her ass, bringing her against his erection. He rubbed her against it to create some sweet friction. He wanted her to know how she affected him. Her tongue responded to his and the kiss deepened. For a moment, he didn't think he could ever stop.

He left a trail of nibbles and kisses on her jawline, and she angled her head to grant him more access and moaned. "How do you know all my sensitive spots already?"

His teeth slid down her throat; his mind a haze of sexual need. "Baby, I'm going to take delight in learning all your sensitive spots." His mouth covered hers again, more masterful this time.

She ran her tongue over his neck, and he nearly dropped to his knees. She bit his earlobe and his eyes damn near crossed. God, she could turn him on. "Am I off your shit list now?"

"Do I get to stay for supper?" She sucked his bottom lip.

"Only if you sit next to me."

She leaned back and stared into his eyes. "What if someone teases me about that red bra? It wasn't like I hadn't worn a top over it. I did."

He smiled before pressing his lips to her ear. "And a mighty fine top it was too."

CHAPTER TEN

While she sat next to Boyd on one of the sofas in the TV room, Graci-Ella went over the permission forms signed by the wives and significant others, paper clipping them to the pictures she'd taken of the fire personnel the other day, so she knew who all she'd have to work with. "Darn, I'm two short." She went through the stack again.

Boyd had his arm around her shoulders. Being so close to him was a great feeling. "I've got an idea if you don't mind a suggestion."

"From you, of course not." Her insides still trembled from their previous kissing session. She'd have to hang her panties from her radio antenna to get them dried before her meeting with a client, though where she'd pull over and shimmy back into them, she hadn't a clue. Sweet heavens, she'd never had a man take command of her mouth like that and yet be tender enough to give her what she wanted.

He fingered through the stack of photos and tapped at one. "Well, when Wolf moved into a townhouse next to Becca, his wife now. Her German shepherd, Einstein, used to steal a pair of her thongs and carry them over to Wolf every chance he got. It was damn comical the ways that dog would think of to sneak a pair of Becca's thongs to their new neighbor, like he was a match-making canine or something. If you could get a shot of Wolf next to Einstein with a pair of Becca's thongs in the dog's mouth, like maybe red for Valentine's Day or white with red hearts. That might be cute."

"Oh, I love it. Do you think I could talk Wolf into it?"

"Are you kidding? You saw how he was the other night. Since he found out they're expecting, the man's in seventh heaven. He'll agree to most anything. He's also commander of the marine rescue unit, so a pic of him in that capacity would show him in a different light. Use *him* twice."

"What a great idea." She gazed into Boyd's gray eyes that crinkled at the corners when he smiled. "Do you always kiss a woman like you did me a little while ago?"

He twirled his fingers around her hair. "You're the first woman I've kissed since a month or more before my ex-wife moved out. At first, I was so filled with anger, I didn't want another woman in my life. I barely talked to a female, except for my aunt Jinny. By the time I'd worked through all that, we were in the middle of preparations for a custody hearing. I've been so worried about losing Matt, I haven't dated, even though my ex lives with another man. Then I met you and I changed my mind. I most definitely want a relationship with you."

She smiled and ran her hand down his arm and traced his pronounced veins with a fingertip. A slight shudder went over him. She bet he really missed the feminine touch.

"How come someone as special as you isn't dating anyone?"

"I've been too busy with work since I moved here from Columbia, Maryland."

His phone played the Sesame Street title song, and he reached to tug it out of its scabbard. "That's Matt's ring." He swiped the screen. "Hey buddy, what's up?" There was excited conversation from the other end of the line. "Aunt Jinny is absolutely right. She's only doing what I told her. Don't you 'oh Dad' me! Either you take an hour's nap now or you go to bed an hour earlier tonight. Be glad I'm giving you a choice. You're still recuperating. So am I.

"Know what I've been allowed to do at work today? Shine the chrome on an ambulance and help out in the kitchen. No assisting with marine rescue or fires for *two* whole weeks. I know you're bummed about the nap thing. I'm pretty bummed about work too. Life's not always fair, is it? Now, tell me who's the best dad?" A little boy's giggling began. "You better tell me or I'll start singing. You know I will." Boyd grinned. She'd lay bet this was a game they played often. "I'll sing the Grinch song."

"No! Anything, but that!" The young voice filtered through the phone. He must have answered properly amidst all the laughter, because Boyd smiled. "And you're the bestest son in the whole world. I love you and have a good nap." He ended the call.

"Will he take the nap or give his aunt a hard time?"

"If he wants the use of his electronic toys, he'll listen. Once he hears me lay down the law like I just did, he behaves very well."

She laughed at his macho bragging.

His eyebrows rose. "What?"

She elbowed him in the ribs. "You did not lay down the law. That usually involves yelling. And once you've yelled, you've lost the argument."

"Right. I didn't yell, I told him what his options were and why, therefore I won." He smiled which made her heart skip a beat.

"We're having more company than you for supper. Our station—for better or worse—has adopted two elderly gentlemen. One, Sam is Barclay's father-in-law."

"Barclay is…Ghost. Right?"

"Yeah. And Sam is Hell's Bells, because he uses that expression a lot. He's in the early stages of dementia, but he and Milt, or Gas Ass, are the best of buddies."

She pulled back a fraction. "Excuse me. Did you say 'Gas Ass?' Why would you give a man a nickname like that?"

"He's got a bit of an intestinal problem from not eating right. He manages the little grouping of vacation cottages Barclay owns. He's comical as hell, but once he takes you under his wing, he'll

74

do anything for you. He's a widower and damn lonely, so we're all his boys."

A few of the firemen joined them, greeted her and asked if she minded if they played Wii until supper was ready. She wanted to point to her eyes and tell them to look at her there when they talked to her and not her boobs, but would it do any good?

Boyd leaned forward. "Guys, the lady has eyes and a lovely face. Look at them when you hold a conversation with her. I'll not have her disrespected."

Kissy Lips sneered. "Hell, Tiny, I was only trying to guess what color bra she has on today, or did you find that out already? Let me know so I get the next poster right."

"You ignorant bastard!" Boyd dove for the smartass kid. The other two guys jumped out of the way. The sofa fell backwards and the sound that cracked through the TV room was more flesh hitting flesh than sofa smacking tile floor.

The captain and Ivy Jo charged out of his office. The captain and Quinn pulled Boyd off Kissy Lips who spat blood on the floor. "You think so much of her, but I bet I'm in her pants long before you."

Ivy Jo grabbed him by the neck of his shirt. "You'll clean that blood and your language up. I put up with the language because I'm one of the guys, but Graci-Ella is a guest here. Show some damn respect." She waved a handful of posters at the captain. "This is what comes from your 'old boy system' thinking. I found your locker room humor as insulting as I'm sure Graci-Ella has. I've got a red bra too. So, how was I to know he wasn't referring to me?"

The bloody mouthed kid had the nerve to spout off, "Because the skin wasn't dark enough." Ivy Jo gave him two blows to his face so quickly her fist was like a blur of motion.

"Darryl, in my office! Now!" The captain glanced at his squad which had assembled in a hurry once the word of the fight spread. "We'll be having a meeting over supper. Graci-Ella, I hope you'll stay to hear my apology, for I utter damn few."

Graci-Ella had seen her share of females fighting during and after basketball practices but, damn, this was a little different. Darryl's expression when Ivy Jo smacked him was priceless. So were her remarks to the captain. Graci-Ella wanted to stand up and cheer both times. Maybe she and Ivy Jo could become friends. She'd collaborate with her on how she wanted photographed, because she'd really like to showcase Ivy Jo's strength—inner and exterior, for she had both in large quantities.

Boyd and Quinn upended the sofa in its rightful position and checked to make sure the back was still securely attached so it could be safely used. The two men exchanged words in a low tone. Quinn glowered at the office door. "I'd have strangled the bastard if he said something like that to Cassie. Wasn't he taught a lick of manners?"

Graci-Ella stood, not sure if she should declare she could take care of herself or simply thank Boyd for sticking up for her. But when he turned around, his expression was nearly feral, as though someone had tried to take something precious that belonged to him. The realization hit and hit her hard. She wanted to belong to him. Not just in a flirtatious way, but in a serious relationship.

She glanced at her watch. Crap, she was going to be late for the meeting with her clients. She gathered her forms and papers and stuck them in her large purse. "Boyd, I have a meeting with clients in twenty minutes. Would you walk me to my car?"

"Do you really have a meeting or are you running from the fight zone?"

"Oh, please. I've seen worse fights that that." He held the door open for her and followed her outside. "I should have chosen a better time to stop, but who knew I'd have an argument with the captain, one fantastic kissing session, a nice snuggle on the sofa and ringside seats for a fight? Nothing scared me except for that kiss. I've never had a smokin' hot one like that." She pointed to the small white SUV.

Boyd wrapped his arm around her and tucked her to his side

as they walked. "I'm sorry you have to rush off. Can you come tomorrow? You'll need to plan your calendar shoot and I'll need to see you."

Reaching into her purse, she removed some tissues and dabbed his bloody lower lip and nose before she handed him the Kleenex. She rubbed her hand over his pecs. "I'll be here."

He wrapped his arm around her and pulled her close. "Drive careful, Sweetness." He pressed his nose to her neck to inhale her fragrance, groaned and kissed her below her ear. An act that made her shiver and yearn for more.

Tires squealed as an old Cutlass sped onto the lot and zipped into a parking spot. The car looked like it was more duct tape than metal.

Boyd took her hand. "Come on. I'll introduce you to Gas Ass. This car is his pride and joy."

She was trying her best not to laugh. The vinyl top was covered with a good three inches of duct tape. One side view mirror was heavily taped to the car. So were both front and rear bumpers. Was this ride even legal?

A skinny man in a Hawaiian style floral shirt and shorts slid out from under the duct taped steering wheel and tooted a few times. "Who you got there, Tiny? She sure is a pretty thing."

Time for some feminine charm. She extended her hand and shook his as he passed more gas. "Sir, my name is Graci-Ella Santana and I haven't seen one of these in shape like this in years." She waved an open hand to his car. "It's a seventy-six Cutlass Supreme, isn't it? Classic orange. What's it got under the hood?"

The man's pigeon chest was all puffed out. "A classic V-8 that purrs like a kitten." His bottom did a little purring too. "Don't often run into a young woman who knows much about cars."

"My daddy runs a garage for classic cars in Maryland. I used to be his right hand man." She gave the poor old Cutlass another once over and lied like many a lawyer. "You've got a beaut, let me tell you. What did you say your name is?"

"Milt Garland." He jerked a thumb over his shoulder to a man wearing a t-shirt that read, "My Tin Roof's Rusted." "My running buddy is Sam Devon."

"Well, I'm pleased to meet you both, but I have to run or I'll be late for a meeting. I hope to see you again."

Boyd walked her to her car. "You know how to schmooze an old man."

"Comes from working in a garage over the summers." She glanced at her watch again. "I really need to hit the road. I'll see you tomorrow. My schedule should be lighter and I'll be here earlier." She hugged him again. "Thank you for defending my honor." She waved at the two old men who were obviously standing chaperone duty, side by side, hands clasped at their waists and all eyes so as not to miss a thing.

All of the squad was settling around the table when Boyd stepped inside. They each welcomed Milt and Sam with boisterous greetings that pleased the old men. Boyd explained Graci-Ella had a meeting with a client and was afraid of being late, so she had to head off.

"Did you see Darryl leave?" Captain Noah took some chicken off the platter and passed it on to Wolf, seated next to him. "I fired him and he threatened Graci-Ella and you. His remarks about Ivy Jo and Graci-Ella were out of line. Illegal."

Boyd's gut rolled. "He can come after me all he wants, but if he tries to harm a hair on Graci-Ella's head, he'll find me breathing down his motherfucking neck, hot and heavy."

The captain nodded. "I figured you'd say as much. Our squad's a tight knit group and that's how I like it. There's a big difference between giving someone a raft of shit and being plain insulting. Kid was lazy. He just wasn't fitting in. I noticed other episodes of verbal sparring he'd started." Noah sighed and looked directly at Ivy Jo and then Emily. "We need to remember women work here now. I don't want them to have a hostile work environment. Ivy

Jo, you've always been a good sport about our joking and teasing. Same for you, Emily. I apologize."

From that point on, normal supper conversation flowed. Boyd's phone chirped. He tugged it from his jeans and saw Graci-Ella's number. He swiped the screen and left the table. "Hey, Sweetness."

"Is Darryl, the guy you got in a fight with, still at the station? A big black pick-up is following me awfully close, and I swear the driver looks like him."

"No. The captain fired him." A banging noise sounded and Boyd's heart stuttered for a few beats.

"That ass just rear-ended me!" There was a repeat of the same noise. "He...he did it again!" There was fear in her voice this time.

Boyd rushed into the eating area. "Hold on a sec." He glanced around the table. "What kind of vehicle does Darryl drive?"

"Truck. Black Ram," the captain replied. "Why?"

"He's following Graci-Ella and has rear-ended her twice." He thumbed a button and spoke into the phone. "Baby, where are you? I have you on speaker so everyone at the table can hear you."

"On CR 896, heading into Tarpon Springs. He's coming up beside me. Dear God, he's hitting the side of the car. You should see his eyes! The man's insane!" As she yelled, metal banged against metal.

"He's trying to force her off the side of the road." Boyd had never been so freaking angry. He should have beaten the hell out of the kid when he had him down on the floor.

The captain stood and pulled out his cell. What kind of car is she driving and what section of 896 is she on? Can she give us a landmark? I'm calling the police."

"She has an older white Toyota Rav 4. Graci-Ella can you see a business to give us an idea where you are?"

"I passed Pete's fruit stand a while back. Now I'm driving along trees." Her scream, followed by a horrible, loud crash sounded. Then silence. Ice did a free-fall through Boyd's system and, for a moment, he was paralyzed.

"The police are on their way. Team B for ambulance one, take off."

Milt stood and so did Sam. "Boyd, come with us. We'll have you there in no time. I know the area she's in. Pete sells good produce. I been there many a time." Milt rushed for the door, tooting as he bustled along. "Come on, time's a waistin' and she needs us."

Boyd glanced at the captain for permission to leave on his shift, not that he'd listen to a negative response.

The captain waved him on. "Do what you need to do, Boyd. I've got your back."

CHAPTER ELEVEN

Although Boyd had heard many tales of Milt's driving exploits, he'd never ridden with him before. Boyd had barely gotten the squeaky back door shut when Milt shifted the Cutlass-Duct-Tape-Mobile in gear and took off. Boyd reached for the seat belts and Milt told him the seatbelts hadn't worked since oh-four. Pieces of foam peeked out from between strips of duct tape on the seat covers.

As the car pealed out onto the street, there were two loud backfires from the front before the car backfired in return. Milt leaned over the steering wheel, his hands white-knuckled. "That girl seemed awful nice. If that bastard did anything to her, I've got a crowbar in my trunk that'll fit mighty fine up that moron's ass." He passed two cars on the left and Boyd pinched his eyes shut.

Milt cussed at a slow-moving compact. "Buy American next time! Maybe you'll get to where you're goin' quicker." The driver gave him the finger and Milt held up a large Buccaneers Red foam hand with all the fingers stapled down, except for the middle one, and waved it out of the window.

Ben reached for Milt's arm. "Now, you know this kind of behavior isn't good for your heart. Drive with some damn sense. We'll get to her in time. We have to. Poor kid's probably scared to death. My Molly always was when she had car trouble."

Milt leaned farther over the steering wheel. "Is that a black pick-up ahead? Do you see her car?"

Boyd did and his stomach turned. Her car was wrapped around a tree. The ambulance wailed behind them and, thank God, Milt pulled over to let them pass. Sam turned in his seat and gave him a hard look. "You okay, son? You're awfully…awfully…what's that word for white?"

"Pale," Milt replied as he bounced the old car back onto the road again, barreling down on the scene of the accident.

"That's it. You're looking pale, Teeny."

He couldn't bring himself to correct Sam that it was Tiny, not Teeny. Dementia often screwed with one's vocabulary. So, he rubbed his hands over his face, hoping to bring some color to it. "Sam, I just need to know she's okay. Then I'm going to kill the motherfucker for what he did to her."

Milt passed a long string of gas. "Sounds like love to me. Right, Sam?" Milt braked the car, and Boyd was out and running. Dear God, let her be okay. Let her be alive.

Graci-Ella's air bag was deployed, so he crawled over the roof of the car and leaned in while ambulance crews worked. "Sweetness. Sweetness, do you hear me? Don't move. Not yet. Ivy Jo and Jace are here to get you out."

"Boyd?"

"That's right, baby. I'm here. We're going to get you out and to the hospital. I won't leave." And he wouldn't either. He couldn't. The feelings he was developing for her were sweet, yet strong. There was one word to describe them all, but he was afraid to admit it might be something that serious already. But it was time he did. When he wasn't looking for it, didn't want it, couldn't handle it, love wrapped its strong tentacles around his heart. It didn't mean he loved Matt less. It meant he'd finally opened his heart to a different kind of love.

Jace held Graci-Ella's head immobile while Ivy Jo attached a neck brace. All the while they asked her questions.

Boyd slid back off the other side of the roof. He rounded her car, heading toward Darryl who was resisting arrest. The bastard broke free and one of the officers tazed him. While he was down, they handcuffed and put zip-strips on his ankles. Both policemen hauled him to the back of the cruiser and strapped him in. Darryl kept making verbal threats against Graci-Ella for getting him fired and called her a cock tease who needed taught a lesson.

If there was ever a man Boyd wanted to work over, it was this mouthy lowlife. He shook with the effort to retain self-control. God, how he wanted to rip him apart. Going to court for custody of Matt would be a lost cause if he had an arrest for assault against Darryl. And, in the end, Darryl would be the winner.

Boyd spoke to one of the arresting officers. "I have the woman's call recorded on my cell if you need it for court. She called me to ask what kind of vehicle Darryl drove. During the conversation, he started ramming her car." The one officer took his name and pertinent information before they took off with their offender. Another police car arrived to investigate the accident.

Ivy Jo and Jace were placing Graci-Ella onto the gurney when Boyd returned to inquire about her condition. Jace was good at initial assessments. "She has a concussion from hitting her head on the passenger window. You can see cuts where she shattered the glass. It's an older car with no side airbags. She'll eventually have two black eyes, plus she has a broken or sprained wrist from the front airbag deploying."

"It's only sprained. I've had them before. I can tell." Graci-Ella spoke with the knowledge of a full-fledged doctor.

Jace grinned. "Broken or *sprained* wrist, bruised internal organs—not sure about any internal bleeding—and a banged up knee. Could have been much worse."

Rage burned a path through Boyd's body. "This lady hadn't done one thing to that bastard Darryl." Boyd sensed an "I'm not even until I'm one ahead" mentality about the kid, but he never in a million years suspected he'd take revenge out on her, especially to this extent. My God, her head was bleeding and, for all they knew, there might be internal bleeding too.

"Boyd, could you get my purse and sunglasses? See if you can pull down the back seat and get into my trunk for my camera equipment and briefcase? The car's totaled and they'll have to tow it to a junk yard."

"Sure thing." He crawled into her car, saw the blood on what remained of her passenger side window and felt his own blood boil. After slipping her sunglasses in her purse, he removed the CD in her player, figuring it was her favorite, and opened the glove compartment to retrieve her registration papers. He crammed the whole works into her purse. Delving into her rear seat, he pulled the tab to lower the back of the bench and reached into the hatchback for her tripod, camera and briefcase.

He tucked her purse next to her on the gurney while Ivy Jo treated the cuts to the side of her head and face. Graci-Ella was asking about scars. Boyd pivoted and gave the rest of her stuff to Milt, asking him to take care of it. "Will do, son. You know that. Poor sweet darling. I'll put her stuff in my trunk right now."

Boyd picked up Graci-Ella's uninjured hand and brushed his lips across her knuckles. "Do you want me to ride in the ambulance with you?" He didn't want to leave her side. His heart hadn't pounded a normal beat since he'd gotten her call. He'd feared he'd lose her before he'd had a chance to build a relationship with her and Matt. Was such a thing even possible? Maybe she didn't like children. Maybe Matt couldn't handle someone new in their lives.

Their eyes connected and she cupped Boyd's cheek. There seemed to be a connection between them, already, after so short a time. "Yes, please. I want you with me." She blinked. "Both of you. Don't move so much. Sometimes I see three of you, which isn't necessarily a bad thing. How long will my vision be like this?" She started to panic and reached for him.

"They'll do tests at the hospital and make you rest. Slowly things will return to normal."

"Boyd's right. Let's head for the ER. You know," Ivy Jo quipped, "it's really not fair that an accident victim can look as pretty as you. Don't you think she looks pretty, Tiny?" Ivy Jo nudged him, jerked her head toward the woman he'd barely been able to stop staring at and made a facial sign as if to say, "Pay her a compliment, dumbass."

"As scared as I was on my way here, pretty doesn't begin to cover it. You have no idea the horrible scenes that flashed through my mind." He trailed his fingers down Graci-Ella's soft cheek. "There's no word to describe you, but beautiful."

"Huh, the only time he's told me I was beautiful was when I shot a three-pointer at one of our basketball games, and we were on the same side."

Graci-Ella glanced at Ivy Jo and winced. "Note to self: Don't move your head. You play basketball, Ivy Jo? I knew there was a reason I liked you. Did you play collegiate?"

"Two years at Florida State, then momma got cancer, dad walked out on the family and I had to come home to care for her and my brothers. How about you?"

"Oh, Ivy Jo, I'm sorry. What a rough way to go."

She made a time out sign. "I can't dwell on it or I get mad as hell at my so-called dad. Tell me where you played."

"UConn. National Camps four years running. All American point guard." She grimaced and placed a palm on her head. "The rougher the game, the better. Yet, I allowed that nutcase in the truck to scare the bejesus out of me." Pain was evident as she spoke in fits and starts.

"Shhh. You don't have to talk, baby. Your head has to hurt like hell."

Her gurney was locked in place, an IV inserted and Boyd on a seat beside her. Ivy Jo drove and Jace took shotgun, relaying the information to the hospital.

"I need to toughen back up. I was always a monster on the court…and…a bitch on wheels in real life. Now I'm more like modern scooter. What do they call them? Ah…a two wheeled gyroscope."

Her blue eyes focused on Boyd, although even he could tell from his experience, they were out of focus. She was definitely concussed. "I didn't know who else to call, but co-workers. Felt safer calling you. Hope that was okay."

He pressed his lips to the palm of her hand. "Had you called anyone else, I'd have been damned upset. Are you in much pain?"

"Only when I move my head…or think of my demolished car… and how my parents are going to react when they hear about this. That car was my graduation gift from college. They weren't happy when I moved south to the land of year-round sun after I passed the bar and was hired at a law firm in Tampa. Dad kept repeating 'hurricanes and tsunamis' and dire predictions of flooding."

She wrapped both of her hands around his. "Thank God, you came."

His heart did a double flip-flop. "Baby, I'll always come when you need me. That's a given." There was no doubt she touched a hungry part of his heart. "Hey, you guys have an ice pack for her eyes? They're starting to swell."

"Second row, bottom drawer." Jace pointed. "You know how to snap 'em to get them to work."

Boyd gently placed the pack over her eyes. "Are you an only child?" He had to change the topic before his mind went down a road it had no business being on. He hadn't given a thought to Matt growing up and moving away. The little squirt wouldn't dare leave him; he'd built his whole life around his son. Once this damnable custody hearing was over, Boyd needed to build some relationships beyond his son and his co-workers at the station. He could invite couples with kids Matt's age over for a barbeque. Have parties. Date. Date this wonderful woman in front of him.

Graci-Ella lifted the ice pack, a look of sadness passing across her face. "I had a brother, Eli. He was three years older, but he was broadsided by a truck on black ice and died instantly."

"Oh hell, Sweetness. I'm sorry to hear about that."

"Then you understand."

"Understand what?" She was taking him in circles, he was starting to get dizzy, himself.

She fumbled for his hand. "Why my parents can't know about this accident. They don't need to find out, do they? I mean, after losing one child this way. To even hint that I might be seriously hurt, which I'm not, would be cruel to them. They're in Maryland. I'm in Florida. Why have them travel down here in a state of fright over some cuts and bruises? Promise me you won't tell them."

Boyd thought about how he'd feel if Matt had a few cuts and bruises. He'd go purely crazy. "Honey, I don't know if I can live up to a promise like that. I feel they deserve to know."

"But they've been through so much all ready. My parents grieved in their own ways. Dad worked more hours. Mom clung to me as if I were her lifeline. I was a junior in high school and became the sole focus of her life. She nearly smothered me to death. If I wanted to go to the mall with some of the girls, Mom insisted on traipsing along. The same with movies and parties. Soon, I wasn't included in the group anymore. So when a scholarship arrived from UConn, I took it. Dad understood, plus he enjoyed the money he saved in tuition and stuff. He used part of it to buy me that car. Claimed it would be safe. And a truck got it…just like Eli's." A tear trickled down her cheek as the ambulance pulled under the brick cover of the hospital's emergency rooms entrance.

A car horn blasted as it whizzed around the portico.

Jace shook his head and laughed, before reaching back to pat Boyd's shoulder. "You got company buddy. The duct-tape-mobile just streaked by."

"Have you seen Milt's Buccaneers Red foam hand with all the fingers stapled down except for the middle one? If I hadn't been out of my mind with worry over Graci-Ella, I'd have hidden on the floor in embarrassment. Good Lord, the man can go from lovable to batshit crazy in the blink of an eye."

The EMT's jumped out of the ambulance and rolled their

87

patient from the vehicle. They rushed her inside and emergency hospital personnel transferred her to a bed in a curtained off area. Jace handed the nurse his assessment form, and he and Ivy Jo headed toward the door with the gurney. "Call the station as soon as you hear anything." Jace clasped Boyd's shoulder. "She'll be all right. You hear me? I can see how you feel about her. Like I do my wife; falling in love with her was so easy. Time you face up to your emotions, man."

Boyd glanced at her examination area and spun toward the two wild-eyed men, both of them tooting by now, barreling in through the emergency doors, pumping their arms as if to give them more momentum. "Yeah, Jace, I hear ya. Her wreck forced me to face a lot of things. I'm still coming to grips with that." He glanced over his shoulder at the two older men. "Then there are these two to contend with. Think the nurses here will give me some 'nervy-dervies' to handle the Gas Brothers?"

Within a few minutes, the nervous trio sat in the waiting room. Milt offered to go for coffee for the three of them. As soon as he was out of earshot, Sam slid over onto the plastic chair next to Boyd. "Tiny, need to ask you something. We both know I've got this dementia issue. I forget things I shouldn't. Get confused easily. I slip into moods where I act like a scary sombitch." He glanced in the direction Milt had gone. "But don't you think Milt turns crazy as a polka dot patch, in a crazy quilt every time he gets behind the wheel of a car? Tell me I'm not confused in the head about this." Sam's expression pleaded for Boyd to agree with him or at least acknowledge his friend acted odd at times.

Poor old soul. Not to know if what you thought was correct or an errant imagination must add an extra layer of confusion to his life. "Between us, Sam. Milt's a hell of a nice guy. He's got his quirks, but then we all do." Sam nodded. "I don't get it either, Sam. Put that nice man behind the wheel of a car and he turns into a freaking, screaming lunatic."

"Whew. I'm glad you noticed it too. I thought I was imagining it. What do you think I can do to help him?"

Oh boy, this is going to be a case of the blind leading the blind. Boyd ran his hand through his hair. "Well, I did notice when you reminded him about his blood pressure and kind of took charge for a minute, he calmed down some."

"Yeah but, Hell's Bells, if I do that too often, he'll just duct tape my mouth shut."

He didn't know if it was what the old man said or the way he said it, but Boyd laughed until he didn't think he could laugh any more. Once he got himself under control, he told Sam he'd have Quinn talk to Milt about some anti-anxiety medicine—nothing strong—just enough to help with the road rage this nice old coot had.

Sam nodded. "If Milt'll listen to anybody, it would be Quinn. You know they were neighbors for three years. The two of them are close, real close. You'll mention this to Quinn then?"

"I think it's something that needs done, don't you?"

Tension seemed to lift from the old man. "Yes. I do. I love him like a brother, but Hell's Bells some days I want to rip my ballcap off and beat some sense into him with it." Sam glanced down the corridor and grinned. "Well, would you look at this?"

Boyd peered in the direction Sam indicated. Milt was walking— or would one call it strutting—beside an attractive young nurse who held the three cups of coffee. Milt, in his aqua floral shirt, khaki shorts, lime green knee socks and black sandals carried bags of snacks and openly flirted with her. By the blush on her cheeks, she enjoyed his attention. They laughed, and when she leaned down to say something to him, he hip bumped her and danced a few steps.

"What the hell do you think they're talking about?" Boyd might have to take lessons from the old coot on how to charm a woman. Damn, if it didn't look like things were going okay for him.

The two reached the waiting room and Milt placed the snacks on an empty chair before he took the cups of coffee from her. "The dance steps go like this, sweetcakes." He took her in his arms and sang a tune while he stepped her through some moves around the waiting room, executed a twirl and a dip. Others in the waiting room clapped their hands in surprise at the impromptu exhibition.

"See? You're a natural for ballroom dancing." Milt took her hand and kissed it. "If I had your phone number, I could call you about going to a couple dance lessons." To Boyd's shock, the nurse pulled out a slip of paper and wrote something on it before placing it in Milt's hand.

Sam elbowed Boyd. "Did you notice he didn't fart once during that whole dance routine? There's something fishy about his ass. I think he has it trained to make racket on command."

CHAPTER TWELVE

The door opened and a momentary shaft of light stabbed the pain in Graci-Ella's head so fiercely, it went from barely tolerable to hellacious bad. Quiet footsteps and the creak of vinyl echoed in the dark room as someone sat in a chair, peeled off the lid of a container allowing the aroma of coffee to waft toward her nose in the darkness.

"Whoever you are, stop making so much noise and give me a sip of your coffee."

"Are you sure? I like my coffee like I like my women. Hot and sweet. But you're welcome to a sip, or two." Boyd's deep voice soothed her senses; cocooned her in safety.

"And I like coffee the way I prefer men. Hot and mine. Now, prop me up so I can have a sip."

Daddy Boyd came out. "What's the magic word?"

"Please?" She would so get him for this...once she felt human again.

He stood and set the paper cup on her nightstand before he slid his arm under her neck. "How are you feeling, Sweetness?" His voice was low and intimate. His cologne, a mixture of woodsy scents and musk, was so familiar. She burrowed into him and moaned in satisfaction.

"I feel better when you hold me. Maybe I don't need coffee.

Maybe I just need held."

He chuckled. "Oh no, you don't. You're not going to tell everyone how I wouldn't even share my coffee with you. Besides, I bought two cups just in case you woke up, so this one is yours." He reached for the cup and placed it in her hand.

She took more than a couple sips. "What time is it?"

He kept his arm around her shoulders, gently rubbing her arm. "Almost three in the morning. Are you alert enough to hear about the damages?"

"From the wreck?" She sipped more coffee. "Sure. Although I feel most of them."

He took the cup from her and set it on the nightstand again. Before he helped her lie back down, he fluffed her pillows. "Concussion, which will mean bad headaches, dizziness and sensitivity to light and sounds for a few days. Both of your eyes are swollen nearly shut and getting blacker by the minute. If you came by the station now, you'd get the nickname of Raccoon."

"Oh, you're a real deck of cards, Boyd. You ought to be dealt with." Gosh, she sounded like her dad with his dumb one liners.

"You had some glass shards removed from your ear and along your hairline. To repair all that, you needed six stitches and several butterfly bandages. You've got a sprained wrist just as you predicted, Dr. Santana." He placed a gentle kiss to her cheek. "You should have become a doctor instead of a lawyer," he said with a degree of humor. "A bruised spleen and liver from the force of the impact and your seatbelt. No internal bleeding, thank God. A banged-up knee that will be sore for a few days. Sounds like a lot, but it could have been so much worse."

She reached for her coffee and he placed the cup in her hand. After a few sips, she glanced at him through the slits in her puffy eyes. "I guess my part-time modeling gig is out, huh? Gee, and it was the swimsuit issue, too."

He took the cup from her and replaced it. "You better be shitting me on that score."

Graci-Ella, touched by his reaction, cupped his cheek. "I only work on one side of the camera." He leaned his head toward her palm and kissed it. "I was wondering about doing a month in the charity calendar with those two old men your squad adopted. Do you think they'd pose for me?"

Boyd laughed. "Milt would in a heartbeat. Sam, you might have to con into doing it."

She snuggled into her pillows, holding onto his face, kissing him here and there. She raked her fingernails up and down his pecs and around his nipples.

He kissed her as if he was afraid he's break her lips. So she took charge. When she bit his lower lip, he jerked back. "Holy hell, easy! You were just in an awful car accident."

"Gee, good of you to remind me. Now bring those lips back down here and kiss me like you mean it. I need a healing touch."

He came close again, his lips barely touching hers. "Oh, I mean it. Let my lips tell you." This time his lips spoke quite eloquently— and in several different languages. "You've kissed long enough. Go back to sleep. I'll be here or on a coffee run."

"Don't you have to go back to work?"

"Aunt Jinny will come for me after she takes Matt to school. She'll give me a ride to the station. It's all clear with the captain. He said since I can't do much anyhow, I'm as worthless as tits on a boar hog."

"Tits, huh? I'll show you mine after you show me yours!" She flashed him a grin.

"What kind of drugs do they have you on anyhow? Female Viagra? Look, Mr. Magoo, could you even see them if I were to flash you mine?"

She covered both of her swollen eyes with her hands. "No, dammit, just my luck. I'm almost as blind as that old cartoon character."

He laughed. "Go to sleep, Graci-Ella. Sleep and get well, sweetheart."

"What about Darryl?" She grasped Boyd's hand and placed it against her collarbone. "Can he still get to me?"

"He's in jail for attempted vehicular murder and resisting arrest."

"Please find out what judge he had and what his bail was set at. He could still get out on bond and hunt me down. He wants me dead."

He placed a gentle kiss to her lips. "He'll have to go through me first. Suddenly, I have two people in my life I can't live without." He burrowed his face in the crook of her neck and they held each other like that for several minutes. "Sleep. Get well."

A nurse woke her to tell her breakfast was coming. She helped her to the bathroom, and Boyd had been right, her knee hurt to walk. Still she'd injured it worse playing ball. She thought of leaning over the sink to get a closer view of her face in the mirror, but figured she couldn't do anything about the bruises and stitches anyhow. Why stress over it?

"My name is April. I'll be here until seven this evening. Here's an ice pack I want you to keep over your eyes to help with the swelling while you wait for your food. I'll see you get a fresh one every couple hours. Your cell phone is here with a note under it. Want me to read it to you?"

"Sure." It had to be from Boyd.

April snorted. "'Hey, Pretty Raccoon Eyes. Call me. We'll talk about tits and stuff.' I'm not even going to ask." She whizzed out of the room, laughing. "Whoo, that's a conversation I'd like to overhear."

After lunch, her doctor came in and washed his hands. At least she hoped that's what he was doing. Water ran, but she couldn't distinguish his movements that well. Just a shadowy form. "Good afternoon, Ms. Santana." He leaned his hip against her bed. "Tell me how everything is going. How do you feel, top to bottom?"

"Major headache. I can't handle the lights, at all. Sometimes, I sense the room spinning and at other times it's like it's flipping end for end. It's getting worse, not better. Eating makes me queasy. So does moving my head quickly." Graci-Ella rested a hand on her stomach. "I can't see much with my eyes practically swollen shut like this, but my body still feels the circling. The ice packs the nurse makes me use helps with the extreme discomfort a little."

"Anything else that hurts?"

"Some soreness where my shoulder strap went and in my knee where it banged the steering column, but nothing I can't handle."

"So your main problems are the concussion and swollen eyes." He pressed around her eyes and tried to open them further. "I can drain some of this edema to help you see a little better." He fingered around her eyebrows and eyelids, plus the area below. "Yes, I think I better remove some of this fluid." He pressed the intercom and told the nurse what he'd need.

April brought the items in and prepared the needle for him to use on Graci-Ella, who grabbed the doctor's hairy wrist. "Tell me you don't mean to stick that needle in my eyes!"

"No. Only one needle per eye." He swiveled toward April. "Sterilize the area, please. Ms. Santana, look straight ahead and do not move your head."

What if he jammed the needle in too far or at the wrong spot? Thank God, it was a quick procedure that made her sweat. When he was through pressing the area with a gauze pad, she was happy she could see again. While her vision field wasn't as large as normal, it was at least much better than a few minutes ago. He flashed a light in her eyes to check her retina response.

"April, give her about fifteen minutes and then put another ice pack on it for half an hour. Thirty minutes on and thirty off. I'll see you tomorrow, Ms. Santana." He charged out of the room.

"Wait! When can I go home?" She had cases to prepare. Briefs to write. Boyd had used her phone to call Elizabeth, her co-worker at the law firm, explaining about the accident and what hospital she was at. He asked her to inform the bosses that Graci-Ella would be out of the office for a few days and to please call the clients to clear up why she'd never shown for the meeting she had scheduled last night.

The doctor paused a moment. "Go home? Tomorrow at the earliest. More than likely, the day after." The door swung shut as he hurried to another patient for five minutes.

"April, would you mind composing a text to the guy who left me the note? I have his number up on the screen, but looking at small print and buttons makes my headache worse." She extended her cell to the nurse, who smiled mischievously.

"This means I'll get to hear your response to his note. Right?"

Graci-Ella grinned. "How does this sound? 'You talk to the firemen about your tits. I've got doctors to talk to about mine. They have nice warm hands.' Think that'll get him fired up?"

"Ohhh, girl, you are so bad." April's fingers flew across the keys, and she read it back to her. "Should I hit send?"

"Yup! Let him stew on that for a while. He's been so focused on what might turn out bad for him, I want to refocus his mind for a bit."

Her cell dinged and April chuckled. "Well, you certainly refocused his brain cells."

Graci-Ella leaned up on her elbow, wincing through the pain. "Read it to me."

"'Don't make me come over there and show you how damn warm MY hands are.' Oh, girl, you have pissed him off."

"Respond with this: 'Pfffttt.'"

April giggled and then snorted. "I think you've got his number. Are you two dating or just at the circling stage?"

"We've just made the step from circling to dating." Her cell dinged. "What does he say?"

"'Pfffttt, my ass!!!!!!' That's with six exclamation points." April's eyes opened wide. "The most I ever get are three."

"Tell him I love a man with a good exclamation point." By now both of them were laughing. "April, I just got a wild thought. We ought to co-author a book, *How to drive a man insane in eight texts, or less.*" Graci-Ella laughed so hard, her side hurt.

"I better stop dabbling in your love life and get you an ice pack for your eyes. Need anything for the pain?"

"Aspirin or something for my headache would be nice. The throbbing never lets up. In fact, I feel like it's getting worse."

April patted her arm. "Okay, girlfriend, be back in a few minutes." She chuckled as she left the room. "How to drive a man insane. Wheee!"

As Graci-Ella waited, she imagined Boyd scowling and barking at everyone at the station. A slow smile spread. He and the captain would be at each other's throats all day long.

The nurse returned with some aspirins and the ice pack. Graci-Ella had no sooner swallowed the pills than the door opened and one hellacious pissed off fireman stood there, as he practically filled the height and width of the doorway. In his grasp was a vase of roses. Under his arm, a present.

April kept patting Graci-Ella's arm and whispering, "Is that him? Is that him? Mr. Exclamation Point? Sweet Jesus, tell me that's not him. Can I have all that delicious muscle if you don't want it? I don't care how shallow I sound."

He swaggered into her room as if he knew his mere presence was hiking up the temperature by ten degrees—and didn't give a good god damn. "I brought you some roses that reminded me of you. Pure white on the inside and edged with passion red. That's where I was when I got your first text. You're damn lucky I didn't buy you a freaking cactus with lots of jaggy burrs."

"Is it me, or is it hot in here?" April couldn't seem to take her eyes off him and her slow perusal covered every inch of his body.

He sat the vase on Graci-Ella's nightstand and flashed a sexy as hell grin at April. "Will I have to kiss you before you'll move out of the way so I can get to the woman I snuck out of work to see?"

"Yes!" The nurse outstretched her arms and Boyd's eyebrows rose. He stepped back one pace.

"No! I need to thank him for the roses."

"Text him," April quipped over her shoulder.

"Good bye, April. I'm sure you have other sick people to see to." Graci-Ella gave her a gentle shove.

The nurse shook her finger at Boyd. "You're lucky I'm so devoted to my patients." She bustled out of the room.

He glared at Graci-Ella? "Pfffttt? You had the audacity to text me 'Pfffttt'? And to brag to me about doctors and their warm hands on your body?" He braced his hands on either side of her head and leaned closer with each word he spoke. He sat on her bed, lifted her and held her on his lap. Shifted her so her chest was against his six-pack abs. Then he lowered his mouth.

CHAPTER THIRTEEN

Boyd sucked on Graci-Ella's bottom lip and swept his tongue in her mouth to tangle with hers. Kissing her was like charging into a burning building in his boxers. Every cell in his body was scorching with heat. He trailed kisses down her neck and snuggled in the curve where her neck met her shoulder. The place he loved to burrow into the essence of her sweetness.

"Did…did you really sneak out of work?" Her pretty blue eyes rose to focus on his.

"No, I'm at the grocery store picking up food for the station and the pharmacy to replenish our first aid supplies. I'll be so energized when I leave here, I'll run through the stores." He bit her chin. "How's my baby feeling?"

"The doctor put needles in my eyes to draw out some of the fluid so I could open them enough to see."

"Baby, was he rough with you?" He kissed the corner of each eye, as gentle as a butterfly landing on bergamot flowers like Matt and Aunt Jinny had planted in the back yard. "I can't stand the thought of you being hurt." His hand swept up the back of her thigh and over her naked bottom. He cupped her ass. "Now, tell me the doctor's hands are as warm as mine."

"You'll probably have to keep them there for a while so I can make an educated opinion." She bit his earlobe and he squeezed a firm behind. "My man." Two words. Two tiny words that made his heart swell with happiness.

They kept kissing until their mingled heavy breathing filled the room. If he didn't soon stop, he'd have her astride his lap, buried deep inside her. His cock was throbbing and yelling, *Go for it! Go for it now!* He placed his face in the crook of her neck and sighed—probably *not* the best of ideas.

"Sweetness, I brought you a gift."

Boyd gently sat her on the bed, fluffed her pillows so she could sit up and handed her a wrapped present. "It's from everyone at the station."

"Really" Oh, how sweet! I'm touched. So incredibly touched." She was like a child, ripping off the paper and ribbon. Then laughter exploded. "*Rory the Raccoon*? Oh, I know who had a hand in this." She leafed through the pages, admiring the artwork.

"Everyone signed their nickname inside. Straight Up, Wolf, Ghost, Comic. Big Kahunas, that's Ivy Jo, Lil' Wolf is Jace. Oh, Emily is Black Thumb." Boyd smiled as he took Graci-Ella's hand and pressed his lips to her palm. "Believe me, I'm in no hurry to leave, but I do have things to do for the station. Call me later. I'd call you, but I'm afraid you'll be sleeping."

"Wait! Where's your signature?" She waved the book at him as he strode out.

"Look for it, baby. It'll be in a spot you'd least expect to find it."

She found it interesting as she slowly leafed through the book of large drawings, reading the story, to see where each fireperson had signed. A few simply scrawled their nickname in the white area around the pictures. One signed along the stem of a flower. Wolf took the page with the mother and baby raccoon to print his nickname; he was really excited about his wife's pregnancy. Ivy Jo wrote hers on the backend of a raccoon crawling up a tree. One animal by a stream, getting a drink, had a captain's hat drawled on it and Straight Up scrolled down the white part of his chest.

Then she spied it. In a hollowed out tree trunk were two raccoons. The biggest one was in the front of the opening as if he were protecting the smaller one peeking out from around him. On the bigger animal's one paw was printed Tiny and on the other he'd put Boyd. As though he were protecting her from everything bad in the world, he'd printed My Love in the white part under her neck, where he liked to snuggle. He struck her as that kind of guy. Protective of those he cared for. Alpha, yet gentle beneath the rough exterior. She hoped old man Henry did a good job and won the custody case for Boyd. If he lost Matt, she wasn't sure he'd ever recover.

After reading the book and smelling the roses, the walls of her room seemed to close in. Graci-Ella needed to move about. It seemed as if she'd been lying in bed for a week. She slowly got out of bed and walked a few laps around her little room. Maybe a longer walk would do her knee some good—stretch out the muscles and exercise it.

She put on a gown over the one she wore, only backwards so the opening was in the front. It was a poor excuse for a robe, but at least she was able to walk to the end of the corridor and back with her butt covered.

It was a pleasant surprise to find a windowed seating area at the end of the hall similar to a solarium. She loved the various species of palm trees and the vibrant flowers that grew year round in this area. Although she hadn't had much time to make a supportive circle of friends, she'd certainly become enamored of the beauty of the gulf side of the state.

She was on her return trek to her room, moving slower the farther she walked. Although the pain in her knee was doing better, things were spinning again. With every step, she wasn't sure where the floor was; some bastard had made the floor wavy while she'd been enjoying the view. Moisture ran from her nose, and when she wiped it, she saw it was blood. At this rate, she wouldn't be able to return to work for several more days. The spinning increased and she leaned against the wall to keep from falling off the face of the earth. Somehow the floor rose to meet her back and she imagined there were people running a race.

Boyd's phone rang using the tune he's assigned for Graci-Ella—"She's a Lady."

"Hey, Sweetness. How're you feeling?" He poured himself a cup of coffee. Cup in hand, he headed for the empty dining room table, preparing for a long chat.

"Boyd, this is April. We met in Graci-Ella's room earlier today."

"Yeah." He stopped. "What's wrong with her?" Earlier the nurse had been jovial. Now, she was tense, all business. His heart started pounding hard and fast in his ears. "Why am I talking to you and not her?"

"On her admittance forms, she listed you as her primary contact. She collapsed in the corridor. Evidently she went for a walk. There was blood flowing from her nose when I found her. They're running tests, but it looks as if brain surgery might be necessary."

Quinn passed by and Boyd grabbed his arm for support. "How soon will they know? Is she going through the tests now or are they completed?"

Wolf must have heard part of the conversation because he was now standing next to him with a roll of paper towels, wiping up the coffee Boyd had spilled when he'd dropped his cup, which he didn't recall doing.

"She's already had a CT scan. They're evaluating it now. They suspect her severe raccoon eyes were a sign we overlooked. The doctor assumed it came from the deploying of the airbag and her fair skin. Now they're trying to decide if it's a basilar skull fracture, which comes from a blunt force trauma, like when she hit her head several times against the driver's window."

"So, Graci-Ella might have a basilar skull fracture?" Sweet Jesus, Boyd collapsed onto a nearby chair. By now most of the squad stood around the table. Boyd's gaze gravitated toward Jace, the most knowledgeable of the EMT's.

Jace raked his fingers through his hair. "Ask if they're considering an epidural hematoma." He pointed to the side of the head above the ear. "She had trauma to the temporal bone located near the ear. Remember? She needed stitches from breaking the passenger window."

Boyd repeated the question. By now, Quinn rubbed his shoulders in a show of support.

"That is a possibility surgeons are considering. The temporal bone is thinner than the other skull bones, it is also the location of the middle meningeal artery that runs just beneath the bone. Fracture of the temporal bone is associated with tearing of this artery and may lead to an epidural hematoma."

Boyd glanced at Jace again. "She mentioned epidural hematoma."

Jace nodded. "Whichever it is, pal, it's going to require brain surgery to repair. You need to face that."

"Anything else I should know, April? Is she conscious? If I come will she know I'm there?"

April sighed. "As crazy as she is about you, I think she'll feel your presence. She'll absorb some of your strength before they take her into surgery. I wish I could tell you when that'll be. Could be fifteen minutes. Could be an hour or two."

"Thanks. I'm on my way." He ended the call, glanced at the ceiling and muttered, "Brain surgery." If there was one thing he was experiencing besides fear, it was exhaustion from worrying about everyone he cared about. First Matt's asthma and pneumonia and now Graci-Ella's brain injury.

"Don't think for a minute I'm allowing you to drive as exhausted as you look." The captain took charge. "Hell, you're still recovering from some injuries yourself. I'll take you." His gazed around the table. "Wolf, you're in charge until I get back. Okay? Tiny, let's roll."

As the captain sped toward the hospital, he asked Boyd if her parents knew she'd been in a car accident.

Boyd rubbed both hands over his face. "I don't think so. She told me she hated to tell them about the wreck because her brother was killed in a car accident. He was broadsided by a truck."

"Don't you think they deserve to know? Especially with this brain surgery coming up? Do you have access to her phone, so you can find their phone number? Hell, I know how I'd feel if I wasn't aware one of my kids was in pretty bad shape."

"The last I saw her phone was earlier today in her room when I dropped off some roses and the raccoon book."

"I do believe you're falling for the pretty photographer."

He nodded as he looked out the window at nothing. "Yeah, you could say that. She's the first woman I've allowed myself to get close to since Chantel moved out." He'd actually thrown her out after he'd walked in on a scene from one of those triple X movies in his bedroom, on *his* fucking bed. "Granted, Graci-Ella is pretty special, but she's also a lawyer, not my favorite species right now with this custody hearing bearing down on me. But, hell, I can overlook that."

"Life has a way of taking charge, Tiny. She might not be physically ready for much dating till the hearing anyhow. I wonder if she'll even be able to do the calendar to benefit the food bank." Captain eased his convertible into a parking spot a van just pulled out of. "Right now, let's concentrate on getting her well and contacting her parents."

Both men jumped out of the car and ran for the main entrance to the hospital. When they entered Graci-Ella's room, she was unconscious and hooked up to monitors. Boyd kissed her on the inside of her palm and nuzzled the crook of her neck, while he murmured words of love and encouragement to her. "I'm here for you, Sweetness. I'll stay until you wake up. Don't be afraid. I'll do my best to be sure you're taken care of, baby. You have a job to do too." He kissed the inside of her palm again, fighting his nerves. Dear God, he could not lose this woman.

With his lips against her ear, he whispered, "You have to fight.

Don't leave me, baby. Please, don't leave me."

Before he fell apart, Boyd straightened and scooped Graci-Ella's cell phone off the nightstand. He thumbed through her contacts until he found a Santana in Columbia, Maryland. Stepping into the corridor, he made the call. The call every parent dreads receiving.

"Hello." Thank God a man answered. From what Graci-Ella had told him, her mother did not react well to bad news. Right now, with his hanging on by an emotional thread, fraying by the minute, Boyd needed someone more stable.

"Is this Mr. Santana?"

"Yes. Who is this?"

Boyd pinched the bridge of his nose and prepared to break a parent's heart. "This is Boyd Calloway. I live in Clearwater, Florida. Do you know anyone who lives in that area?"

A gasp and a pained sound crossed the phone waves. "Yes. What did you say your name was and how did you get ahold of my daughter's cell phone?"

"Do you have a pen and paper nearby to write down some information?" The man grunted in the positive. Boyd repeated his name, gave him his cell number and told him how he'd met Graci-Ella at Fire and Marine Rescue Station Thirty-two. He explained she came to make preliminary plans to photograph firemen for a calendar that was to be sold to benefit the local food bank.

"Yes, she mentioned that to us. She was excited to use her photography skills again. But why are you calling? Has something happened?"

"After she left from one of her visits with us, she was involved in a vehicle accident."

"Dear God. Not again."

A feminine voice spoke in the background. "Ellis! Ellis, what is it? You've gone pale."

"Hush a minute, Grace, I need to hear what this man is telling me. Then I'll tell you everything. Okay, Boyd, please continue."

"At first, Graci-Ella's injuries appeared minor, except for a concussion. Bleeding has started in her brain and they're going to have to do brain surgery. I don't know how soon they'll take her down to the operating room."

"What hospital is she in?"

"Bay Care Health System. Here's the address and phone number. If you're planning on flying into the Tampa airport, I'll have someone from the fire station meet you there and bring you here. If you're unable to make the trip, I'll keep calling you with updates on my phone. I see the battery on hers is getting low. You've got my number, right? I'm a little rattled right now, Mr. Santana. I care a great deal for your daughter."

"I see. Yes, I have it. We'll be in touch with our flight arrangements. Thank you for the call, young man."

The captain strode down the corridor with a cup of coffee in each hand. "Did you reach her parents?"

"Yeah. I talked to Graci-Ella's dad. He'll call me with their flight arrangements." Both men walked into her room, the monitors beeping and her body lying still except for the rise and fall of her chest. Boyd set his coffee on a table and held Graci-Ella's hand. "Sweetness."

To his shock, her hand opened, her palm up. She could hear him. He had to believe that, had to hang onto that tiny shred of hope. He lifted her palm and leaned over to press a long kiss to it. "I'm here for you, baby."

"My man," she whispered.

"Yes, your man. I've called your parents. They're flying down. Your mom and dad are coming. Can you hear me?"

"Okay." She drifted off again.

Nearly an hour later, orderlies came to lift Graci-Ella from her bed to a gurney to take her to the operating room. Panic seized Boyd's lungs so fiercely; he didn't know if he could take his next breath. He held her hand and walked along until they reached the double doors to surgery. He leaned and whispered in her ear. "They're going to make you better, but you have to fight to stay with me. Don't leave me, baby. Don't leave me. I need you." He kissed her lips and, unless he imagined it or willed it, her lips weakly kissed him in return.

The orderlies pushed her through the doors and Boyd watched her until they closed in his face. He stepped away and bent over, his hands on his knees while he took huge gulps of air. Christ, they were going to drill open the skull of this dear, sweet woman. How had he come to care for her so quickly? So deeply? He watched two teardrops splatter onto his shoes and accepted the truth—he loved her.

CHAPTER FOURTEEN

Boyd finally corralled his emotions enough to stand erect. He paced back and forth in front of the closed doors, loathe to leave her. Which, of course, was a little over the top, but he'd be the same way if Matty was in there. He slipped his cell from its scabbard and called Mr. Santana.

"Boyd, how's our girl. We're packing now. The earliest flight we could get leaves in about two hours."

"They..." he cleared his throat to gain some composure, "they just now wheeled her into the operating room. I held her hand until we reached the entrance. She did show some response to me earlier, even in her unconscious state."

"Oh? How?"

"See, I often kiss the palm of her hand and, every once in a while, she'd turn her wrist over and open her hand for me to kiss it. I told her you two were coming and she said, 'okay'."

"Well, that's encouraging. She evidently knew you were there and what she wanted. But then our girl always went after what she wanted. Thanks for telling me that." He cleared his throat too. "That gives us something to hang on to. Here's our flight plans, son." Ellis gave Boyd the airline, flight number and arrival time and he entered it into his smart phone.

One hellacious long hour and twenty minutes went crept by

before a man in blue scrubs approached Boyd and the captain in the waiting room. "She did well. I fixed the vein that had ruptured, repaired the surrounding area. We'll have her in intensive care and monitoring her closely for the next forty-eight hours, but I expect a full recovery."

Boyd had his cell out, swiping Ellis Santana's number. When he answered, Boyd asked him to hold on. "Doctor, I have her father on the line. They're flying down from Maryland. Could you tell him what you just told me?"

"Certainly." He took the phone and relayed the same information. He also answered a few questions Graci-Ella's dad asked before handing the phone back to Boyd.

When he held the phone to his ear, all he could hear was a man and woman crying. He imagined their embracing each other and sharing a few moments of blessed relief. He ended the call. Let them have their time of breakdown in private. He'd so often felt the same over Matt, only his moments of joyful relief were in private, alone.

The captain clasped him on the shoulder. "While she's in recovery, let's go get a bite to eat in the cafeteria." Over soup and cheeseburgers, the captain kept the conversation going from his son Zack deciding on a college to buying a big screen TV to his wife's moodiness from menopause. "Sometimes, when she's through yelling, I feel like I've been sliced, diced and pureed."

"But you still love her." The captain was a family man through and through.

"Christ, more than anything." He grinned the way he did when he was thinking of doing something evil. "Know what I'd like to do? Replace her birth control pills with aspirins and slip one in on her." He shrugged as he bit into his cheeseburger. "I mean, if the woman's going to bitch..." And he chewed and laughed and choked at the same time. He wiped the tears from his eyes. "God, I love that woman. Susan is one adorable doll baby when she's big and pregnant. Besides, no kids at the house just don't seem right. Even she's been moaning and groaning about being alone so much after Zack leaves for college. Maybe I'll get that little girl I want this time."

"Seems like a topic the two of you ought to discuss—together." *Is he being serious or just handing me a line of bullshit to keep my mind off of Graci-Ella?*

"What, and miss the explosion when Susan finds out she's pregnant? Whoo! That ought to be a doozy. And guess who'll get to calm her down? I've got a sure-fired comforting procedure." Ol' Captain winked. "No, I wouldn't do it. Would be a dirty trick, but I have been talking to her about trying for another baby. I caught a sparkle of hope in her eyes, so I'll keep bringing the subject up every few days. Hell, we're still young enough."

"Well, that's good. Surprise babies happen all the time, but to purposely trick your wife doesn't sound like a good idea to me." He'd been on the receiving end of being tricked and it was a sore spot with him.

The captain leaned back in his chair. "You and Graci-Ella sure hit it off fast. Kinda pleases me. I like the young lady. Just don't put your heart out there too fast."

Boyd wiped his mouth and crumbled his napkin. "I won't deny I care for her." No way would he mention the L word. He was still coming to grips with that emotion himself, waffling back and forth.

How many times had he sworn to himself and others that he would never love another woman again? Standing there as they wheeled her into the OR was a highly charged emotional moment, which no doubt brought about his highly charged emotional reaction. He cared. He cared a lot.

"You haven't been with a woman for damn near a year or more. You need to date some before you hand any woman your heart. Especially with this custody battle hanging over your head."

He stood and snatched their empty plates and bowls. "Hell, captain, you think I don't know that? You think I haven't argued with myself about what an involvement with her could do to my chances for custody, so much so I called my lawyer and asked him straight out? You think the desire for her hasn't eaten at me from the moment I set eyes on her? And who the hell believes in love at first sight, anyhow? Not this guy. Lust, yeah. But love needs a chance to develop." He stormed to the trash containers and tubs for dirty dishes.

The captain studied him with his one eye narrowed in that way he had. "You ain't fooling me, son. You've already fallen in love with her. I bet the thought has you shaking in your shoes." A slow grin spread. "Dammit, I get a charge out of watching my men fall in love and fighting the feeling all the way to the altar. Makes my heart feel good."

"Go to hell."

The captain leaned over and laughed until everyone in the place was staring at him.

As they headed to Graci-Ella's room, the captain elbowed Boyd. "Wolf fell for Becca as soon as he saw her in her backyard, playing with Einstein."

Boyd wasn't playing the captain's game. He didn't respond.

"Quinn flipped for Cassie the first time he saw her at her eighteenth birthday party."

Again, he ground his back molars and kept silent.

They reached the elevator and the doors whispered open. "Barclay got it bad for Molly the first night he met her."

Both stepped onto the elevator. The captain's face was relaxed. Boyd could feel his own was pinched into a sneer. One more remark. One more freaking remark from the captain and Boyd was going to jack his jaw.

"Ivy Jo's eyes lit up the first moment she saw Ryder. The two of them are like magnets now. You see how happy she is?"

Boyd curled his hands into fists to keep quiet.

"Jace took a couple months to work up nerve to ask Wendy out. He was slow in the romance department."

Well, thank God for that.

"But the moment I laid eyes on my Susan at the beach, wearing that red bikini. God, I knew right then."

Boyd whirled on him. "Shut up! Shut the fuck up! Can't you understand how crazy mixed-up my life is right now?"

"Then you need to talk to her, tell her how it is, how you feel."

"Hell, you think I haven't done that, Mr. Aspirin-Birth-Control-Pills?"

"Are you pissed?" The captain placed his hands on his hips and had the nerve to grin like a simpleton.

"Hell, yes, I'm pissed!" Boyd yelled and recalled Graci-Ella's remark that once you began yelling, you'd lost the argument.

The Old Man, as the firemen called him behind his back, patted Boyd's arm. "Then my job here is done. Call when you need your car. I'm going back to the station and deliver the good news to the guys. Smile, man, the object of your lust made it through surgery."

Boyd followed him out the exit door into the bright sunlight. "Don't you dare talk about her that way! She's the sweetest woman I've ever met. I won't have her maligned. Do you hear me?"

The captain whirled. "You need to get a grip on things. Time for you to unwind about this custody hearing and enjoy life. You've lived like a damn monk for nearly a year. I don't know of a man who was meant to be a dad more than you. Or to love a woman."

Boyd stared at the tops of his shoes and blinked to maintain some control.

"Now, either you're in major lust for this lovely young woman or you're falling in love with her. I'm betting on the latter. Now, go back inside and get your shit together." He loosely embraced Brad. "You've got this custody business, son. You got this. Stop obsessing about it and decide on how much Graci-Ella means to you." The captain got in his car and left.

Boyd took a long walk around the parking lot. Walked and thought. Kicked an empty water bottle and evaluated how he'd been living his life. Tossed the bottle in the trash and contemplated some more. He was not in lust with Graci-Ella. His feelings were full-blown love. It was time he stopped questioning himself about it and admit how he really felt.

He headed for the hospital entrance. He was going back to her floor to see if April had heard any news.

April rushed to him as soon as he stepped off the elevator. "Boyd, they've moved her to ICU. If you go down to the first floor, you might get to see her for five minutes. She'll be in and out of it, so five minutes is the time limit."

He hugged her. "Bless you, April." In too much of a hurry to wait for the elevator, he ran down the steps.

Before he was allowed in for his brief visit, he had to put on a sterilized cap and gown. The fastidious nurse handed him a pair of gloves and ushered him in. Boyd glanced over all the machines and monitors they had her hooked up to. It looked like tubes were coming out of every orifice. An arc of her hair had been shaved over her ear. Stitches took up a large portion of that area. She looked so pale and vulnerable.

He leaned over the railing of her bed. "Sweetness. It's Boyd. You're going to be okay, baby."

Her hand rolled over exposing her palm. She'd heard him. She recognized his voice. He lifted her hand and pressed his lips to her palm. They were developing a silent way of communicating.

"I'm only allowed to stay for a few minutes. Then I have to wait two hours. Tomorrow, I can see you every hour. You were so strong during the surgery. You fought. I'm proud of you."

Blue eyes opened and stared at him. What a beautiful sight. "Fought for you."

"Oh, baby. I love you."

"You love me." She smiled and drifted off to sleep.

Thanks to Wolf and Jace bringing his car to the hospital, Boyd was able to meet Graci-Ella's parents at the airport. He held a sign on which Ivy Jo had printed "Santana" for him to hold at the luggage area.

A haggard looking couple hurried over to him. "We're Ellis and Grace Santana," the man said.

"I'm Boyd Calloway, the guy you've been talking to over the phone."

"How's our little girl?" Grace dabbed at her eyes with a crumbled tissue.

Boyd took her hands in his. "She's been upgraded to ICU."

"Upgraded? That's good, right?"

"Yes. She spent two hours in recovery and once she became responsive, they upgraded her. I got to spend five minutes with her in ICU. She rolled her hand over for me to kiss her palm. And her eyes opened. My God, the most beautiful sight I ever saw. She has your eyes, Mrs. Santana."

"Please, call us Grace and Ellis. Did our girl recognize you? I mean, did she seem like herself?" Her father wrapped his arms around his wife's shoulders. Of course they'd be worried about brain damage during surgery.

"I told her she fought hard and I was proud of her. She replied she'd fought hard for me."

"Well, this is all so much to take in." Grace blew her nose.

"Yes, but it's all good. Point your luggage out to me. I'll get it off the carousel."

"Royal blue with a red ribbon on the handles. My, you are a big man."

"Grace, don't drool. You know how testy you get when I stare at skinny blondes."

Boyd wanted to laugh. He bet the two had a close marriage, full of teasing and protection. "Follow me and I'll take you straight to the hospital so you can see her. It'll be scary at first. She's hooked up to a lot of machines and monitors. Part of her hair has been shaved. Her eyes are black and blue. But the sweetness in her soul is still there."

He placed their luggage in the back of his Mustang. "Grace, do you mind a back seat? There should still be room with Matt's car seat. Ellis you can sit up front with me."

Grace glanced in his vehicle. "You have a child?"

"Yes, a first grader. I currently have primary custody, but I'm trying to get permanent custody. Matt suffers from asthma and should not be around cigarette smoke. My ex smokes both legal and illegal cigarettes. Every Monday or Tuesday after spending the weekend at her house, he gets a severe asthma attack and often ends up in the hospital."

"Oh, how awful. I teach second graders and every year have a few with asthma."

"I've had a rough week or more. Matt had an asthma attack that turned into pneumonia. I'm a firefighter and marine rescue team member. I had to go back into a burning building to retrieve a kid who'd snuck back in to get his dad's ball glove. His dad's fighting in Afghanistan and that glove is his only link to him. I had him and the glove in my arms, and we fell through the steps and a floor to the basement. I ended up in the hospital for a couple days. Then Graci-Ella's car wreck. If I don't make a whole lot of sense at times, just overlook me, please?"

"You strike me as a strong man. I bet you tackle anything thrown at you. Look at all these palm trees, Grace. What water is this we're crossing?"

"It's the Intercostal Waterway, the bridge is called the Clearwater Memorial Causeway. It's a major evacuation route during hurricanes."

As soon as he eased into a parking spot at the hospital, the three of them hurried toward the entrance. Boyd led them to the ICU. He spoke to the head nurse, explaining who Grace and Ellis were and that they'd just flown in from Maryland.

"There are rules to be followed regarding visitation. But your daughter is progressing very well. Her vitals are good. If you promise no crying in front of her or doing anything to upset her, I'll allow you to go in now, ten minutes early. I know you're dying to see her. I would be if it were one of my kids. Follow me. I'll show you the sterilized gowns, slippers and masks to wear."

"Thank you so much. She's our only remaining child." Grace dabbled at her eyes. "Don't worry. I won't cry in front of her."

Boyd wasn't so sure he believed that.

Ellis pivoted and grabbed Boyd's arm. "Come along. The family stays together."

In response, Boyd wrapped an arm around each parent's waist and walked them in. When Grace gasped, he leaned down and kissed her forehead in a show of comfort. "It's a lot to take in. All these machines, but they're helping her. If you'll look at the area over her ear, you'll see where they operated. Let me see if I can get her attention."

He took a couple steps away from the parents and they moved closer together as if to lean on each other. Boyd leaned over the railing, her parents shifting to stand beside him. "Sweetness. Sweetness, how are you?" Her hand rolled over, exposing her palm and he kissed it. "You mom and dad are here. Can you open your eyes to see them?"

"Mommy? Dad?" Her speech was a little slurred.

"Graci-Ella." Her mother dabbed her sodden tissue at her eyes and Boyd smiled.

Blue eyes opened. "Mom, are you crying?"

Her mother spun into her husband's embrace, burying her face against his golf shirt. Her shoulders shook with sobs. "No."

Graci-Ella smiled a little. "Mom, five dollars in the lie jar. Right, Dad?"

"Whatever you say, Tiger. Are you in any pain?"

"No. So many drugs. Isn't my man the best?" She looked at Boyd. "We're in love." Her eyelids started to droop again. "Mom, Dad, thanks for coming. Stay at my condo. Third floor. Parking lot entry code forty-eight twelve. Extra key in my make-up kit in purse. Sleepy…" Her eyes drifted shut and she slipped into deep slumber again.

"I feel better. Don't you, Grace? She recognized us. Knew you'd cry."

Grace chuckled. "Yes, and she remembered that five dollar lie jar. That's a detail you wouldn't expect so soon after surgery."

"She remembered where her extra condo key was." Her dad shook his head, his eyes filling with tears. "I didn't expect her to be this alert during the short times she was awake."

"Ellis, are you crying?"

"Hell yes! Grace, you're not getting my five dollars in that damn lie jar." He glanced at his watch. "Our time is almost up. We should leave."

Graci-Ella flipped her hand over and Boyd leaned to press a kiss in her palm. In her ear, he whispered, "I love you, baby."

"My man," she mumbled.

CHAPTER FIFTEEN

The next week seemed extra busy for Boyd. While the Santanas took taxis back and forth to the hospital from Graci-Ella's condo, he still made his visits as often as his work schedule and time with Matt could allow. She'd been moved from ICU to a regular room which was a big help as far as time management went. He could see her whenever he wanted. The physical therapy team had her walking, using a walker. Her parents were delighted with her progress. So was he.

While Matt was in school, Boyd stopped by the florist to get her some red roses and white daisies. Graci-Ella was slowly walking around her bed when he opened the door to her room. "Don't you look pretty in your clown nightgown?"

She yanked on some of the material. "This…*this* is a sore subject. Obviously my mother picked it out. I haven't liked clowns since I was a little girl." She stilled and shook her head. "Oh, Boyd, we had an argument over this gown that turned nasty."

"That doesn't sound good." He set the flowers on her nightstand and she inched over to smell them.

"They're beautiful. Thank you. Could you lift me into bed? Do you know it's five miles from it to the bathroom right behind me? Or so it seems. God, I hate being weak. My physical therapist stepped things up today and gave me quite a workout." She was out of breath, which he didn't like to hear, so he scooped her into his arms and kissed her. She clasped her arms around his neck. "I wish I could snuggle against you for an hour or two. You always make me feel better."

He carried her over to the big leather chair and sat with her on his lap, curving her against him. "Do you want to talk about the argument?"

She kissed his neck and kept her face against it. "Years of my trying to live up to my brother's image came to a head. Eli could do anything. All A's in school, captain of the basketball squad, track team star and had a bright future ahead of him. He wanted to go into law and he'd have been great at it."

"Sounds like big brother was your hero." It also sounded as if she'd tried to take his place.

"I can't say my parents ignored me before Eli's death, but he was always their main focus. Discussions at the dinner table focused on what Eli had accomplished that day. I didn't mind being in the background, because I adored him. After his death, Dad worked more hours, Mom tried to insert herself into my life and I did all the things Eli had done or was going to do to help lessen the loss my parents felt."

"Which is why you played basketball and went into law." His hand stroked up and down her back in a show of sympathy.

"Playing basketball was *my* way of keeping him close. He'd taught me how to play and allowed me to tag along to pickup games in the neighborhood. It turned out I was probably a better player than he'd been. Soon, my dad started to notice. His spirits lifted a little because of what I was doing. So, I tried harder and harder to excel."

"I'd say you did that very well."

"To a degree. I had an aptitude for photography and took classes in it in college. My parents tolerated my little hobby, but told me law was where I belonged. So, I worked hard at it to make them proud because I was all they had left. And yesterday when Mother gave me this nightgown, I didn't show the proper gratitude. Dad growled me for it. I fired back. Long story short, in a matter of minutes I told them how I was worn out from being both Eli and me. That I hated being a lawyer and wanted to go into photography. They accused me of being jealous over Eli's memory, blah…blah…blah."

He held her closer. "Baby, I'm sorry."

"I hurt my parents. What kind of person does that make me?" She swiped at some tears.

He pressed a kiss to her palm. "One who wants to be her own person. You helped them through their grieving process. Now I think it's time you do whatever it is you wants to do."

She shifted on his lap and made eye contact. "That's just it. I don't know what I want to do. At times I'd like to open my own law practice, but I don't have enough money set aside to keep me afloat until I pick up enough clients to pay the bills. At other times, I'd like to go into photography. Either way, starting a business takes money, and I have to buy a new car. First, I have to smooth things out with my parents."

He trailed the backs of his fingers down her face. "They love you. They'll come around."

"I should call them and apologize. I can't bear having them upset over an argument."

"That sounds like a good idea. I'll put you back in bed and head for home. Then you can talk to them in private and work things out."

After Matt got home from school, Boyd decided to talk to him about Graci-Ella and to see how he reacted to someone else being included in their lives from time to time. This was the first he'd introduced a woman to Matt. His stomach was a mass of jitters.

They were lying on the floor, building spaceships with Legos. "You know mommy has a boyfriend."

"Yeah, and he's mean to me sometimes." They'd had this

conversation before, so Boyd didn't pursue the matter. He knew how the jerk acted.

"What if your daddy got a girlfriend?" He watched Matt's face for any reaction.

"A nice girlfriend or a mean one?" Matt pressed on a red block.

Boyd picked up a blue one. "You always come first, buddy. If she's mean to you, then she won't be my girlfriend any more. Unless you're misbehaving on purpose." He set the blue block on their spaceship. "But I think you're too smart for that."

"Yeah…I am. So, when are you going to get one?"

He played dumb for a minute. "One what?"

Matt smiled and rolled on his side, slinging his arm over his eyes. "Dad! What were we just talking about? You must be getting 'sepile'! A girlfriend."

"That's senile, buddy. And I've already got one. She's in the hospital right now."

Matt sat up. "Why? Did she have an asthma attack? Does she have to use inhalers like me?"

"No, she was injured in a car accident and had to have brain surgery. But she's doing much better. Sometime soon, I'll take you to see her."

The boy snatched his sneakers and slipped them on. Tugged on his shirt, examining it for any spots. "Think I need a clean shirt, Dad? You know it wouldn't hurt you to put on a clean one and shave. I'll go brush my teeth." The six-year old tornado was up and gone in an instant.

Boyd shook his head. He'd agonized for two days over telling Matt about Graci-Ella. When he'd mentioned going to see her sometime soon, he didn't mean in the next ten freakin' minutes. He stood and went into his bathroom to shave and freshen up. He came out of the bathroom to find a grey t-shirt with aqua, pink and lime surfboards across the chest lying on the bed. Matt had one just like it; was he wearing his too?

In less than three minutes the surfboard duo was headed to

the car. "What is she like?"

"Well, she's a really good basketball player. She made All American."

"Wow," Matt's voice was full of awe.

"She's a photographer, a lawyer and she likes to tease me." And she's got the sweetest pair of lips in the whole world.

"Dad, we need to stop at the grocery store. The one that has a big flower section."

"That's okay, buddy. I've already gotten her some flowers."

"Shouldn't I take something? I want to make a good 'imbression' so she likes me." Matt pointed. "Here. This is the store."

Boyd could hardly keep up as Matt charged to the flower section of the market. His son marched up to the florist. "Do you have any basketball holders for flowers or plants?"

"Well, let me see. I used to have a few." She rummaged around under her counter and retrieved what Matt obviously had in mind for his face lit up.

"Do you have any plants? Aunt Jinny says plants last longer than flowers."

The lady pointed out a few and Matt chose two. She asked him if he wanted some flowers stuck in vials of water to brighten it up and he asked for pink daisies. Boyd paid the bill and watched with pride as his son carefully carried his purchase to the car. Graci-Ella would love it.

Boyd offered to carry the planter into the hospital for Matt and his son gave him such a scowl, he quickly backed off. When they opened the door, Graci-Ella was setting up in her bed, her feet dangling over the sides.

"Up for some company?" Boyd placed his hand on Matt's head. "I brought my son with me tonight. He was eager to meet you."

She opened her arms and Matt gravitated toward her as if he were skateboarding downhill. "I am so glad you came. Your daddy talks about you all the time."

Matt held out the planter. "I picked this out for you because

Dad said you were a really good basketball player." He spoke rather softly and shyly.

"You picked it out?" She gave Matt one of her heart-stopping smiles and put her arm around him.

He leaned into her, all signs of shyness gone. "I asked the florist if she had any basketball planters and she did. Then...then I picked the plants. The real flowers were her idea, but I got to pick the colors. Girls like pink."

How does my six-year old know this?

Graci-Ella waved her hand around the room. "Do you see all the flowers I've gotten?" She held the basketball planter up and slowly examined it. "I do believe I like yours the best."

Matt's face split into a grin. "Dad told me we were getting a new girlfriend."

Hey, where did this we stuff come from?

"Dad said you had brain surgery." He looked over her head. "Where?"

She pulled her long hair back and showed him her shaved spot and stitches.

"Did any of your brains fall out 'cause that would be cool for me to take to school for Show and Tell."

Boyd slapped his hand over his eyes and slowly peeked through his fingers. You just never knew what the kid was going to say. Graci-Ella was laughing and hugging Matt. "Sorry, no extra brain cells. I need them all."

"So, when do you get out of the hospital, Graci-fella? We need to make room for you so we can look after you until you're all better."

She scowled at Boyd. He held up both hands in a surrender gesture. "I never mentioned that to him. *That* was his idea."

She planted a kiss on Matt's hair. "Honey, I have my own condo. My mother's going to stay with me for a week after I go home. My dad's flying back to Maryland tomorrow. So, I'll have my mom to help me when I first get home."

The door opened and her parents walked in. Both were smiling, so Graci-Ella must have straightened out the argument. Both went to her for kisses and long hugs.

"Mom, Dad, this is Boyd's son, Matt. Look at the beautiful planter he bought me. Isn't he adorable? Matt, could you set it on the window sill between the two flower arrangements? Please?"

He quickly did as she asked, shoving the other two flowers toward the glass, so his stood out. When he returned, he looped his arm around Graci-Ella's. "I think Graci-fella is the most beautiful woman in the world."

"Well, I see flattery runs in the family." Graci-Ella winked at Boyd who stared at his shoes. Damn, he hadn't expected his son to put on such a show. He glanced over at her father whose shoulders shook with laughter.

After several tries, "Graci-fella" tumbled from Ellis's lips. "Son, come here. You are a tonic after these last ten days."

On Matt's way by, he saw Graci-Ella's feet feel around on the floor for her slippers. Matt dropped to his knees and wiped each soul of her foot off and reached for her slippers to put them on—the wrong feet. "There," Matt brushed his hands together to indicate a job well done. "Now you can walk without stepping in someone's chewing gum or doggie poo." Boyd had a feeling Ellis had had a few drinks this afternoon, because he got another fit of giggles over that.

Graci-Ella glanced down at her slippers, pointing in the wrong way and shrugged. She walked toward Boyd. "If the mountain won't come to his woman for a kiss, then his woman will have to chase him down for one." She wrapped her arms around his neck. "Thank you for bringing Matt. He is adorable, simply the sweetest kid." Then she kissed Boyd.

Matt leaned against Ellis. "See that? He didn't bring her a stinkin' thing and he gets the big kiss. Life is strange, ain't it? Sometimes you catch the elevator and sometimes you get the shaft."

Ellis covered his mouth as he nearly fell out of his chair in hysterics. Even Grace, her face red and her eyes twinkling, oozed,

"Oh, isn't he just too precious?"

Five days later and Graci-Ella was getting ready to go back to the hospital, her mother fussing and fretting behind her. "It's too soon, darling. Let me go, while you stay home and rest." Graci-Ella just wanted to go out on her patio and scream. She was almost glad her mother was packed for her return trip to Maryland tomorrow. She loved her mom like crazy, but the woman had her ways that drove her up the freaking wall.

If Graci-Ella rested any more per her mother's orders, she'd turn into a boneless blob. She needed exercise. She needed fresh air. She needed to spend time with someone who didn't sprinkle wheat germ on all food items and sanitize every surface in her condo, including the outside of her patio doors. Her mother didn't just hover; she nestled like a momma hen over her eggs.

"Mother, please stop. Matt came to see me twice while I was in the hospital and brought me a beautiful basketball planter he'd picked out himself. Now, he's in with another attack of pneumonia and no one or nothing is going to keep me from spending some time with him.

"I'm cleared to drive, after all I got my stitches out yesterday and I have to go back to work in a couple days. On our way, I'll stop at this children's book store I know of and pick out some books for him."

"Someone is over-doing," her mother replied in a sing-song voice.

"Stop trying to run my life!" Graci-Ella cupped her mother's cheek. "I don't mean to be sharp with you, but he's a little boy whose mother never comes to visit him when he's in the hospital. He doesn't have a fantastic mom like I do. He needs us, he really does."

Her mother gasped. "She never comes? But why? How far away does she live?"

"I'll tell you on the way to the bookstore. Grab your purse. Let's go." Graci-Ella had a rental compact, supplied by her auto insurance, that she could barely fit her long legs into. First chance she got, she was buying another car that sat higher with more leg room. As she drove, Graci-Ella explained Matt's world to her mother.

"How much effort would it be for her and her live-in to walk outside and smoke? It's not like you get a foot of snow down here. Certainly, the boy's health is more important." She sniffed as she got out of the car at the bookstore.

Graci-Ella asked for books for first and second grade reading levels and the shop keeper directed them to the correct section. She found one on space ships and another on forest animals, since Matt had shown such an interest in her raccoon book. Her mother was looking elsewhere. Both brought their purchases to the register about the same time. Graci-Ella spied a round container of gummy bears and grabbed those too.

While the saleslady wrapped their purchases, Graci-Ella elbowed her mom. "You don't fool me, young lady."

"What?" Her mother plastered on her patented innocent look.

"I saw the books you got him. One of Maryland and another of famous women basketball players, that just happens to have my picture in it. I'm surprised they still have that book out."

"Well, when you and Boyd bring him to see us, I want him to know something of the state."

She planted her hand on the hip of her capris. "When Boyd and I bring Matt to see you? What makes you think we're getting that serious?"

"Young lady," her mother quipped, "don't you use that patented innocent expression on me! I see how you two look at each other and kiss. There's more than humidity in the air around here." She picked off an imaginary piece of lint on Graci-Ella's plaid cotton blouse. "Your father is looking forward to having Matt for a grandson and he thinks Boyd can do no wrong. Boyd took him on a tour of the fire station. He said everyone calls Boyd Tiny, which he found quite funny. He got to sit behind the wheel of one of those big fire trucks like a kid. So, you certainly have our blessing."

"Well, we need more time." Good God, the woman would be choosing wedding patterns next and wedding gowns. Graci-Ella glared at her mother. "Don't you *dare* go shopping for a wedding gown for me! I know how you work."

Her mother blinked in that innocent way she pretended. "Who, me? Why, I would never conceive of doing such a thing. Although I do think white would look better on you than ivory. Something plain to emphasize your height since Boyd is so tall. A long sheath, perhaps with pearls and lace at the neckline."

"Mother!"

"What? I didn't say a thing!"

CHAPTER SIXTEEN

Boyd finished cleaning his gear from a garage fire. He couldn't explain how good it felt to be back at work on a full-duty status. A man had to be next to crazy to find happiness in charging into a burning building, but there you had it. He was a fireman and damn he loved his job. Being able to fight one of the elements was a heady feeling, to say nothing of saving people's lives and their possessions.

He stowed away his items and headed for the shower, peeling off his sweat-soaked t-shirt on the way, tossing it into the squad's large washer. After his shower, he flopped onto his cot and called Matt. It was almost past his son's normal bedtime, but the hospital always had him off schedule.

"Dad! Guess who was here to see me! Just guess." Well, someone certainly had the kid wound up.

With the trial date getting closer, now would be the time for Chantel to start playing the devoted mother. He always made it a point of calling her when Matt was admitted to the hospital. In response, she made it a point of not coming to see him. He had yet to figure out why she was fighting for custody, unless it was pure spite.

"Your mom?"

"No! Better! Graci-fella and her mom. They bought me presents!"

On one hand, he was surprised and, on the other, he wasn't. Not really. Graci-Ella really cared about people. She had a special friendliness, a warmth about her. "They did? Did you thank them?"

"I hugged and kissed them both, was that thanks enough?"

Boyd laughed. Oh, this kid of his; was there even a way to measure his love for him? "Yes, I suppose so. What did they get you?"

"Grace, and she said I could call her that…ooor grandma. Graci-fella elbowed her on that remark. Anyhow, Grace gave me a book about 'Maryland,' that's the state they live in, like we live in Florida, and she gave me a book about famous women basketball players and guess what! You'll never guess in a million years!"

Boyd smiled and rubbed a hand over his heart. "What, son?"

"It has Graci-fella's picture in it! Is that cool, or what? She's got on a uniform and everything. Her hair's in a ponytail and she's jumping high to make a basket. She's famous!"

"Hey, that is cool. You'll have to show it to me, son."

"I will. Graci-fella gave me a book on spaceships and one on animals in a forest. I can read most of the words in that one. She also gave me a tub of gummi bears, but I can't eat more than four at a time. She made me promise."

"Sounds like a good promise to me." He'd have to thank her for her kindness to his son.

"Aaaand, she gave me a stuffed raccoon to remind me of her when her eyes were black and blue. I'm going to sleep with him while I'm here. She said that's not being 'babyfied,' that's keeping someone special in your thoughts. She is special, isn't she, dad?"

A warmness wrapped itself around his heart, thawing it after all Chantel had done to him and Matt. But who was he kidding? The melting of his heart had begun the moment Graci-Ella aimed those vibrant blue eyes at him. Every time he saw her, heard her laugh, smelled her perfume and held her lush curves against him, the speed of the melting increased. "Yes, Graci-Ella is very special."

Matt was curling into his sleeping position, the sounds of blankets and sheets rustled. "I'm naming my raccoon Fella after her." He yawned.

Boyd tried his best not to laugh. He'd soon have to work with his son on the correct pronunciation of her name but, damn, it sounded so cute the way Matt said it. "Sleep well, buddy."

"I love you, Daddy."

"Love you more." He ended their connection and dialed Graci-Ella's. He wanted to tell her how nice it was of her to go see his son and brighten his lonely evening.

"Hey, handsome. How did your day go?"

"Not as good as my son's. He got to see you. I believe he even mentioned hugging and kissing."

"What's wrong, big guy, feeling left out? Want me to drive to the station and tuck you into bed?" She laughed in that low, sexy way she had that aroused him in an instant, but then everything about her turned him on.

"Is your mom in bed?"

"Yes, she flies out early tomorrow and has a taxi reserved to pick her up."

"Then we can speak freely. Baby, if you come out here to tuck me into bed, you'd be in bed with me. You need to think if you're ready for the next step in our relationship, because it's going to be as physical as you can think of—and that's no lie. The only thing that will hold me back is you saying, 'No.' Is that clear?"

He detected a hitch in her breathing. "I'm ready, big guy. Have plenty of condoms on hand." His erection stretched another painful inch. God, what this woman could do to him.

"I'm going to have to say goodnight and take another shower. This shower will need to be cold…hellacious cold."

"Now, you know that's an oxymoron. Nothing about hell is cold."

"I hate a smartass lawyer. Love you, baby."

An idea popped into Graci-Ella's mind. She could make it work. Her mom was asleep, and she could sneak out once she changed clothes. She'd leave her a note in case she woke up. Graci-Ella rummaged through her skimpy wear drawer until she found a red stretchy tube top and a pair of black very brief running shorts she could adjust the ties on the side to pull the material up higher at her hips. Tonight, she was going commando. She rubbed her signature lotion on her arms, chest and neck. Then she covered it all with a short red satin robe with a tie belt and red mules she wouldn't put on until she got outside.

Ten minutes later, she strutted to the side door of the fire station and rang the bell. Wolf answered, his eyes widened as he glanced up and down her outfit. "Honey, we don't allow overnight guests or my wife would be here."

"I just want to tease Tiny. I won't stay but five minutes."

Wolf glanced over his shoulder at the guys watching a game in the TV room. "Are you wearing anything under that robe? 'Cause you're going to create one hell of a scene in here."

"Of course, what kind of person do you think I am?"

He grabbed her arm and pulled her inside. "One condition." He held up an index finger. "You stand at the entrance to the TV area, so we can all get a look at Tiny's reaction when he sees you. He'll probably beat your ass—in a nice way, of course."

A case of nerves moved into her stomach. "I thought I could do this privately."

"Privately?" his voice rose. "Around here? Ain't happening. Come on. You're putting on a little show for him. Right?"

A show? She was almost too embarrassed to smile. "Y…yes."

"Guys, hold down the noise until Tiny gets out here. Graci-Ella has a surprise for him."

"But we can watch. Right?" The eyes nearly bugged out of a young man called The Virgin. His Adam's apple bobbed when he swallowed.

"As much as Tiny will let you see. I just wanna watch his jaw drop. He's always in such control. You know how he is." Wolf pressed the button on the in-house intercom. "Tiny, you're needed out in the TV room. Tiny, get yer lazy ass out here."

A door slammed. "What in God's name do you want, you bossy son of a…" His voice trailed off as soon as he saw her. Of course, it was kind of hard to talk with your lower jaw hanging down to your waist. He wore blue plaid sleep pants and Nike sandals.

"Tiny," she purred, "your official tucking in service has arrived." She loosened the tie-belt on her short robe, just a little, and shifted her shoulders so the robe slid down revealing bear skin, but not the tube top.

The guys hooted and whistled.

Tiny strode four or five steps closer to her and then crooked his finger for her to come to him.

She shook her head and laughed. Her long hair swinging back and forth.

He pointed to the floor in front of him. Crap. He didn't seem too happy with her surprise.

"Are you going to smack my ass?"

His dark eyebrows were furrowed. "You have no idea."

She grabbed her purse off the dining room table and waved to the squad. "Sorry to run, guys, but I've got an ass to save." She made a beeline for the door.

Footsteps barreled down on her before strong hands lifted her into a fireman's carry and a palm struck her bottom. He shoved open the side door of the building and headed for the parking area. "What the hell, Graci-Ella! You come out here half naked, show off skin that only I should see."

"Why should only you see it?"

"I can't believe you even need to ask that question. Not as close as we are." He set her on the ground and walked away from her, while his lecture continued. "I've told you I love you over and over. You said the same thing to me. That creates a bond, dammit." He turned and she had her robe dropped to the parking lot.

132

"I'm not naked. I would never do that to you or myself. We were teasing each other and I thought with the stress of worrying about Matt and the court date coming up, you could use a good laugh." She bent to retrieve her robe and shook it out before she put it on, yanking the tie belt. "You better go back inside before the guys think we're out here doing the deed. I hate that I made you angry."

"Baby, I'm sorry. I want you for myself. Exclusively. When I thought you were naked under that robe, I saw green. Hell, the top of my head nearly blew off, I was so jealous."

"Don't you think you should know me better than that? Yes, I was teasing you, but not at the cost of my personal dignity—or yours." She unlocked her door, got in, started the little car and spun out.

Well, I certainly botched up that idea. Still, he didn't have to be so caveman about the whole deal.

She'd just stepped into her condo when the first text dinged. *We need to talk.* Oh, he was not getting anywhere with orders like that.

Is that an order, Mr. Caveman?

Call me.

I didn't see the magic word. She snorted and hit send.

She changed into a nightgown and brushed her hair and teeth before crawling into bed.

His next tweet was *PLEASE!!!!!!*

She swiped his number. "I'm really not in the mood to talk. As you so kindly pointed out, I made a fool of myself tonight, when I was only trying to cheer you. It was an error in judgment. One I won't ever make again. Now, you macho, arrogant caveman, I'd like to lick my wounds and go to sleep." She ended the call.

Her phone dinged an incoming text. *I was thinking of a conversation. U know. U talk. I talk. Then U talk. What U gave me was a damn monologue.*

She called him back. "What would you like to say? I put on extra perfume for your enjoyment, and you never got close enough

133

to smell it. I wore no underwear and you never touched me to find that out."

"Baby, may I please have a chance to say something? I'm sorry I over-reacted. What's worse, I hurt your feelings." Her tears started. "Sweetness, I love you. I cherish you. Don't cry."

"I'm tired. Today was the first day I've driven. I know I'm making a bigger issue than I need to. I just need sleep. Mom's taxi comes early to take her to the airport. Good night."

Quite a few tears were shed before she drifted off to sleep. After a few hours, her alarm went off. She made fresh squeezed orange juice, coffee and rye toast for her mother. "Think I could talk you and dad into moving here after you retire?"

"We might buy a condo in this town to rent during the summer when it gets really hot, but live in it ourselves during the winter to escape the snow and ice. Ellis likes it down here. We'd see you more often, which would be grand."

Graci-Ella got a text and was almost afraid to look at it. No doubt, Boyd was up and ready to start his texting marathon. Thank goodness, this was the taxi service announcing its arrival at the condo gate. She gave him the security code and the number of her condo. "Your ride is here, mom. Let me help you with your luggage."

"Nonsense! That's what I'm tipping the driver for." A flurry of hugs, kisses and good-byes, and her mother was gone. Graci-Ella felt lonely, yet relieved. Today was a good day for sulking.

Someone knocked at her door. Had her mother forgotten something? She unlocked and opened it to stare into Boyd's grey eyes and a t-shirt stretched tightly across muscles.

"Is your shift over? Why are you here? To bitch at me some more for doing something I thought you'd enjoy?"

Boyd sauntered in, cupped her cheek with one hand and her ass with his other. He pulled her against him. "I will not have this distance between us." His lips covered hers, and she didn't think she could stand up for the onslaught his mouth gave hers.

"I wasn't angry with you. The timing yes, because I needed you so badly and when I saw you like that I didn't think I could take my next breath. I wanted to take you on the floor, up against the wall, over the dining room table, on the kitchen counter, but we had an audience. And I won't have anyone else looking at you."

"Well, you could have fooled me."

"Yeah, I can act like an ass pretty quickly. Not with Matt. And I'd hoped not with you, but this sexual desire I have for you that's slowly driving me insane is playing havoc with my moods." The backs of his fingers ran down her cheek. "Because you're flawless and I adore every bit of your perfection."

"No one's perfect."

"Ask a man in love who desires a woman more than his next cup of coffee or his next breath of air or to hear his next heart-beat." He leaned in and kissed her forehead. "There is this astute mind of yours for starters." Kisses feathered on her eyes. "Then, you have these beautiful azure eyes that see things others miss. Eyes that take my breath away."

Her mouth drifted open and a nervous tongue moistened her lips just before he kissed her.

"I think you already know what I think of your lips. The gracefulness of your neck and the delicious way it smells draws me like a magnet." By turns, he gently bit, soothed with his tongue and kissed her neck. "A man could feast here forever, but then he'd miss the rest of the delights your body presents." As he talked and seduced, he asked which way her bedroom was and she silently pointed.

His voice kept up its sexual purr as he continued with the compliments until he had her backed against the bed. He reached back with one hand and yanked off his t-shirt and toed off his boots. She pulled off her nightgown and lay on the bed. Waiting. Watching.

He tugged three rubbers from his front pocket, laid them on the nightstand and then unbuttoned his jeans. He shucked his boxers, leaving him completely naked.

Her gaze feasted on his cock, which was a turn on in itself. "There's nothing tiny about you, is there?"

A blush heated her skin as he took a long, slow gaze over her body. "My Sweetness." Her bed dipped as he crawled in, lying half over her. His fingertips lightly skimmed her face, neck and breasts. Her nipples peaked in response. "God, I love your large breasts." He lowered his head and circled her points with his tongue while his hand applied gentle pressure in a caress to her breast. "A freakin' work of art."

He drew her nipple into his mouth and sucked while her back bowed toward him. She gasped and scratched his back. "Oh my God. Don't you dare stop!"

Eyes gazed at what he obviously wanted to devour when he raised his head to look at her. "Stop? Oh, baby, I don't intend to stop for years. You better believe I'm just getting started." His palms slowly stroked the skin of her thighs to the shaved lips of her labia as if they were the last thing he wanted to touch in his lifetime. "Pure silk. Sweet satin. Sensual skin a man dreams of."

He reached for a condom and tore open the foil. "A warning. This first time will be fast. I've got it for you so freaking bad, I won't have much control."

"It's okay."

"No, it won't be. I want you to come first." His lips were like warm, breathy caresses showering her body with the purity and strength of his emotions. "My love." While he sucked at her breasts, his one hand slid between their bodies, first one finger and then two entering her while his thumb circled her clit. Her body tightened. Her muscles quivered and her core spun into a coil of desire. His lips traveled down her abdomen while his fingers created a rhythm she could not resist.

"I want you in me when I come. I'm so close. I want our first time to be together."

Boyd slipped his hands under her legs and bent to circle his tongue around her nub until she started to climax against his fingers. He withdrew and shoved his cock into her, pushing her legs higher over his shoulders. Her climax rolled through her body and she trembled, screaming his name. A few more strokes and he groaned her name against her throat. And limbs around limbs, skin to skin, heart to heart, they meshed and melted into the fissures and jagged pits of each other's souls.

CHAPTER SEVENTEEN

They both must have dozed for over an hour, according to Graci-Ella's clock. She woke with the weight of a thick thigh over her legs, a muscular arm around her, holding her breast in his hand and a mighty fine erection, lying in wait in the crack of her butt cheeks. Her gaze zeroed onto the remaining two condoms on her dresser. Did she have the stamina for two more rounds?

"I may have been selfish with grabbing three. I wasn't giving thought to what you've been through the last few weeks. His large hand released her breast and knocked one foil packet onto the floor. "I felt you stiffen when you woke up and looked at them. Want me to toss the other one too?"

His voice was so sexy when it was heavy with sleep. She snuggled back against him and he moved her hair to the side to kiss her neck. "Baby."

"Put the rubber on and take me this way. Play with my clit like you did before, while you slide into me from behind. As big as you are, you can reach my opening with no problem."

He reached for the condom. "I like a woman who knows what she wants."

"I read about it in a book. It sounded interesting. I want to see how it feels."

"Is this classified as legal research?" After he'd sheathed himself, he nibbled and kissed her shoulders. With one arm under her shoulders and his other slipped under her one elbow, he plucked at both nipples, giving them a gentle twist every so often. He moved his hand to lift her leg over his thigh and began working her clit. As soon as he slid in, she started moaning. "So good. So, so good. I had no idea."

"How do you want it? Fast or slow?"

"Slow, big guy." She reached under him and fondled his balls.

"Hell, Sweetness, much of that and I'll be out of my freaking mind." How nice to know some of his sensitive spots. After all, one didn't make All-American without knowing how to work a ball.

"After Chantel left, I never thought I'd love again or trust another woman. Then I found you and my heart opened to both emotions."

Chantel? Why did that name sound familiar? She ran into all kinds of names in her profession. Chantel Calloway certainly had a ring to it. The way he was nibbling and kissing her shoulders while he circled her bud with his thumb erased whatever she was thinking. All she could do was concentrate on the onslaught of her building climax.

"Boyd!" Her climax was growing, stronger and stronger.

"Come for me baby. Need me faster? Harder?"

"No, don't change a thing!" Her muscles contracted and her core unspun like a child's top...and she screamed, convulsing around him.

He came within a few more strokes, telling her over and over how much he loved her as he held her close, almost as if he were trying to absorb her into his skin. Eventually, he released her and went into her bathroom to dispose of the condom.

Not that she was one to stare, but he did have a fine, naked behind. And he seemed comfortable in his own skin. Could she walk around naked in front of him? Or would she reach for a robe? Her previous relationships were less intense than this one. From the beginning, their interaction had been different, more teasing on one hand and quite powerful on the other.

She trusted him. He was a good person, full of integrity and caring ways she found deeply appealing.

He strutted back in her bedroom and stretched on her bed, leaning his head against a hand upturned at the elbow. "What are your plans for the day?" His other hand skimmed up and down her side. "Visiting hours start at one in Matt's ward. Would you like to go with me? We could shower and stop for a soft shell crab sandwich on our way."

She studied his eyes. "Would Matt like sharing you with me? Kids have a way of being very possessive of their parents, especially the one they depend on the most."

"I think it's time he sees us together as a couple and come to think of the three of us as a unit, don't you?" He took her wrist, bringing her palm up so he could press a kiss on it.

Acid rolled in her stomach. "A unit of what? What are your thoughts about our future?" She swallowed loudly in the quiet room. "Exactly."

He bent to kiss both of her breasts. "I'm thinking of a long relationship. But I'm not sure how you feel about a child becoming a large part of your life? Or knowing you'll always come second to Matt. His mother pushed him aside. I won't." His jaw was set with determination.

He'd been honest with her. Now it was her turn. "I understand that's your reality. My reality is I'm a lawyer who works long hours five days a week. Sometimes, I bring cases home with me to do legal research on and write briefs. I'd planned on a marriage and a couple of children in a few years, when my career is more settled."

"Are you telling me your future is non-negotiable? That there's no room in your heart for the destiny of two strangers meeting and falling in love?" Her man was so open and truthful about his emotions. Was she understanding him correctly?

"But you're not talking about our moving in together, are you? That might be too much for Matt to accept after all he's had to deal with at his mom's. This hearing is going to be hard on him. We have to give him a space of time with no changes, where he can become grounded in his security again."

Boyd rolled onto his back and laid an arm over his eyes. "I know. We've had child protective services at the townhouse. They interviewed him. So has a child psychologist." He chuffed a laugh. "Poor kid. He was scared to death to say something wrong. He was afraid the incorrect answer would take him away from me. We had a lot of long talks about being truthful opposed to saying what we think people want to hear. I kept telling him to be honest about everything. That it was okay to give a wrong answer now and then. He even developed a stutter for a month or so."

"Oh no, poor baby." She'd seen a few kids traumatized by the trial process.

"I called the child psychologist and explained. I asked if she could interview him in a playful environment rather than a sterile room. She said she'd work something out. When she called his mother to verify what I'd told her, Chantel claimed Matt had no stuttering problem. So, who do you think was believed? Surely not me. My son was a basket case when the interview was over and within hours went into a full blown asthma attack."

He rolled and sat on the edge of the bed. "Wish you could have heard how happy he was after you and your mom came to visit him yesterday. Thanks for your thoughtfulness, by the way. Last night, he slept with the raccoon you gave him. He…ah…named it after you." He glanced over his shoulder at her and grinned. "Fella."

"Fella? Ohhh! He calls me Graci-Fella. I think it's so cute how he does that. I'm honored he named Fella after me. I would never mind coming second to him as long as you could handle coming second to my career."

A strange expression played across Boyd's face. His eyes narrowed for a few seconds and the muscle in his jaw twitched. His phone rang and he glanced at her as he dug it out of his jeans on the floor. "It's the hospital's ring." He swiped it. "Boyd Calloway speaking." There was a slight pause. "Awesome. We're on our way in about half an hour. Thanks." He ended the call. "Matt's lungs are clear, he can come home today. I'd like for you to come along, but only if you're good with that."

She kissed him and shoved him back on the bed. "I get dibs on the shower." She grabbed some clean panties and bra from her dresser before charging for the bathroom.

Boyd paced through her bedroom while she showered. What the hell kind of agreement had they just arranged? They would see each other, but not live together—which was probably best for Matt. Her career would always come first, as would his son. But what about the two of them? Where was their love in all of this? What about their future? Did she want a future with him? A lawyer and a fireman—and another woman's biological child. *Fuck!*

They hadn't settled a damn thing. All they'd done was muddy the waters because he hadn't mentioned what he truly wanted. Her. A marriage. At least one more child. A house with the damn picket fence he'd have to paint every year—and God how he hated painting. But he'd do it for her…for them.

Graci-Ella charged into the bedroom, wearing a set of blue lace underwear and her hair brushed into a ponytail. "Shower's all yours." She started slathering on that great smelling lotion that set his libido into overdrive.

He snatched his boxers from the floor and headed for the bathroom, evidently it was the room with the steam still rolling out of it. Barely warm water sluiced down his back as he soaped up and sulked some more. There was no doubt in his mind he loved her. She'd told him she loved him, but were they talking about the same kind of love? And what exactly had she said that put him in this pissy mood?

He turned around to rinse off his front. He'd just had two mind-blowing orgasms. He'd had his hands all over her, his lips too. She'd agreed to go along to pick-up Matt. So, what was up with his mood?

He turned off the water and reached for a towel. She was looking on this as a casual relationship. He wanted permanence.

When he returned to the bedroom, she was applying some make-up. She had on jean shorts and a blue t-shirt with a basketball sailing through a net and the slogan, "String Music" in pink lettering. She looked fabulous and he was getting angrier by the minute.

"I go back to work tomorrow. This is the last day of my medical vacation."

"Guess that makes you happy." He jerked on his jeans and buttoned them before snatching his t-shirt off the floor and shaking it out. He rammed his arms into the sleeves and yanked it over his head, then ran his fingers through his wavy hair to make sure it wasn't sticking up.

She stopped whatever she was doing to her eyes and turned. "Boyd? Are you upset about something? The tone of your voice is different, clipped. I can almost sense your anger vibrating from here."

He sat on her bed to put on his boots. "I thought you understood what I was fumbling around, trying to say earlier. I want an exclusive, serious relationship with you." He jerked on his shoestrings. "I'm not into casual, especially the way I feel about you."

"Neither am I." She stepped between his spread legs and cupped his face. "My man, I love you. I've never loved another man before, and I'm pretty scared about this new emotion in my life. Sure I dated. I lost my virginity years ago. So, I suppose one could say I've already done casual. But you're so intense, too forceful to look on as casual. With you, there's safety and an abundance of love I find I need. I need you, sweetheart."

Somewhat mollified, he forged ahead on a burst of breath. "But for how long?"

Her eyebrows wrinkled. "How long, what?"

"Baby, I'm thinking forever. I want it all with you and Matt and whoever else comes along."

She swallowed in that loud way she had when she was nervous. "Wh...what do you mean by forever?"

Damn if he hadn't allowed her to box him into that corner. He glanced away to think how he needed to phrase this—obviously, very delicately. "I want us to work toward a future that includes marriage, because that's how strongly I love you. I'm not ready to propose yet. As you said, we need to get Matt straightened out first. But I want to be up front here." He sliced the air with the edge of his hand. "One day, I want to put a wedding band on your finger. Maybe six months from now. A year, or more. Whenever we're both ready. Take a few days to think about it, to see if you want to work toward the same thing."

She nodded as if he'd knocked her speechless.

He couldn't go into it anymore. First, he needed to get his temperament smoothed out. "I don't know about you, but I need to stop at a drive-in somewhere for coffee and a sandwich. Or I won't have the energy to handle that boy once he's home." He placed his hands on the backs of her thighs. "Sweetness, I love you to a degree I can't begin to explain. You need to think and gauge how much you love me. We need to make sure we're on the same relationship page."

"I will. Thank you for sharing your feelings. Your honesty is one of the many things I admire about you." She extended her hand. "Come on, my man, I'm starving too."

Later they walked into Matt's room to find him dressed and his books in a bag. He clutched to Fella and was nearly in tears. His arms outstretched to Boyd.

"Hey, buddy, what is it?"

"I...I'm afraid they won't let me go home once...once I tell them how bad my feet hurt."

Both Boyd and Graci-Ella looked at a pair of sneakers tied onto the wrong feet. Boyd covered his mouth, spun and started laughing. Graci-Ella backhanded his ass.

144

"Oh, that sneaky raccoon. Did he make you put your sneakers on the wrong feet?" She crouched and untied his shoes, removing them. "Raccoons are tricky like that."

Boyd turned just in time to see Matt run the heel of his palm over the end of his nose. "I...I didn't know."

Graci-Ella reached for a tissue and handed it to him, without missing a beat. Then she kissed the top of each foot before she put the sneakers back on him. "It was just a little mistake. We'll forgive Fella this time. Okay?"

Matt smiled. "Okay. I wish you were my mom. You make me feel good." He pointed to the area of her surgery. "Let me see your scar. Is it any better today?" His fingertip trailed the incision. "I think it's healing."

"Probably because of that kiss you gave it yesterday." She gave a huge sigh. "If only I could get another kiss, I know it would feel better."

"Didn't my dad hug and kiss you today?"

"I think that's none of your business wise guy." Boyd tapped the end of Matt's nose. He was growing up too fast or witnessing too much at his mother's place. Boyd didn't even want his mind to go there.

"To be honest, Matt, he did. But I'm not sure if he does as good a job as you do."

Matt heaved a sigh just as she'd done a minute earlier and held out his little arms. "Okay then." He kissed her incision and hugged her until she grunted. "Dad, what's wrong with you? She smells so good. You should be hugging her a lot."

Graci-Ella flashed Boyd one of her heart-stopping smiles. "Yeah, Dad, you should be hugging me a lot." Then she had the audacity to wink. Oh, she would pay.

A member of the hospital auxiliary pushed a wheelchair into the room. "Do we have a young man in here ready to go home?"

Once they were all buckled in the Mustang, Matt started. "Graci-Fella, are you a good cook? 'Cause I was thinking. You could stay

145

at our place this evening and cook us some shrimp pasta and then watch a movie. Do you like Transformers? I've got all their movies. And do you put a lot of shrimp in your pasta, 'cause I like a lot of shrimp. We could all snuggle on the sofa—Dad, you, me and Fella—just like a real family. How's that sound?"

"Sounds like you better take me to my place so I can pick up my rental and buy some shrimp at the seafood store. I do have to get up early for work tomorrow." She glanced at Boyd as if measuring his reaction.

"Will this be too hard on you? I'm not wild about you driving home late at night. We could order in pizza."

A six-year old groan sounded from the back seat. "Not pizza *again*. Can't we just drive her home when it's bedtime, Dad?"

"We'll still need to stop at the market so I can get the ingredients. You guys get what you want in your salad."

Boyd glanced over his shoulder to Matt in the back seat and nearly exploded with laugher at Matt's widened eyes. "Salad comes with the shrimp pasta, buddy."

"If she makes it, I'll eat it. Well, a bite, anyway." There was a pregnant pause. "Hope I don't throw it back up."

They carried in their groceries, and Boyd ordered Matt to bed for a nap after the kid showed her his bedroom, decorated with spaceships and fish.

"Why don't you lie down with him and let him show you his books, while I make the salad and wash the vegies for the shrimp pasta?" Her warm blue eyes waited for his reply.

"Make the salad and then come in his room and snuggle in with us. We'll all three take a nap." Would she think that was too much togetherness? He didn't want her to overdo if she was starting back to work tomorrow—a week too soon in his opinion.

From behind them came a devilish little voice of wisdom. "The family who naps together stays together."

Boyd whipped his head around as did Graci-Ella. *Where does he pick up these sayings?* He guessed now would be a time for her

146

to make another step or hold her ground. Hell, he was just happy she'd agreed to cook for them and watch a movie.

He looked at her shocked expression. Her gaze traversing from Matt to the kitchen to him. "Give me ten minutes."

"Yes!" Matt gave a fist pump and charged back to his bedroom.

Boyd slid his hand across the small of her back. "Sweetness, do you want me to talk to him? I'll tell him relationships move at a slower pace. He gets being pushy from his dad."

Her gaze rose to meet his. "Gee, who would have guessed?"

CHAPTER EIGHTEEN

Ten minutes after her male escorts brought her home, hugged and kissed her goodnight, Graci-Ella was in her pajamas looking for a new car online. She'd loved her Rav-4 and wanted another one with a sun roof and side airbags, preferably in white. A couple dealers in Tampa had what she wanted. She printed out their addresses to visit after work tomorrow. It would feel odd to walk back into the firm again after being on sick leave for so long.

She crawled into bed and smiled over their cocooned snuggling in Matt's double bed. When she lay down, the little guy was against the wall, big guy was in the middle and she clung for dear life to the edge of the bed. Boyd suggested they all lay on their sides, so everyone had enough room. Matt's little hand barely reached his dad's arm. Boyd's arm with the nearly full-sleeve tattoo wrapped around her and settled on her breast. She traced his design with her fingernail.

The closeness didn't take her long to drift off and, at one point, the bed shifted and Boyd's hand moved off her breast for an instant. A sigh filled the room followed by a whispered, "Now I feel like an Oreo cookie. I'm safe. No one can make me sit in one spot for hours." Boyd grunted and she figured she'd dreamed the whole thing until an hour or so later when she woke to find Matt on his side snuggled securely between them, his one little arm around Fella.

Early morning brought the music from her clock radio and her usual hurried routine. She strode into the office building, a large cappuccino in one hand and her briefcase in the other. The black sheath she wore showcased the weight she'd lost during her time off. Her pink and black dotted scarf and pink stilettoes brightened the dress. She stepped on the elevator and pressed the button for the fourth floor. Across the door to her office was a banner that read, "Welcome Back!" She peeled it off carefully and walked into her office, expecting to find all her plants dead from lack of water.

To her surprise, they were all green and healthy looking. There was a new flowering plant with a card. "I took care of your green babies until you got back. The wife picked out this new one for you. Sure have missed your smiling face around here. Jo-Jo."

She smiled and rubbed her finger over his shaky scrawl. He was the nicest man.

As quickly as she could, she went through her back mail, tossing away ads and legal magazines she wouldn't have time to read anyway. She turned on her computer and logged into her email. She went through her files to prepare for court, thankful to see someone had taken at least half of them. Taking note of the cases going to court in two weeks, she removed them from the top of the pile. Once she'd emptied the worst of her two-thousand plus emails, she'd scan over these files.

She deleted the emails about meetings she'd missed and the cartoons everyone felt compelled to send to everybody in the office. Those emails from the partners, she read. Next she skimmed through the messages from the junior partners.

By now, her cappuccino was gone and her head was pounding. She emptied two prescription pills in her hand and strode up the hallway to the water dispenser. On her way, a couple people hurried by and blurted, "Welcome back. How are you feeling?" Since they never stopped to hear her response, she figured they weren't all that concerned. She rounded the corner and got a cup

149

of coffee and a pack of Oreos from the snack machines. Matt and his cookie analogy. Just what did he mean by having to sit in one spot for hours? She'd have to talk to him privately. Maybe he'd open up to her.

She went back to her office to attack the remainder of her emails, deleting many. Then she saw two from the same email address: kissylips@mugo.com. Her heart rate kicked up. One was written three weeks ago. She opened it and read the message: "I was out of jail long before you'll get out of the hospital." No signature. No threat. So, she opened the second one. "You look a little cramped in that faded red compact you're driving. Wait until I push it off the road. Maybe off a bridge somewhere."

Okay, now I'm freaking.

She swiped through her phone contacts, but had nothing for the officers who investigated the accident. She could call Boyd, but he'd go into his protective mode. So, she called Ivy Jo to ask if she had any information about the policemen who arrested Darryl at the scene of the accident. Meanwhile Graci-Ella wiped damp hands on her skirt. How did he know her work email or what kind of car she was driving? Shivers made a round trip through her system. So did a strong dose of fear. He must be watching her—the crazy man who'd run her off the road, trying to kill her—was watching her.

"Gee, hon, that was over a month ago. Give me a second to think. Sorry I'm so slow on the ball. Today is my yearly mammogram and pap smear, and I'm concentrating on that. Okay, I remember now. Lieutenant Lithgow."

Graci-Ella scribbled his name on a legal pad. "Thank you, friend. Sorry to bother you on your day off. Good luck with your tests. Bye now." She ended the call and phoned the police department, asking if Lieutenant Lithgow was in. Her first question, when he came on the line, was if Darryl Weir was out on bond.

"Yes, he is. His family made bail…" papers rustled. "Two days after his preliminary hearing."

"And no one thought to tell me? I had to find out in two creepy emails from him on my first day back at work? Somehow he found out my work email address. He's been watching me; knows what kind of car I'm driving and is making threats." Anger and terror both raced like swimmers through her veins.

"Ms. Santana, can you forward those emails to me? Don't delete the originals. Here's my address." She forwarded them both to him. "Reading them now. Do you want an escort to and from your law firm?"

She took a deep breath and fought to gain control of her runaway emotions. Her fingers ran over the side of her head where her headache was having one hellacious bang of a party. "No, but thanks for the offer. It seems a little excessive, doesn't it? No doubt he'd just trying to scare the bejesus out of me, which he did. I can take care of myself if I know what I'm up against. The last person I expected to hear from was him. It really threw me off guard. Do you have the name of his lawyer and the trial date?" She made notes, crossed out her nervous scribbling because even she couldn't read it and rewrote everything more legible.

She fingered the folder on top. Trial date was November third. Last name, Calloway. *Dear God, no!* "Look, Lieutenant, I have to go. Thank you for the information." She flipped the cover of the folder and stared at the client's name until it became forever etched in her mind—Chantel Calloway.

Graci-Ella fought her tears.

She was being watched by the deranged man who'd tried to kill her.

She was in love with a wonderful man who loved his son more than anything.

And she was the lawyer assigned to represent the ex in a case to take Matt away from him.

She flipped through the pages in the file, skimming over the typical legal jargon and concentrating on the pertinent details of the case. Chantel had certainly portrayed Boyd as a completely different man than the one Graci-Ella knew. She read over the private investigator's report, which read more like the man she loved.

There was no way she could represent Chantel. Graci-Ella was having sex with the accused—talk about a conflict of interest. She groaned and laid her head on the desk. What a great day this way turning out to be.

Her office phone rang and it was the receptionist telling her flowers had just been delivered for her. She smiled and strode toward the firm's entrance. They had to be from Boyd or maybe her parents. Bethany, the firm's receptionist, glanced at her oddly and pointed to the vase of white lilies and black roses. Graci-Ella's mouth went dry. She knew before she read the card who they were from.

Touching only the edges of the card, she read, "With deepest sympathies for your upcoming funeral." There was no signature, of course, but she knew. She removed the plastic card holder.

"Bethany, would you please throw these away? They're from the man who ran me off the road. He's out on bail and sending me threats."

The pretty blonde's jaw dropped. "Oh, Graci-Ella. How awful! Have you called the police?"

"I did after I got threatening emails from the whack job here at work. Looks like I'll need to call again." She pulled her cell from her dress pocket and dialed Lieutenant Lithgow. He told her he'd be by to get the card with the message. She thanked Bethany one more time and prodded back to her office, stopping at the snack machines to buy a bottle of water. Time to quit thinking about Darryl's scare tactics and work on the really important issue—the custody trial that was about to destroy so many lives, including hers.

She peeked into Patrick's office as she passed by and knocked on his door frame. He spun around. "Hey, look who's back! How are you doing?"

"Not so good. I have a case Elizabeth gave me that's a direct conflict of interest. I'll trade it for three of yours."

His eyes narrowed. "What's wrong with it?"

"A custody case. I never looked at the name on the folder when Elizabeth handed it to me, except to check on the trial date. I'm dating the ex-husband. It's gotten serious and I'm very close to the child they're fighting over."

"Hell, that certainly comes under the heading of conflict of interest. When's the trial date?" He opened his calendar.

"November third." She crossed both of her fingers.

"Can't. I've got two trials that day too. Did you ask Joe?"

She exhaled a sigh of disappointment. "No, but I will. Thanks, anyhow." She pivoted toward her office and ran into one of the senior partners, Sterling Hughes. "Oops! I'm sorry."

"Jesus Christ!" He yanked off his glassed her boobs had crashed into and knocked out of kilter. He scowled as he wiped the lenses with his handkerchief. Was it her fault she was so tall and he wasn't quite average height? "I was on my way to your office. We need to have a discussion."

Was she getting fired? She'd been off work for over a month, and the firm had a strict policy about not missing a lot of time. Well, this would certainly take care of her conflict of interest, wouldn't it?

She led the way into her small, but pretty office space and offered him a seat. He glanced around. "Last time I peeked in here, it was a hovel. You've worked hard to make your space very nice." He nodded and sat in one of the leather client chairs she loved so much. "Very nice, indeed."

He glanced at her for a minute with glasses that now sat crooked on his nose. "You've lost weight. The scar from your brain surgery is bigger than I expected. I understand you're getting threats from the man who ran you off the road. Bethany thinks a lot of you and she stopped me to tell me what happened with the flowers. She said there were more threats. Care to tell me about them?" He unbuttoned his suit jacket as if settling in for a long conversation. "Did you know him before the accident?"

She reminded him of the firemen's calendar she was photographing of the top notch firefighting unit. Sterling Hughes nodded. As she gave him the short version of the story, he frowned. His lips narrowed when she told him about Darryl running her off the road into a group of trees. She asked him if he wanted to read the emails she got from him.

He stood and moved behind her as she brought the first and second email on her monitor for him to read. "Have you called the police about this? The second one is a blatant threat."

"Yes, and I called him again when I got the flowers this morning."

"Call me when he comes. I want to sit in on this meeting. You're also going to want a restraining order against this Darryl Weir."

"Yes, you're right. I was hoping he'd still be in jail so I hadn't given it much thought."

"I'll set it up for you. You'll still need to sign the forms. We'll want it for personal, phone, email, texts and anything else you find harassing. No one should have to go through this. My daughter was hassled by a male student at college. She damned near dropped out of Yale over the no good bastard."

"Oh, that's awful. Has he stopped?"

"With Daddy Sterling on his ass, you better believe he stopped!"

"Mr. Hughes, I have another problem I could use your advice on." She held up Chantel's folder and told him it was one Elizabeth has asked her to take over when she was given her first important case. Then she felt the heat of a blush as she explained she'd been dating the ex-husband and things were very serious between them, causing this conflict of interest.

"All the lawyers in our firm are very busy. Call the woman who filed the custody case and tell her we can't represent her. Tell her you've been in the hospital and haven't been able to properly prepare for her side of the argument. Tell her we'll refund her deposit, but she'll have to find another attorney." He stood.

"Remember, call me when the Lieutenant shows up."

"Yes, sir." Although, frankly she was more concerned about Chantel Calloway than she was Darryl Weir. Sterling Hughes left her office, and she opened Chantel's file to locate her phone number. *This conversation ought to be pleasant.*

"Chantel Calloway?"

An annoyed huff sounded over the line. "Yes, who the hell is this? I'm in the middle of a pedicure. No, not that pink. It's got an orangey tint to it. I told you hot pink. Now, who did you say you were?"

"This is Graci-Ella Santana, the attorney assigned to your custody hearing for your little boy."

"What happened to Elizabeth? I liked her." The woman certainly had whining down to an art form. No, it was more like fingernails scraping a chalkboard. Her voice was the type that grated on one's nerves.

"Elizabeth has been given a larger, more important case."

There was a gasp over the phone line. "More important than *my* case? I resent that!"

Resent it all you want lady. "Unfortunately, I'm not going to be able to handle this legal affair for you, either. My senior partner has authorized me to inform you of our decision to withdrawal as your legal representatives and to refund you your deposit of the lawyer's retainer fee. You'll have to find yourself other legal counsel. I wish you good luck. Good bye, Ms. Calloway." Graci-Ella hung up in the middle of the woman's screaming rant.

She called the finance department of the law firm, told the person in charge what Sterling Hughes had told her what to do and gave her the name and address of their former client, as well as the amount paid as a retainer fee. She closed the file and placed it on her narrow cabinet.

Her headache was growing worse, accompanied by some dizziness. No doubt it was coming from stress more than her car accident. She rummaged in her purse for some strong headache medicine, washed it down with her bottled water.

Another glance at Chantel's file lifted her spirits. Thank God, she'd gotten out of that mess. She checked her emails again and found another from Darryl. *No one messes with my life. Gotta say I enjoyed watching you and Tiny screw yesterday morning.*

Someone knocked on her open door and she jumped.

"Sorry. I'm Lieutenant Lithgow. We talked earlier."

She took a sip of her water and motioned him in. "I just got another email from Darryl." She stood and moved out of the way so the Lieutenant could sit and read. "I'm supposed to call one of the senior partners when you get here. He'll want to hear about this latest email. Although I can't say I want him to read it." Her stomach turned. She was exactly happy to have a strange policeman read it either. She made her call and Sterling said he was on his way.

Both men agreed Darryl possessed a danger to Graci-Ella. Plans were made to have him arrested again. They discussed how they would handle the case. Sterling knew the district attorney and several judges quite well. Many of them played golf together. He'd handle things on his end.

Lieutenant Lithgow phoned the captain of Boyd's squad and asked him if he knew of some places Darryl hung out or who his buddies were. Evidently, the captain asked why because the policeman filled him in on the threatening emails and flowers Graci-Ella received. "He's been watching her apartment, her rental car and her private life. The threats aren't overtly cruel, but bad enough she needs protection and he needs arrested again. This time, with no bail." After a few more minutes of conversation, the call was ended.

She hated being talked about as if she weren't really there. But the way her head and eyes hurt, she wasn't so sure she was. Sometimes, the room spun and at others it turned blurry. ·

Sterling, leaned toward her. "How are you? Your baby blues look they could use some rest. I think one of us ought to drive you home. Tomorrow is another day for you to start fresh. You've always given this firm your very best and we've noticed. We especially noticed when you were gone so long."

Lieutenant Lithgow offered to drive her home and see that she had a policeman drive her to the office tomorrow morning. She could get her rental car then.

"Who is your insurance agent?" Sterling plucked a pack of sticky notes from his pocket and a pen. "I'm going to call him and tell him you want a different car. Did I hear you mention compact with your long legs? You need an SUV." He waved an open hand. "I'll take care of it. The different car will be in your parking space tomorrow morning and the keys with Bethany." He stood and nodded to them both. "I think we're through here." He pointed to her. "Sleep the rest of the day."

CHAPTER NINETEEN

Boyd dialed Graci-Ella's number and handed the phone to Matt at the kitchen table so he could talk. Meanwhile, he loaded the dishwasher and wiped off the kitchen counters. He'd missed his love all day and, at times, Matt missed her too. The guys decided to pick up some take out and carry supper to her condo.

"Hi, Graci-Fella. This is Matt. How's work going?" There was a pause. "You sound strange, like you're sleeping at work." She must have spoken again. "How did you get home?" Boyd froze. "A policeman?" Boyd's heart rate increased.

He asked Matt for the phone. "Baby? What's going on?"

The bed clothes rustled. "I got a bad headache at work. Then dizziness hit."

"Did you pass out?"

"No. But my whole day was rather bizarre. I was sent home early. One of the senior partners is having my auto insurance company swap the older compact they gave me for an SUV. It's supposed to be in my parking space tomorrow morning."

His temper flickered. "Why didn't you call me for help? Taking care of you pleases me. Didn't your time in the hospital teach you that? Matt and I would have come to the law firm to pick you up as soon as you called."

"Because I didn't want to drag Matt out and have him overdo.

Why have him wear down quickly the way I did. I had to have a policeman drive me home and I went straight to bed after I closed all the blinds."

Damn her headache must have been bad. "How are you getting to work tomorrow? I'll be at the station. Are you calling a taxi?" Something more was going on. She was hiding something from him.

"I have a ride."

His temper raised a notch and his fingers clamped the phone. "With…?"

"My man, I want to tell you and I want you to hold me, but I know you'll probably overreact and scare Matt." She sounded like she was crying. She needed him.

"Matt, go pick out a movie for tonight, but not one that's too loud. In fact, get three and we'll let Graci-Ella choose. I'm going outside on the patio to talk to her."

"Okay, daddy. Give her a kiss for me too." He squealed and giggled as he trotted into the living room.

He sat on one of the patio chairs. "Talk to me."

"Did you know Darryl is out on bond?"

He jumped out of the chair and paced. "What the fuck? No, I didn't."

"I didn't either until I was wading through all the emails, deleting old ones, etc., and found two from an email address, Kissy Lips. The first one was just his normal smart ass thing. The second was a threat."

"What do you mean threat?" He'd kill the bastard.

"He knows the type of car I'm driving now and he threated to drive it off a bridge, with me in it, of course."

"He motherfucking what?" He stomped through his yard.

"I called Ivy Jo to see if she remembered the name of the arresting officer at my accident." *Ivy Jo, but not me?* "She gave me his name and I called him. He asked me to keep the original emails and forward him copies. I figured Darryl was just trying to scare me. Then the receptionist called to tell me I'd had flowers delivered. I figured they were from you. As soon as I saw the lilies and black roses, I knew."

"Oh, Jesus, baby," he whispered. How many times could he beat someone for scaring this sweet woman?

"The card read something about sympathies for my upcoming funeral. I kept the card, touching only the edges in case there were any fingerprints on it and called Lieutenant Lithgow again. He said he'd come right over. By the time I got back to my office, another email from Kissy Lips was waiting. He said he'd enjoyed watching us have sex yesterday morning. He's been watching me, the car I drive and my home." She blew her nose with a tissue. "And, no, I am not crying!"

"Did I say you were?"

"No. You were getting ready to lecture me on not relying on you more. On calling Ivy Jo and the police and having the police take me to work tomorrow. Honey, you have a sick child to look after. I'll get through this on my own, one step at a time."

She couldn't have jabbed his heart or his male ego any harder. "Are you punishing me because I told you Matt would always come first?"

"What? Is that the kind of woman you think I am? Petty? Childish? Vindictive?"

He ran his hand through his hair in frustration. "No. That would be my ex-wife. She would go to any lengths to make me pay for something I thoughtlessly said. You've taught me not all women are like that." He bent to pull a weed from the flowers Matt had planted.

"Well, you adorable idiot. I'm telling you he should come first. I'm also telling you I'll take care of myself. I filed a restraining order against him for any type of contact."

"I don't like it. Why can't I take care of you both?"

"If we were already married and living together, you'd have no choice. But neither one of us is ready for that. We both have responsibilities right now that take precedence."

"Hell you sound like a damn lawyer. Do you or do you not want to have supper and a movie with us tonight?"

"Yes. I need to see you, big guy. I want hugged so bad, I ache for it. I know I said I can take care of myself, but that doesn't mean I don't need your strength and support at times too."

"You mentioned having blinds in your bedroom. What about the rest of the condo? I don't want that bastard spying on you again. What does he use? Binoculars? Hell, you're on the third floor."

"Beats me. And how did he get the code to enter the parking lot? This whole business creeps me out. You're right, I'm in the habit of opening them when I get up, but until he's in jail for a good long time, I'll keep them drawn all the time. I never asked how Matt's feeling today?"

"Better. He'll go back to school tomorrow when I go back to work. These are the choices the kid gave you for supper. Soft shell crab sandwiches and curly fries…or pizza," dragging it out in bored way Matt did.

"I'm guessing soft shells would be the correct answer to that. You two want to eat and watch movies over here? Can I just stay in my pajamas? Tell Matt to wear his. We'll have a pajama party. She cleared her throat." She was waiting for him to jump on the pajama band wagon. *Ain't happening, sweet cakes.*

"I am not going into Pete's Soft Shells in a pair of freaking pajamas."

"Why, do you sleep naked?"

This woman would be the death of him. "You know I don't with a child in the house. But thanks a hellofa lot for the mental image of you and me naked in bed."

"What do you mean? I didn't say a thing."

Cripes, what the hell did she think was happening to him… outside…in the middle of his damn back yard…with her breathing in his ear?

"Pack a bag, *big* guy."

An officer knocked at Graci-Ella's front door the next morning. She was more rested than she'd been the day before and didn't even care it was raining. Since the officer was fairly quiet as he played escort duty, she immersed herself into thoughts of last night. The guys set the table while she chose a Disney movie. After they ate and threw away their paper plates, Boyd slipped into the bathroom with his bag and came out wearing green check sleeping pants and—heaven help her greedy female parts—no shirt.

She stared at him and swallowed. Her tongue wanted to lick every mountain and valley of his pecs and abs.

Boyd whispered in her ear, asking what was wrong.

"Would Matt notice if I crawled up your body like a cat in heat?"

He glanced toward Matt trying to figure how to work her Blu-ray. "Save that thought for another time." He rubbed his hand over her ass before he strutted away and sprawled out on her tan sofa sectional, his one knee raised. She lay against his chest and crotch. And Matt wiggled between both bodies, so he could have an arm around each of their necks and grinned. "I love being the icing in an Oreo."

He was such a sweet kid. Thankfully, he was more like his father than his mother. He must have kissed her scar three times during the course of the movie while Boyd fingered her hair. It was an exceptionally tender night after such a rough day.

The officer dropped her in front of the building's doors, and she thanked him for his kindness before she slid out of the squad car and ran the short distance through the rain, her navy strappy heels getting wet in the puddles. She did get a few strange looks from co-workers as they hurried into the grey and black glass building. *What? Didn't everyone come to work in a squad car?*

Bethany motioned her aside. "I just wanted you to know the IT department did some work to your computer. Minor on your end, but any emails coming from that weirdo, no matter how many IP addressed he's using, will go directly to Lieutenant Lithgow's office. You won't even see them again. Some new technology the police department is testing out."

Graci-Ella felt such relief. "Oh, Bethany, I could hug you to pieces. Thank you for telling me I won't have to be afraid of my emails anymore. You're the best."

Bethany leaned over and whispered, "Well, it was something Sterling Hughes and Lieutenant Lithgow worked out together." The young girl always did enjoy being in the know, but she had a heart of gold along with it. "Oh, before I forget." She reached into a drawer. "Here're the keys for your Murano. It's parked in your assigned spot, all ready for you."

The elevator trip to her floor seemed to fly, the great mood Graci-Ella was in. She strode into her office and called Boyd on her cell.

"Hey Sweetness."

"Guess what? You'll never guess in a million years!"

The man started laughing. "Boyd, what's so funny?"

"Matt asks me the same thing almost every time he calls and now you. 'Guess what? You'll never guess in a million years!'"

She turned on her computer. "Oh, shush. Consider yourself doubly blessed. Let me tell you what the police department had the IT department here rig up on my computer. Is that awesome, or what?"

"*That* is very awesome, Sweetness. I'm glad to hear that." A loud alarm, followed by an address and size of fire blared over the loud speaker. "Gotta go, love. Duty calls." He ended the call.

She began her normal routine at the office, checking emails and reading over the file for her next trial. Within the hour, she was writing her brief, two legal books open on her desk.

Sterling Hughes knocked on her door frame. "How are you feeling today?"

"Much, much better." She smiled. "I'm relieved I don't have to worry about threatening emails. Whatever you had to do with that miracle and the restraining order, I thank you, sir."

A brief smile nearly touched down on his lips, almost like a bee on a blossom. "We like to take good care of our staff here, especially one of our up and coming litigators. Keep me informed as to this Weir fellow. Have a good weekend."

"I will and thank you, sir." He nodded and moved on.

After only an hour of overtime, she closed down her computer and snatched her purse. Boyd had told her weeks ago her tripod and camera were stored at the fire station. She'd go out to pick it up and maybe take a few pictures if the men were back from the fire. Thanks to her injuries and surgery, she was really behind on this project.

She had to admit, she enjoyed driving the Murano. It was much roomier for her long legs than that compact. As she drove around the fire station, several guys were hosing down fire trucks and ladder equipment. She parked next to the side entrance and knocked on the door. Quinn opened it and smiled.

"Hey, you're just in time to make hamburgers and spaghetti or something. Come on in, I've got an apron to fit over that navy outfit."

"I didn't come to cook. Boyd told me my camera gear was in storage out here. The two old men took off with it after my accident."

"Gas Ass and Hell's Bells? Lord only knows what they did with it. Hold on." He went to the intercom and pressed a button. "Boyd, could you report to the kitchen please? We have an uncooperative cook here, wearing navy stilettoes, who needs your attention."

Within minutes, he sauntered toward her wearing untied boots and jeans with the first two buttons undone. He was like someone had set a block of chocolate with very big nuts in front of her. She wanted to bite and lick him all over. The way his grey eyes darkened, he had to know what she was thinking.

"I…ah….came for my camera equipment."

He backed her against the wall in the eating area. His eyes locked on hers. "Don't we say hello first?" He leaned his face against her neck and inhaled her fragrance, before he nibbled and sucked it.

"Well…ah…sure, but I figured you'd be busy."

"Confucius say woman should never speak for man." He bit her jaw, working his way toward her mouth.

She tapped his shoulder. "What does he say about a crowd watching?"

Boyd gazed over his shoulder and then glanced back with an evil smile. "Confucius say fuck 'em." And he kissed her long and hard.

"What the hell is going on in my fire station? A course in sex ed?" The captain stood next to them with his hands fisted on his waist. "Hell, you two are going to have everyone horned up." His yelling bounced off the walls.

Graci-Ella broke away from Boyd. "I came for my camera equipment the two older gentlemen brought back here after my accident. I'd like to start taking some pictures for the calendar. Boyd was just showing me his tripod." She blinked innocently, trying her best to channel her mother.

Boyd and the onlookers burst into laughter. The captain scowled at her for a minute before his lips turned up at the corners. "I watched your mother do that with your dad. Don't think I'm going to fall for it like he's evidently been doing for years." He motioned. "Follow me. I locked it up in a closet." He inserted a key and opened a door. "You let me get it now. Heard you had a rough day yesterday in a lot of ways." He leaned her camera equipment against the wall. "Any time you want to talk about it. I'm here."

"Talk? To another man? With an alpha hot on my trail?" She glanced around for Boyd. "I had no clue a man could be like this."

"Hell, neither did my wife." He started to laugh and the marine rescue alarm went off. A sea-cruiser had hit come coral reefs, tore a couple holes and was sinking. Coordinates were given. Wolf yelled orders and Boyd, Quinn and Barclay were on their way to change into water gear.

"I'll finish making supper while they're all gone. Are you okay with that, captain?"

He grinned. "Baby doll, you help yourself. My men have had a rough day. Whatever you make will be appreciated, or I'll damn well know why."

She looked over the packs of hamburger Quinn had just opened. She searched through the cabinets and refrigerators for ingredients and started mixing eggs, dry bread crumbs, onions and spices into a large bowl of the hamburger. She rolled her mixture into Italian meatballs and placed onto a baking sheet to slide in the oven. She sent Jace to the store for submarine rolls and sliced provolone. She peeled potatoes and cubed them to cook for potato salad. Eggs boiled too. She mixed two cakes—one chocolate and one strawberry—to put in the oven as soon as the meatballs were baked. Pulling down the three crockpots, she filled them halfway with her mother's special Italian sauce. Once the meatballs were baked, she drained the grease off and put them in the sauce.

Jace brought in the rolls and cheese and saw her put the cakes in the oven. "Great guns, if you ain't a whiz in the kitchen. What all have you made?"

"Well, you're having meatball subs with provolone cheese on top, potato salad and two cakes." She looked at him. "Will that be enough?"

"Yes. Now, time for you to sit down. I've got some new pictures of my son I'd like to show you."

When she woke, curled on the sofa alone, Jace's pictures were on the coffee table and the cakes were cooling on racks. She put icing on them both and decorated the strawberry one with sprinkles into the number 32. On the chocolate cake, she put white icing and "Too Hot to Handle" in chocolate icing. She placed them in the middle of the big dining table, did a quick headcount of the people there and set the table.

After she carried her photography gear out to her car, she headed for home. She was due for a bath and several hours of sleep. At least she knew her man would have a good meal. *Oh God, look at me, the lawyer in the Betty Crocker apron. What is wrong with this picture?*

Once she'd showered, she'd just settled between the sheets when her cell rang. "Hello."

"Which bridge do you want me to push you over, bitch?" Heavy breathing followed.

Oh my God! She trembled so badly, she could barely swipe her screen to cut the call off. Something inside made her stop. Was this how an All-American reacted? Hadn't she gone against the best and roughest female basketball players in the States? And no one could be stronger and rougher than a team of women. She put the phone back to her ear, laughed and trash-talked him. "Your shoelace is untied. Your daddy's a wimp. Is that the best you got?"

"Huh?"

"Go away, kid. If you can't make a basket, ride a bicycle." She was getting in the swing of things now. She had years of basketball court trash talk and she was only getting started. "If you can't scratch with the big pussy cats, get out of the sandbox."

"You're crazy." He hung up.

Now that Darryl's surprise call was over, Graci-Ella began trembling. Her basketball game of trash talking ended and the questioning began. How had he gotten her phone number? Was he outside one of her windows now, peeking in along the sides or a little crack in the blinds? She asked herself again how he'd gotten her number. She crawled out of bed and turned on a light in her living room.

In the side pocket of her briefcase, she kept the papers she'd created for signing up to be part of the firefighters' calendar. There on the bottom of the sheet was her name and phone number. Well, that solved that little mystery. She'd have to block his number and pay more attention to the caller I.D's when her phone rang. In fact, it was time she started being more observant of her surroundings and paid more attention to people in her life. She would not be a victim.

CHAPTER TWENTY

Her phone chirped again. This time she glanced at the I.D. on the screen and saw it was Boyd. "Hello."

He hesitated for a few seconds. "Are you okay, Graci-Ella?"

"Yes. Calming down, I guess." She paced around her room and thought of turning on the heat. The chill of Darryl's surprise call went clear to her bone.

"Why? Did you fall again?" Concern was heavy in Boyd's voice. "Baby, is that why you didn't stay to eat with us after all the work you did? The guys really appreciated it, by the way. The meal was great."

She crawled back in bed, hoping the weight of one blanket would stop her shaking. "I just had a call from Darryl and it scared me."

"Son of a bitch! What did the bastard say?"

"He…He asked 'Which bridge do you want me to push you over, bitch?'"

"I will kill him. No one…*no one* threatens my woman. Hold on." She could detect footsteps and knocking. "Captain, I've got Graci-Ella on the phone. Even with the restraining order against him, that lowlife, miserable, bastard Darryl called her tonight and asked her which bridge she wanted him to push her over."

Hearing the captain's response would have been a little hard over Boyd's phone if he hadn't been yelling. "The man's fucking insane! Has she called the police? I'm calling the Fire Chief now. He needs to know his nephew is facing harassment charges on top of everything else. Hell, he can't lie his way out of it, not with cell phone records from towers."

"Baby, have you called Lieutenant Lithgow?"

"No, you called right after Darryl. I haven't had a chance. I'm shivering so badly from nerves, I can't get warm. I'll hang up now and call him."

"Call me back when you're through, I'll sing you to sleep." He was trying to lighten her mood. "I'll even go so far as to sing Matt's favorite lullaby."

She groaned. "I'm afraid to ask. How do I know you can even sing?"

"You'll have to trust me, baby. I noticed you have a security system. You do have it set, right?"

"Yes, as soon as I get home. It's a habit."

"Oh, I do love a smart woman. Call me and tell me what the officer says, okay Sweetness?"

After her phone call to the officer, who would soon think she had a thing for him if she didn't stop contacting him every day, she called Boyd.

"Baby, I'm pulling into your condo complex now. The captain told me I had more than enough personal time, even with taking time off for Matt, to come spend the night with you as long as I'm back by six. He did make me promise not to sing. Claimed you'd had enough trauma for the day. Look out your front window now and see my rear lights. I'm parked across from your parking space."

She jumped out of bed and ran for her patio door. "I can't believe you're here!" She peeked out through the blinds and saw his lights. They *were* his, right? "Turn them off and on again." He did. "Okay, my man, sorry to be so paranoid. It's gonna take a lot to calm me down."

After turning off his lights and engine, he unfolded from his

Mustang. Like him, the car was all power and speed. He jogged across the drive toward her and she unlocked the door. No sooner had he stepped across the threshold than she was in his arms and her face was buried in the crook of his neck.

"I got you baby." His arms were wrapped tight around her and her toes barely touched the floor. "I got you."

"Why? Why has he started this vendetta? It's not like I damaged his truck or kneed him in the nuts."

He carried her into her bedroom, stopping for her to turn out her lights as he went. "He's a bully. Has been all his life, from what I can gather. He's used to pushing others around, either verbally or physically." He laid her down on the bed as he sat and began to undress. He aimed a cocked eyebrow at her when she just sat there in her pajamas. Once she got the hint and took them off and slid beneath the covers, he continued talking as he removed his jeans and boxers.

"Our unit intimidated him a little. None of us are small, nor do we take being pushed around. Yeah, we tease, but good-naturedly, but we've always got each other's six." Condoms flopped on her nightstand. "He had to spend a lot of time in the gym, working out to get rid of his excess flab and build up some strength."

He lifted the covers and the mattress dipped as he snuggled in next to her. She rolled into his arms and he stroked her back while he talked. "Darryl had this dream of being a fireman. One of our highly trained squads. Trouble was there were certain situations he was scared of and he was lazy about work around the station. He bluffed the newer guys with his know-it-all mouth, but the rest of the team avoided him. So when you rejected him for this calendar deal, he flipped out."

"Figures. Me and my big mouth. I guess my trash talking to him tonight didn't help him any. All I did was make him think I was nuts."

He squeezed her bottom and his eyebrows dipped into a V. "What do you mean?"

170

She repeated the conversation and his eyes widened and his jaw dropped. "You're shittin' me. Right?" He laughed and held her closer, pressing her head against his neck. "God, woman, you are one piece of work. I have never met anyone like you. As the guys say, 'You are off the chain.'" He nipped her jawbone.

"Sweetness, the ass was treading the line of unstable behavior long before you came along. He figured you're a weak target or he did before you gave him a dose of sass tonight. Still, he has no clue who all has your six, your back. Nor does he know the captain has put out the word to every fire station across the country about him. He'll never get another job as a fireman. And it's not your fault."

She stroked his semi-erect cock that hardened almost instantly. "Is this my fault, too, handsome?" She rose and scooted on her knees to lean over him, took him in her mouth, her curtain of hair falling and blocking the magic she was doing with her lips and tongue. She traced his slit and he groaned from the bottom of his marvelous chest.

She swirled her tongue around the head of his cock, he fisted his hands in her hair and his hips rose. "Good God woman!"

Slowly she took him into her mouth, not sure she could handle him all, but knowing she could drive him crazy with what she could. She created an in and out rhythm with two swirls of her tongue around his head every time she pulled his shaft out. With her fingertips, she gently scraped his balls.

He grabbed her upper arms and pulled her on top of him, his eyes nearly wild with the need of her. "My addiction to you is your fault, baby, because you're perfect."

She straddled him and braced her forearms on either side of his head. Her pelvis moved rhythmically over his hard-on as she stared into his grey eyes. "My man, I am far from perfect, but I'll gladly be your addiction because you and Matt are mine. Put on a condom and love me. Love me like your heart can't beat without me."

"It can't. Don't you know that?" He forked his hands in her

long hair and brought her face down to his so their tongues and lips could trace and meld. "Put the rubber on me, love, and we'll see how many times you can come tonight."

She tore the packet open and rolled the latex on his engorged cock.

He slipped a finger inside her. "You're plenty wet for me already, Sweetness." He pushed within her and moaned. "So tight. So sweet. No one touches you, but me. To hurt you, they have to go through me. Dammit, Graci-Ella, from the moment I looked in your blue-eyed gaze, I was one fucking goner." He hooked his heels around her calves and together they rode their own sweet ride to nirvana.

They made love two more times between rounds of talking and then finally snuggled together to sleep the rest of the night.

When his cell phone's alarm went off at five-thirty, Boyd quickly turned it off. She brushed her hair out of her eyes and moaned. It was Saturday, a day for sleeping in. He dressed quickly and quietly the way some men are able to do. Then he leaned over and brushed his lips against hers. "I love you."

"See you later when I come to take pictures."

He smacked her bottom. "Get up and lock the door behind me. I want to hear the deadbolt click too."

She stuck her tongue out and crawled from their warm nest of covers. "Text me when you get to the station, so I know you made it safely." She ran her palm up and down his chest in a caress.

He kissed her again so sweetly, it made her heart ache. "It's been years since anyone's cared if I've gotten anywhere safely." He wrapped his hands around her head and pulled her to his neck. "You are…" And, as if he couldn't finish what he wanted to say, he buried his face in her mussed hair for a minute before striding out the door into the early morning mist.

When the car dealership opened, Graci-Ella was there ready to shop. She'd worn red capris, a white tank top over a red one and her lucky red sequined ballet shopping shoes. When a salivating car salesman approached her, she waved him off just like her daddy had taught her. She even used his exact words. "I'll let you know when I'm ready and pull your nuts up now, 'cause we're going bare-assed deep on the negotiations." She breezed by while the slack jawed salesman stood frozen to the spot with the strangest expression on his face.

She knew the options she wanted on her new car. Nothing more. If this dealership didn't have it or want to deal with her on the price, she'd get in her rental and drive a few streets over to another dealership. Her white baby all but winked its headlights at her. Sunroof, check. Right engine size, check. Front and side airbags, check. Tan leather seats, check. USB ports, check. The door was unlocked and she sat in it. Felt solid, safe and exactly what she was looking for.

She motioned the salesman over and jotted the pricelist on her notepad. "Let's go inside and diddle on this car. See that puny luggage rack up there?" She pointed. "I don't want it and I'm telling you right now, I'm not paying the three-hundred your company is trying to stiff me for it. Now, follow me." She led him into the showroom as if she owned the place, mentally figuring the highest she would go.

Two hours later, she walked out papers and keys in hand. She'd called her insurance company and told them they could come by the dealership to pick up the Murano. While waiting, she transferred her camera equipment and other personal items into her paid for, creamy white RAV-4, with its free luggage rack. *Did my daddy teach me well, or what?*

Of course it hadn't hurt that the police called while she was in the middle of negotiations to tell her they had Darryl behind bars. "Thank you, officer. So, that man who thought I was an idiot he could push around is in jail without possibility of bond?"

He laughed. "Yes, ma'am."

For some reason, negotiations went easier after that.

She slipped in her Bluetooth and called her dad, taking joy in his laughter when she told him she used his line about negotiations on the dumbfounded salesman. She couldn't tell him about the trouble she'd been having with Darryl. Why worry them when the whack job was in jail again? No doubt her parents were just calming down from their visit here after her surgery. They still carried too many painful memories of losing Eli.

Then she called Boyd. "Guess what!"

She was positive she heard a snort before he asked, "What?"

"Darryl is behind bars. No way is he getting paroled this time."

"Thank God, baby."

"There's more. I bought a new car and I got the luggage rack for free. Listen, I'm coming over to the station to start taking pictures for the calendar. Could I go by your place and get Matt? I thought he might get a charge out of being my helper. He could spend the night at my place if he has a sleeping bag."

"Well, I'm sure he'd love both of those things. You'll have to borrow the car seat from Aunt Jinny. Let me make sure they're home. I'll call you back in a sec."

She pulled into a strip mall that contained a craft store. If they had children's ball caps and iron-on letters, she'd have them make a helper hat for Matt.

Boyd called back and said they were just hanging out at his house and Aunt Jinny said she'd transfer the seat for her. Matt was already packing an overnight bag and to be prepared. His excitement level was in the stratosphere.

"Great, I have a couple little things to do and then I'll pick him up."

"Yeah, well, just remember the longer you take, the more he'll pack. Oh, and do you want him to wear his pajamas now?"

"You're joking, right?" She laughed and jumped out of her new SUV, charging for the craft store. She grabbed the first employee she saw. "Quick, do you have children's ball caps and iron-on letters you attach to the hat here in the store?"

She held a plastic bag to her when she rang Boyd's doorbell.

Matt nearly wrenched it off the hinges as he hugged her around the legs. "I'm packed!" He jerked his thumb over his thin shoulder.

Her gaze fell on a sleeping bag, Fella, two pillows, a stuffed duffle bag and an overnight suitcase on wheels. "I...I see. I brought you a helper's shirt and cap. Since everyone at the station has a nickname, I gave you one. Flash, like on a camera." She handed him the bag.

He glanced in and ripped off the shirt he had on. He shoved his hands into the navy tee with "Photography Helper" arched across the top and "Flash" across the back. Then he examined the white hat with his nickname across the back opening and the same words as the shirt in smaller letters across the front. He bent the bill and socked it on backwards. "Okay, let's roll." He grabbed his duffle bag and Fella and marched out.

"Was his father like that?"

The woman everyone called Aunt Jinny grabbed the pillows and sleeping bag. "The spitting image," she declared as she threw back her head and laughed when she passed Graci-Ella.

Just my freakin' luck. She snatched the overnight suitcase's handle and followed the gang to her new car.

Graci-Ella loaded her back hatch while Aunt Jinny transferred the booster seat for Matt. He kissed his aunt goodbye and turned to his new boss. "Am I only getting minimum wage? How about insurance and vacation pay? What about stock options?"

There was no way he knew about this kind of stuff. *No way.* "Your daddy told you to ask me these questions, didn't he?"

High-pitched giggling confirmed her suspicions.

"Well, I'm going to need your social security number and see a resume." She picked him up and strapped him into his seat. "You're the first person to ride in my new car."

"Really? This is cool. I sit up nice and high compared to the 'stang." As she backed out, she saw him swipe a number on his cell and then whisper, "Dad, she says I'm going to need a social security number and a copy of my 'rezu-mery'. Do I have those things?"

"You can't get ahead in life without 'em, buddy." Graci-Ella turned her steering wheel to exit the complex. Just to aggravate Boyd some more, she added, "And it ought to have a notary seal on it too."

"Dad, I'm in deep crap. I need a 'rezu-mery' with a naughty seal on it to get ahead in life. Do you think this seal has to be alive?"

"Stop laughing and guess what? Just guess!"

Matt snapped his fingers. "Ah, shoot! How did you guess I was in her new car? Do you two tell each other everything? Well, bet you don't know I have a work uniform. It's got my new nickname on it and everything."

CHAPTER TWENTY-ONE

Graci-Ella helped Matt out of his car seat. "Now, as my helper, you will walk beside me and not run ahead. We'll stick close together so you can hear me when I tell you I need something done. Sometimes I mumble when I shouldn't. Understand?"

He nodded.

"Let me teach you one of your most important jobs and that's to measure distance from the firefighter to my elbow. That helps me take a better picture, sharper and clearer, if the lighting inside isn't what we really need." She pulled her hyper-focal distance tape measure from her camera utility bag and showed him how to use it from her tire to her elbow and a window in the fire station to her elbow.

In this instance, accuracy wasn't paramount; her digital camera, a Christmas gift from her parents, was pretty top notch. What was important to her was Matt's feeling involved and essential.

"Can you put the tape in your pants pocket? Now, can we sling this camera case over your head and shoulder just like I'm carrying the other one? Excellent! You're a fast learner. Now, let me get my purse and accessory bag and you can ring the doorbell once I tell you. After all, you're my assistant."

The smile he flashed at her was a heart stopper. She placed her palm on his upper back. "You're the best, Matt. Don't let anyone else tell you any different."

He scuffed his sneaker at the base of the step. "My mom and stepdad do."

She wanted to beat them both. Anger and protectiveness for this child roared through her veins. "Honey, even adults can be wrong. I believe in you, just like your daddy does."

He leaned against her leg and wrapped an arm around it. "I love you." Grey eyes like his dad's stared at her as if he were starving for her affection.

She took off his hat and leaned to kiss his dark hair. "I love you too, Flash. You know everyone in this unit has a nickname, so make sure you tell them Flash is yours." She returned his hat and he socked it on with the bill in the back again. "What's my dad's?"

"Tiny." She tried not to smirk.

His cute grey eyes widened. "No way!"

She nodded. "Way. Now, ring the doorbell, Flash."

Barclay opened the door and grinned at Matt. "Hi Graci-Ella. I see you brought your camera equipment, but who's the helper?"

"This is my helper, his nickname is Flash. Flash, this is Ghost. Do you want your picture taken first? How about in front of one of the fire trucks?"

"Sure, come on down. I see we're on nickname basis today, huh?"

"Yeah, I thought it would help me keep the theme of the calendar if I focused on the personality of your nicknames."

"Well, then Raccoon and Firecracker, follow me."

"Where's Tiny?" Matt was looking around.

"Ah, Tiny's shining the chrome on one of the trucks." Barclay smiled and winked at Graci-Ella. "My Sammy cut his first tooth last night. Thank God. He's had a fussy week. Have you seen my son? He's something else." The man's chest puffed out with pride.

They walked into the vehicles garage, and there were shouts of welcome for Raccoon. Graci-Ella placed her hand on Matt's shoulder. "This is my photography assistant. His nickname is Flash."

178

Boyd jumped from the top of the fire truck, grinning. "Flash, huh? I'd say the name fits. Hey, nice shirt and hat."

"It's what all the photography assistants are wearing, Tiny." Matt started to giggle and hid behind Graci-Ella. "You can't tickle me when I'm working."

Boyd was bent over and his big hands were wiggling like claws. "You're full of yourself, aren't you?" He glanced at her. "How about it, Raccoon, do I get a kiss?"

Matt stepped out, his little hands on his hips. "Really, Tiny? *Really*? We don't have time for the mushy stuff. We've got photography work to do. You can kiss Raccoon boss lady later."

Hoots and hollers went up from the firefighters. Captain Steele leaned against the block wall and folded his arms, shaking his head. "Thought you said your son was kinda shy, Tiny."

"Looks like the *kinda* part is shrinking." Boyd was all smiles, obviously enjoying the show his boy was putting on.

"Flash, I'll need you to call out the person we want to photograph first. Call for Ghost, please." Graci-Ella changed the lens on her camera.

Firecracker leaned back like a rooster and crowed, "Ghost!"

Barclay laughed so hard, he could barely walk straight. The whole squad made a large semi-circle around the photography circus. "Run over to him and ask him to stand next to the step of the fire truck. I'll want his left foot on the step, too, Flash."

Her little helper positioned Ghost's foot.

"I'll need his shirt off. Have him hand it to you."

Barclay pulled off his red tank top and passed it to Flash, who tossed it over his shoulder, hitting Quinn's face in the process. "Hey!" Quinn, known as Comic, yelled. Boyd bent over at the waist and laughed. The rest of the gang joined in.

"Tell Ghost to beef up a little while you do your measurement with your hyper-focal distance tape measure."

Displaying all the self-pride and importance in the world, little Matt tugged the tape from his pants pocket, slipped the end under

Ghost's boot and pulled it to her elbow. He did a perfect job reading her the numbers.

"Excellent. Most excellent, Flash." She'd already made the adjustments on her digital camera, but she wanted him to have the feeling of accomplishment, of a job well done. After about six shots, she kneeled next to her helper. "I've got an idea, but I don't know if it'll look good or dumb. So, as my partner, tell me what you think." He covered his chin as if he were thinking deep thoughts. "I've got some different shades of powder in my kit, along with a brush. What if I show you how to apply the right amount and we make his face look like a ghost?"

Flash shot off, jumping straight in the air. "Yes! That would be awesome!"

Ghost pointed to him and looked at Boyd. "Your kid's making me nervous."

She opened her kit and laid out the colors she had.

"The whiter, the better, boss lady."

Oh God, she could hug him to bits. She chose the undercover brush and showed him how to brush off the excess. She explained it wouldn't hurt to put a light layer on first, because he could always add a layer or two more. "Now carry the make-up and brush over, slowly, and ask Ghost to sit on the step so you can reach his face. If the guys make you nervous with all their wisecracks and laughter, just yell 'quiet on the set.'"

"Gotcha." He slowly walked over, carrying his items as if they were precious gold. Ghost sat when Flash asked and nodded when he explained what the powder was for. The little boy went through the steps she'd explained and began lightly brushing over Ghost's forehead and working down.

As she suspected, the guys started teasing, and Flash looked at her over his shoulder, a nervous expression in his eyes. She nodded. He nodded in return before rearing back like a rooster once more and bellowing, "Quiet on the set!"

Instant silence, except for a few who covered their mouths and sniggered. Graci-Ella put her hands on her hips and scowled at them. They stopped in a hurry. She gave them a thumb's up sign for their cooperation.

As soon as Flash had the first layer of powder over Ghost's face, her helper glanced at her. "I think he needs more on his forehead and cheeks so he looks like a skeleton."

Graci-Ella nodded. "I think you're right." Gosh, Ghost did look menacing. When Flash was done, she told him to have Ghost stay seated, place his hands on his knees and lean forward. She snapped a few shots and was quite pleased. "Tell him we're done with him and bring the make-up back. Oh, hand him his shirt, please. Then call for the Virgin."

"Need a Virgin," Flash yelled.

The guys shoved a blushing young man toward them.

"Flash, have the Virgin get his ax and we'll stand in front of the smaller fire truck for a little variety. Oh, and ask him to take his shirt off."

One virgin t-shirt flew through the air over Flash's shoulder before he did his measurements. She had him hold the ax in a couple different poses until she found the one that showcased his muscles and then shot several pictures of him in that position.

"Hand the Virgin his shirt and tell him he's all done." She glanced around. Ivy Jo had a bright yellow sports bra on. "Flash, next up is Big Kahunas, and I want her standing at the open doors at the back of one of the ambulances."

Rooster reared back again. "Big Kahunas! Please report to the back of one of the 'amlances' with both back doors open." His head swiveled between Big Kahunas and her. "Do you want her shirt off, boss lady?"

The squad hooted and whistled.

The captain growled one word. "Harassment!"

"No. But ask her to show more of her—" heck how did she say cleavage or boobs to a six-year old? "—pecs and please ask her politely."

After his request, Big Kahunas turned her back and made some adjustments. She wouldn't need much. Like Graci-Ella, she was a big busted woman. Big Kahunas turned around and Flash pivoted to Graci-Ella. "She's got pecs now!" Out of the corner of her eye, she chanced a glance at Boyd, who had slapped a hand over his face.

"Ask her to sit with one hand balanced on the floor of the ambulance and the other on her hip. We want her to lean forward. Then do your measurements for me." He did and Graci-Ella snapped a few shots.

She walked over to the ambulance. "Ivy Jo, I want one of your back, lifting or doing something heavy that shows your strength. Your back muscles are every bit as strong as a man's."

Her remark earned her a huge smile. It was obvious she worked hard for her muscles and was very proud of them. "I know just the thing. I'll carry one of the men."

She struck a pose so Flash could take his measurements. Then she yelled, "Wolf, fireman's carry!" He stood in front of her and Graci-Ella started snapping as soon as Big Kahunas began lifting Wolf from the floor until she had him draped over her shoulder.

"Got it. Tell them 'cut.'"

"Cut and wow!" Her assistant was obviously impressed by the woman's strength.

She placed her hand on Flash's shoulder. Every employee gets a break. She pulled some bills from her pocket. "Wolf, would you take my assistant for an orange soda and whatever he wants from the snack machine? He needs a rest."

"Don't do Tiny until my break's over!" He glanced at his dad with a kind of longing. She bet he wanted to impress him.

"Chief, you're next up! Take your shirt off please and grab a fire hose." She showed him how she wanted him to hold it and she also ruffled his hair into sexy disarray. Her hands gently smoothed the hair over his chest and stomach. She could almost feel Boyd scowling at her. "Is he getting pissed?" she whispered near the captain's ear.

Captain laughed. "Oh, you have no idea."

She took several shots of him from different angles. Then she called for Beer-meister. She wanted him to hold a fireman's hat and drape a fireman's coat over a shoulder.

A few minutes into his posing session, with her positioning his leg, he kept glancing at Boyd. "Look, I love the attention, but much more and your man is going to jack my jaw."

She winked and snapped a few pictures of him. "Lil' Wolf, you're next."

"No way in hell. Not until Tiny's blood pressure drops several degrees, and you do not get to touch me. I want to live to play with my son and wife tomorrow night."

If the guys were talking about it, she'd evidently gone too far. What possessed her to try to make her man jealous? That was high school behavior. She walked to stand directly in front of the raging inferno. "I'm sorry, my man. I didn't mean to go overboard with my arrangements. Guess I just figured you'd know I wasn't interested in any of the other firefighters, that I was only prepping them for the pictures."

"What the hell, Graci-Ella! My ex would do shit like that to see how mad she could make me. I thought you were better than that." His face was red and his grey eyes narrowed and nearly stormy grey than their typical silver color. "Would you like me to stroke other women?"

"No. I'd hate it." Her gaze dropped. "For some crazy reason, I thought it would be funny. We were all having a good time with Matt." She lifted her gaze to lock on his. "I was wrong and I'm sorry. It won't happen again. I'll take a break until Matt's ready to come back as my helper."

"Yeah, that might help calm the beast inside me, because I'm not in the greatest of moods right now. Dammit to hell!" He grabbed her forearms, lifted her and laid a lip-lock on her that practically melted the red sequins off her special shopping shoes.

"I turn my back for one minute and you've got your hands all over Raccoon boss lady? We've got work to do and all you can think about is mushy stuff?"

Boyd had his hand on her ass pushing her against his erection. She'd lay bet he was thinking about more than mushy stuff because there wasn't a soft spot on his body. He was trembling with anger or need. Either way, he pivoted so his son couldn't see his hard on, and set her down on the ground.

"We'll do you as soon as you go put on those button-down jeans and nothing else but your boots, unlaced."

His jaw jutted in a pugnacious manner. She really had pushed him too far. "I meant what I said, Graci-Ella."

She cupped his cheek and stared into his eyes. "And I meant what I said, sweetheart. I was wrong and I'm sorry."

Boyd nodded and pivoted toward the dormitory area. She breathed a sigh of relief. For a few minutes she feared she'd lost her main pin-up.

Graci-Ella looked at Flash. "Our next person to photograph is Black Thumb."

Her little rooster reared back and hollered, "Black Thumb!"

Black Thumb was known for killing every plant she bought. She held one up with a hopeful expression. "I brought a prop, if you think it'll look cute."

Her helper took Graci-Ella's hand and walked her a few steps away. "Boss, that's a dead flower she's holding. How's it gonna look cute?" Flash glanced back again and shook his head. "Man, it's beyond dead. I've got Legos with more life than that plant."

"That's why everyone calls Emily Black Thumb, because she somehow kills every plant she gets. People who can grow anything are said to have a green thumb."

"Okay, but if you ask me, it looks creepy. I could powder the look of death out of it, but I don't think you've got that much powder."

"We could always have her go up the ladder and hold it as if she's pulled it from a burning building."

Flash gave her one of his father's "are you shittin' me?" looks that made Graci-Ella want to laugh so hard, she was afraid she'd insult him. "Let's get one of her up on the ladder with a hose. That'll be the main picture. Then, down in the corner, we can have a small image of the dead plant."

He nodded. "Now, that I can see. Maybe have her hand pointing to it or something."

Graci-Ella snapped a few photos of Black Thumb wearing fireman's pants with suspenders over her orange tank top and a fire hat. She dragged a hose over her shoulder as she climbed the ladder.

Graci-Ella showed Flash how to work the camera hanging around his neck. He took six pictures of the dead plant. He even laid down and propped his elbows on the concrete to snap a few. You'd have thought he'd been given every toy in the store. He was one happy kid.

CHAPTER TWENTY-TWO

Boyd tried his best to calm down while he changed into what Graci-Ella had asked. Seeing her touch other men so freely brought back memories of Chantel's taunting and, later, cheating on him behind his back. He wouldn't go through it again with another woman. Not even the one he loved to distraction.

Still, maybe he was overreacting. Graci-Ella had provided Matt with a fantastic day. God, he'd been so comical and, yet, so sure of himself. She had a way of bringing that out in him, unlike his mother. When Matt yelled "quiet on the set," Boyd thought he'd piss himself laughing.

He stepped into the vehicle area in time to see his son on his stomach, camera in hand, inching around Black Thumb's dead plant to snap a photo from every angle. As he did so, Graci-Ella took pictures of him—the novel shutterbug. She moved next to him and pressed her hand on his back. "Excellent job, Flash. Next person up is Tiny."

His son jumped up, his chest puffed out and roared, "On deck is Tiny." *Where had he learned that expression?* Then Matt and Graci-Ella did a fist bump. Well, that answered that question.

Flash marched toward him and pointed to the front of the newest fire truck. "Tiny, we'd like you standing in front of the truck's grill." He got into position just as Flash requested.

Graci-Ella sauntered over. "I'll do the higher part, Flash, and then I'll turn the rest over to you." She took each of Boyd's arms and stretched them across the top of the chrome grill, stroking and murmuring sexy words to him. She ran her fingers through his hair the way she did when they made love. Then warm fingers trailed over his pecs and abs. He was two heartbeats from being hard as a rock.

"Why are you breathing so fast, my man?"

"You just wait until I get my hands on you. I'm tying your arms spread eagle to the bed just like you've got me spread out here."

"I've always thought handcuffs would be such a turn-on." Then she had the audacity to wink at him. *Oh, I will so make her pay.* She sat a fire hat on the hood behind his elbow. On the other side she laid a fire jacket in a haphazard fashion. Then she stepped back.

"Firecracker, have him spread his legs apart about the length of Fella and flip up one of the cuffs of his jeans so he looks a little sloppy. Then do your measurements."

By damn the kid was good at following her instructions. Once he'd given her some numbers, she told him to unbutton the top two buttons of Tiny's jeans. He unbuttoned the top one, turned to her with a quizzical look on his face and yelled, "Will his peepee show with two buttons open?" The guys in the squad turned in a collective group, their hands over their mouths and their damn shoulders shaking in laughter. She smiled and shook her head. The click and whirl of her camera sounded around Tiny.

"Flash, have him put one toe on top of the other. Tell him something to make him smile, he looks so serious."

"Guess what, dad!"

Darn if his son didn't know how to work him. He smiled.

Graci-Ella removed the coat and hat from the hood of the fire truck. She told him to place his hands at his waist. She positioned his broad shoulders

Boyd heaved a sigh. "I feel like such a piece of meat."

She leaned in, her lips at his ear. "Well, how does this man like his woman's naughty parts? Shaved bald? Shaved with a little beard? Or au 'natural? Think on that while I take a few more pictures."

He knew her well enough to guess what her sexual questions were aimed to do—give him a smoldering expression she was looking for. No doubt he was giving it to her because he was thinking of doing the shaving of her pussy himself. She'd be so sensitive, he could get her to come with just a few well-placed licks. The thought even made him smile...and thank God the pictures were only from the waist up. His buttons were straining and ready to pop.

The alarm went off and the dispatcher announced the location and type of fire. Graci-Ella and Flash gathered their stuff and stood on the sidewalk in front of the station to watch them in action, yet be out of the way.

"Which fire truck will my daddy be on?" Matt's eyes were wide as he watched the organized confusion.

"I think he usually rides on Quinn's truck. That's the one we had him leaning against to take his pictures."

Matt nodded. "Okay. I'll watch for him."

"I think they're usually the first truck out. It's a race thing with Quinn."

Matt pointed. "Look! Quinn's changed his clothes already! Here comes Dad and Wolf. There's Lil' Wolf. And...and that Black Thumb lady."

Quinn fired up the truck's engines and Matt covered his ears. "Did you know they made so much noise?"

When the truck roared out, all the firefighters waved and yelled, "Flash!" He waved back as he leaned against her leg. She hoped she hadn't overextended the kid. With his being in and out of the hospital, his stamina levels couldn't be that great. Maybe she'd take him home and con him into a nap.

Two minutes down the road, she glanced in her rear view mirror. His chin was on his chest. He was exhausted. She lugged him into the elevator to her condo and laid him on the sofa. He sighed and snuggled under the afghan she placed over him before she ran outside for his overnight cargo and her camera equipment.

Her skin was sticky and sweat trickled down her back. While he was sound asleep, she took a quick shower, braided her wet hair and put on pajamas. It was barely after six. She opened a bottle of water and turned on her computer. She was eager to see Matt's and her pictures. Using her photo shop program, she downloaded the cards from both cameras. She studied every picture and made a notation of the frame's number that snagged her eye as being particularly outstanding.

Choosing the front picture of the calendar, the one that would sell it, came easy. The one of Boyd, his eyes hooded with desire after she's asked him how he'd like her private parts shaved. The muscles and massive fire truck would draw in the guys. Boyd's "I want you now" expression would pull in the women. She tried various sample lettering for the year and Fire and Marine Rescue Station Thirty-two's Hero Calendar. She certainly didn't want to cover up any of the man, her man. Damn, he looked good.

Next, she put Black Thumb for the month of September. With her high up on the ladder, it left a blank space in the corner for Matt's picture of Emily's dead plant. Graci-Ella went through the ones he'd taken, chose the best, resized it and placed a black frame around it. Overlapping a corner of the plant picture, she placed one she'd taken of Flash on his stomach, snapping a picture of the plant, highlighted with the same black frame. On a diagonal between the ladder shot and the two small pictures, she used a special font and wrote, "Black Thumb—Plant Killer Extraordinaire." What a great combo. She was pleased.

She was also getting bleary-eyed and the bed was calling her for a nap. She closed down her programs and went to bed. After all, with Boyd here with her last night, she hadn't gotten much sleep. Not that she'd minded.

Not soon after she'd shifted and scrunched around to find her comfort spot in bed, there was a slight dip in the mattress. The orange, tan and yellow of the afghan came into her peripheral vision and a skinny form snuggled against her back, but not before tugging her blankets down enough he could kiss her forehead. "I want you for my mommy," he whispered. "I'm safe with you." Then he rolled up in his crocheted blanket and went back to sleep.

He would be safe with her, too. For she'd fight all his demons if he'd let her. It's what her parents had done for her and Eli. It was what every child deserved. She had to talk to Boyd about having Matt seen by a child psychologist she'd used in court already. Dr. Zapotocky would know how to speak to Matt and find his secrets that worried him so. Her breathing fell into a pattern with his and, before long, her eyes drifted shut.

She woke up to a stuffed raccoon in her face. "I'm hungry and so is my human."

"We could order in pizza."

"The way my human likes it or the way his dad likes it?" Glass eyes and a black nose nearly touched hers.

"How does your human like it? They don't make it with candy on top."

The giggling started. "Extra cheese and mushrooms."

"Hey, that's how I like it. You got a deal. I'll order while you take your shower and put on your pajamas. Then we'll eat and watch a movie. Did you bring some?"

The kid flashed her a fiendish gleam. "What do you think is in the suitcase with wheels?"

It was nearing three in the morning when a text dinged on her phone that the firemen had just gotten back from the fire that consumed two buildings. Boyd was going to crash for as long as he could. Would Matt be okay with her?

She replied Matt could stay as long as needed. He was fine and sleeping soundly, just as his dad should be.

Hours later, once they were up, she began mixing pancake

batter. "Hey, do you want to call my dad and tell him what a big helper you were to me yesterday?"

She picked up her landline phone and dialed her parents. "Dad, do you have the time to talk? I have a young man here who wants to tell you about his big day yesterday." She handed the phone to Matt who regaled her dad for twenty minutes with stories of the photo shoot. "I wish you coulda seen the dead plant this woman brought. She actually thought it would look cute in the picture. Ellis, it was dead six ways from Sunday as my neighbor Pete would say. Guess what they call this woman at the station? The Black Thumb. They shoulda called her the Kiss of Death!"

Her father's boisterous laughter came through the phone line.

"Graci-Fella is making me blueberry pancakes. Dad was out at a fire until early this morning. I saw pictures of it on the news. It was a bad one. What are you going to do today? Play golf? Yeah, a lot of old people do that down here. They say it's for exercise, but they ride around in cool looking little cars. Where's the exercise in that?"

Her dad busted with laughter again.

"Me? I'd like to go see Graci-Fella's office. I never saw where a lawyer worked before. She just set a plateful in front of me. I gotta go. Don't hit your balls too hard. Bye."

Once they were full of pancakes and dressed, she drove him to Baker, Brannock, and Hughes law firm. She flashed her badge to security personnel and told him she was bringing in a potential future lawyer for a looksee of her office. The security guy hung a badge on a black cord around Matt's neck and handed him a pen and tablet.

"Wow, I get a badge and everything." The kid was aptly impressed and kept staring at his badge. When they got to the elevators, he couldn't believe they had six. "Which one do you use?"

"The one that's open or about to open. Pick one and press the button."

"Man, these are better than the ones at the hospital." The fourth

191

side was all glass opening to the lobby full of plants below.

"I couldn't agree more." They got off and she showed him to her little office. Her plants looked a little dry, so she pulled out her plastic watering can and filled it in the ladies washroom while Matt stared at her basketball pictures. She watered the hanging plants and he took over the job of watering the potted plants. He put the empty can back where she'd gotten it."

"You know there's a great ice cream place up the street. Do you feel up to walking to it? They make great chocolate and gummi bear sundaes."

His little face lit up. "Okay, let's go." He took her hand and they headed for the elevators.

Being with him was something she could easily get used to. "You know you might have to give back the badge for security reasons."

"So the bad guys don't get in?"

"Yeah." Then she thought of some of her clients and shook her head at the irony.

Not long after they got home, Boyd came to pick up Matt. His looked haggard. His eyes were sunken and wrinkles lined his face. He hugged Graci-Ella hard and whispered in her ear. "I pulled out two dead children last night. One was a baby and the other wasn't much older than Matt. It'll be a while before I get over it. I just want to go home and hug my son."

"Of course." She began gathering Matt's things while Boyd held his little boy, talking to him about yesterday and how proud he was of him. Why did she suddenly feel excluded? She was being childish. They had only talked about becoming a unit, hadn't really worked at making it permanent. So, in times of stress, things would naturally revert to old patterns. The man, who adored being a father, was traumatized and rightfully so.

She went into the bathroom and picked Matt's clothes from yesterday. She put his toothbrush and toothpaste into a baggie and his comb and Elmo shampoo into another baggie. She rolled up his sleeping bag and gathered his two pillows. Within a few minutes, she had all of Matt's belongings at her front door.

Boyd thanked her for everything. He and Matt scooped up his stuff before they left. No hugs or kisses goodbye. The two were clearly a private unit that from time to time allowed a stranger into their lives. Now they had closed ranks. Maybe her time was over already, no matter what Boyd had said to her so many times before. Who knew? The only thing she was sure of was her confusion—and her hurt, no matter how she tried to rationalize it all out.

Why, in God's name should she feel so empty?

CHAPTER TWENTY-THREE

Graci-Ella was choosing her clothes and jewelry for the next day when her cell rang. It was Boyd. "Hey handsome. How are you feeling now?"

"I have two questions for you." Was he ill? He barely sounded like himself; his voice shook. "Where is Fella? And do you work at Baker, Brannock and Hughes because my son brought home some of their pens and a pad of paper?"

Why was he interrogating her in this tone of voice? "No, I don't have Fella. The last time I saw the raccoon, Matt had it in my office. But, now that I think about it, he didn't have it at the ice cream parlor we went to afterward. At my office, he was helping me water my plants so he must have lain the stuffed animal aside and forgot about it. He thought it was a big deal to be where I work."

She sat on the sofa and wrapped the afghan around her shoulders. There was a definite chill from his end of the conversation.

"So you do work at that damn law firm, the one that's trying to take my son away from me?" His anger was almost a palpable force reaching through the cell waves to crush her heart.

"Yes, I do. But we are no longer representing your ex-wife."

"What the hell do you mean by that? I trusted you!" He bellowed so loud, she held the phone away from her ear. "You were spending time with me to get anything derogatory to use in court."

"That is not true and you know it."

"Do I?"

She exhaled a deep sigh and hoped she could make him understand. "The attorney who handled your divorce and then the subsequent custody case was Elizabeth Stone. Elizabeth was given a promotion and larger profile cases. She had to divvy up her caseload between the three newest lawyers, of which I'm one. I ended up with Chantel's custody case. I never looked at it, I put a court date sticker on it like I did the others Elizabeth turned over to me and put all of them in my caseload pile, in order of date to court."

"Am I supposed to believe that shit? You know I wondered from time to time why you snagged onto me out of all the single men in the squad." He expelled a harsh bark of laughter. "I guess now I know why."

She jumped from her seat on the sofa and shook with anger. "You've got some paranoia issues, Boyd Calloway."

"Why wouldn't I when the woman I trusted had planned all along to take my son from me. And how? Legally? No. By buttering up to me. Getting me to fall in love with you so I'd let my guard down. Tell me, did you have cameras in your bedroom filming us? Now I've posed for that damned calendar, turned on like some horny teenager. The one thing…," his fist hit a surface. "The one thing who means everything to me and you worked your charms to make sure I'd lose him!"

"Listen to what you're saying. It makes no sense. Cameras in my bedroom? *Really*, Boyd? And just how could I use the video? Illegally in court? So I could be disbarred?"

"I don't want to see you ever again. Stay away from us. Do you understand?"

"Daddy, does she have my Fella?" Matt was crying. And while the father had her livid, the son was tearing at her heartstrings.

"Tell him, I'm going for it now. That in fifteen minutes, he should start looking out the window for me. As for all the things

I want to say to you, my father taught me never to argue with an idiot." She hung up on him, grabbed her keys and purse and ran out the door.

The man had flipped his gourd, lost his twizzle stick, gone off his meds. "Whatever," she growled as she started her car. Thank God she saw the true man before she got in too deep. Before she fell head over heels in love. Or before she began wedding plans. Or, worse, got pregnant.

But she *had* fallen in love with him and his son, and right this minute her heart was breaking.

Yes, he'd gone through a terrible event during the night, pulling two dead children from a burning house. That would push anyone over the edge for a while. Shove him or her into a depression, perhaps a deep one. But did everyone around that person have to pay too?

Even on a Sunday evening, she pulled into her assigned parking spot on the empty lot and ran inside. She showed the security guy her pass and explained her son had left his favorite stuffed toy in her office. The elevator was halfway to her floor before she realized she'd called Matt her son. That's when the tears started. Dammit!

Fella was on her desk chair waiting for someone who loved him to come claim his stuffed raccoon ass. "Don't worry, you'll soon be with your owner. As soon as I stop the waterworks and get control of my emotions."

A few minutes later, she eased her RAV-4 in front of Boyd's townhouse. She leaned her face against the steering wheel and took three deep steadying breaths. *Let's get this over with.*

Her hand wrapped around Fella, and she strode toward the Calloway's front door. It opened and Matt ran toward her, his arms outstretched. "Graci-Fella!" He jumped into her arms, wrapped his arm around Fella and snuggled his face against her neck. "Hold me."

"You've got your raccoon. Now, you can go to sleep and dream of taking pictures."

He nodded against her neck. "I love you."

"Oh, sweetie, I love you too. You are the best boy in the whole world." She kissed his forehead and both of his cheeks. "Time for me to head to bed too. Goodbye, Matt, my special boy." He slid down until his feet touched the sidewalk, and she turned for her car, knowing she'd probably never see either one of the guys again. Boyd was so angry, he hadn't even looked out the window or door, much less walked out to greet her. *The chicken shit ass.*

Maybe in time she'd understand and stop hurting so much. Right now, she needed a crying jag—and God help anyone who got in her way because she was one pissed-off woman.

She walked into work the next day with eyes that looked like she'd cried all night, which she nearly had. Except for her eyes, she had her game face on. Millions of women across the globe had been dumped by someone they loved and survived. She would too. Now she would understand why women so often cried when they came to her to file for divorce. It was the end of their dream, their emotional security as part of a couple.

The appointment she had with her neurosurgeon after work went well. He pronounced her healed and told her she didn't need to come back. When she asked if she could begin workouts at the gym again, he said he thought that would be great if she started slowly.

However, she didn't go to the gym. She went home to see if any flowers had been delivered, just as she'd waited all day at work for a bouquet with the words "I'm sorry" attached. When there were none and no phone calls, the emptiness in her heart grew and she spent another night crying.

About eleven the following day, someone knocked at her office door. "Come on in." She was searching through a law book for a precedent, making notes for a brief. She shoved the pencil behind her ear and spun her chair around to see who it was.

Boyd stood there, his fingertips tucked in the front pockets of his jeans. A blue golf shirt stretched over his muscles, looking so good he almost took her breath away. She couldn't look at him, not with her emotions floating like crushed ice in a sea of pain. She glanced at the tiny print in the book, blinking away tears that burned her eyes.

"If you came by my office to tell me once more what a lying, lowlife you think I am, I really don't have the time. I never represented your wife."

"No, that's not why I'm here." He made a tentative step into her inner sanctum.

"Although, if you want to get picky, yes, I suppose I did." She pointed to the red file on the cabinet with the word "Closed" stamped on it. "During my time off from the accident, files were removed from my stack according to when they went to trial. My first day back to work, the day I got those emails from Darryl, I also saw a red file at the top of my list that had Chantel Calloway's name on it. I kept telling myself it wasn't the same Calloway, but when I opened the file and read the first two pages, I knew it was."

He made another step toward her. "And you never thought to tell me?"

"No, because I told my boss, Sterling Hughes, that I was dating the respondent in the case and for me to represent her would be a direct conflict of interest. He told me to call her and tell her we could no longer represent her. He had the finance department cut her a refund check for the retainer fee she'd given Elizabeth."

"I came by to thank you for bringing over Fella the other night. Matt adores that thing. Almost as much as he adores you."

"You're a strange person, Boyd Calloway. You break up with me over the phone and, yet, make a special trip to my office to thank me for returning a stuffed toy. Now, if you'll excuse me, I have work to do."

"I was hoping you'd have lunch with me so we can talk."

She jerked the pen from behind her ear and tapped her notepad. "Gee, isn't eating lunch going to be a little difficult for you, wearing a blindfold since you said you never wanted to see me again?"

"I'm sorry about that."

"Besides, I have lunch scheduled with a client."

"What about supper? I could ask Aunt Jinny to keep Matt."

She shook her head. "No. That would look too much like a date. What if someone saw us together and figured you were ignoring your son? As it is, I'm starting back at Marcus's Gym today. I need something to fill my evenings. If I ever have a man in my life again—and that's a big if after the pain I'm feeling right now—I want a man who trusts me." She looked at him for what would probably be the last time, except for finishing a few more pictures at the station.

"You don't have a lot of trust, do you? You don't have any trust in the lawyer you hired to win your case for you, which is why you wouldn't date. And we both know you have zero trust in me because I work here. You accused me of making you fall in love with me. Meanwhile I'd fallen in love with two people, so I'm hurting doubly as bad because I've lost twice as much. I don't need your kind of love. It hurts too much. Just leave. I'm not supposed to have personal meetings at work."

Boyd did one of the hardest things he'd ever done. He turned and walked away from the woman he loved. He'd really screwed things up with her and their future. How was he going to straighten this mess? Her eyes were swollen no doubt from a lot of crying last night and he hated he'd been the cause. But she was right. He didn't trust easily. Not after Chantel.

He walked out into the Florida sunshine and slipped on his wraparound sunglasses. He fired up his Mustang, drove to Beach Bum Burgers, a local sandwich joint known for its gigantic burgers. He ordered one and a large icy drink. In a few minutes he sat at a bench under some palm trees along the Gulf Boulevard. He watched the waves roll in as he relived every moment of his time with Graci-Ella, the woman who had brought him back to life.

Leaning forward, with his elbows on his knees and his face

planted in his upturned palms, he faced his own errors in his loss. She'd never once hidden the fact she was a lawyer, but he'd never asked her if she had her own practice or worked for a firm. When all that business was going on with Darryl and she talked about her boss helping her, he'd never asked who her boss was. But once he found out, he'd jumped off the deep end with accusations and telling her he never wanted to see her again.

He leaned back, his face to the sun. "Crap, I am such an ass."

A car's brakes squealed and jerked into a spot next to his. Two doors squeaked opened. Someone farted. *No. Please no. Not the Bald Brothers. Not today.*

"I knew it was him. Didn't I tell you that was Boyd's Mustang?" Milt put-putted over to one end of the bench and sat. Sam took the other end.

"Son, what's wrong? You look like your horse done died." Milt passed gas again.

Sam patted Boyd's arm. "Is your son sick again?"

"No. He's in school. I screwed things up with Graci-Ella though. Night before last, I told her I never wanted to see her again."

"Why? You nearly died when she had that car wreck last month." Sam's forehead wrinkled.

Maybe if he used these two old men as sounding boards, a solution would present itself. "I could really use some advice guys. Do you have a few minutes to give me?"

Milt's pigeon chest puffed out. "We got all the time in the world, don't we Sam? Especially for one of our boys."

Boyd gave them the short version of his marriage and divorce.

Milt farted. "Wait, you came home to find your neighbor *and* his buddy in bed with your wife? She was boinking two men at once?"

"They call that a ménage a train." Sam nodded.

"No, Sam, *ménage a trois*. He's not into sex games the way I am." Milt winked and elbowed Boyd.

What the hell made me think this would be a freaking good idea?

He proceeded with how he was served with papers after the

divorce suing him for custody of Matt. How he'd hired an attorney who advised him to lead a clean life to show the court he was a good example for the child and thus the most desirable and dependable of the two parents. He explained how he refused to be part of the firefighters' calendar, fearful even that would classify him as an unfit father.

"But you met Graci-Ella and fell for her hard. Damn near love at first sight, just like Barclay and my Molly." Sam pulled off his Grandpa ballcap and wiped the sweat off his bald head with his handkerchief.

"I just couldn't seem to stay away from her. Then the accident and the operation." He sighed. "I was a goner, even though she never made a secret about being an attorney. I just never asked where."

"Oh Christ, don't tell me..." Milt farted.

Boyd continued with the tale of how Graci-Ella ended up with Chantel's custody case. How he found out about it and acted like an ass over the phone. By the time he was through with the telling of his romantic misery, both of the old men had an arm around his shoulder, patting him in male commiseration.

"This is gonna take all three of us putting our heads together." Sam nodded.

Boyd's balls drew up in fear. *Hell, I'm in deep shit.*

A string of gas erupted. "Whew! You stepped in a pile of crapola with this one. I'm tellin' ya, no one can hold a grudge like a pissed off woman." Milt jabbed his bony chest with his thumb. "I was married to one. I know. A bouquet of flowers will never undo this hell of a mess. Maybe a combination. Leave a note at her door every day. A card. A poem you wrote. A picture of you and Matt. Give us her address and we'll take it by on days you work. Do it six days a week, so she wonders on the days you don't. You told her you never wanted to see her again? Man, you hurt her to the core with that statement. It's gonna take a while for her to get over it."

"Ring her doorbell, hand her one perfect flower and give her a short kiss. Then leave without saying a word. Keep her off balance. Invite her out on a date. Eventually, she'll forget why she's pissed at you." Sam nodded at his sage advice.

"She'll have me arrested for stalking her."

Milt gave him his one narrowed eye look. "Not if you skip a day, now and then. Does she go to a gym to work out? Show up there. Anything to keep her thinking about you."

"Do you want to hear the real joke in all of this? The night Graci-Ella brought over Matt's raccoon, I was on the phone with Chantel. She wants to drop the custody case. She's pregnant and says she can only handle one kid at a time. She agreed to give up all rights to Matthew. I was at my lawyer's this morning to have him draw up the papers for her to sign. Of course I won't believe her change of heart until I have her signature on the agreement and it's filed with the court. So, looks like I get the boy, but lose the woman. How's that for a kick in the ass?" Boyd ran his fingers through his hair. "Of course I'll be holding my breath Chantel doesn't change her mind before everything's official. Stable, she's not."

"So, what are you gonna do, son?"

"Guess I'll go shopping for some cards and check into a visitor's pass at Marcus's gym. You two have been a big help. Thanks to both of you." He got up to leave and so did they. He wrapped an arm around each old coot. "I'm sure glad you stopped."

"You know all you need to do is ask." Milt farted again. "You're one of our boys."

"Wish my dad was half the man you two are. He ditched the family when I was twelve. Thank God for Uncle Toby, Aunt Jinny's husband. He was a good man. Now I've got you two."

Both men wiped their eyes and glanced around as if they hadn't been crying. "Good luck, boy." Sam waved before he got into Milt's Cutlass. Milt grabbed Boyd in an impromptu hug. "It's you boys at the station that keeps me alive. You make me feel needed." He got in the car, fired her up and backed onto Gulf Boulevard.

CHAPTER TWENTY-FOUR

Graci-Ella worked like a fiend the rest of the day, trying to forget her earlier visitor. A handsome man, with piercing grey eyes and muscles that felt both safe and exciting when wrapped around her, who stood in front of her, contrite with apology.

Apology, my ass.

He'd accused her of warming up to him on purpose, of chasing after him to win his heart and working deceitfully to take his son away from him. Hadn't he come to know her any better than that? Was there no real attraction? No enduring love? No truth in his words about their future?

Forking her fingers through her hair, lifting it off her neck, she groaned. She *had* to stop this. Otherwise she'd be on the verge of tears for days and she refused to give into that weakness. Which was why she had to begin exercising at the gym again. A good workout always reduced her stress levels. The way she felt today, she'd be there until closing.

In the dressing room of the gym, she changed from her office wear into a mint Lycra tank, grey Lycra shorts and sneakers. She grabbed her water bottle and sweat towel before she strode out to the gymnasium where she hopped on a stationary bike and began a slow pedaling, increasing her speed every few minutes.

Fifteen minutes later, she moved to the treadmills and chose one between a man and a middle-aged woman. Graci-Ella blotted the sweat with her towel as she punched in the speed and incline of the treadmill, starting off at a fast walk. She'd just increased the speed for the second time when the guy, next to her, shut down his machine, wiped it off with disinfectant and moved onto the weight machines. The lady on her other side engaged her in some polite conversation when someone stepped onto the empty treadmill and powered it up.

A combination of events told her who the person was. The middle-aged lady's visual reaction and her whispering, "My God, I think my ovaries just rolled over in pure joy. Check out the hunk next to you." Graci-Ella didn't need to. Every hair and hormone in her body was standing at attention. It had to be Boyd.

"What are you doing here?" She shot him a scowl.

"Working out." He flashed her a grin. *The ass.*

"I thought you used the weight room at the station."

"It's my day off, so I thought I'd give this place a try." As he glanced around nonchalantly, pretending to check out the equipment, her pinky accidently touched the speed button on his control panel—three times. He nearly stumbled to keep up with the sudden acceleration.

"While you're here, maybe you can educate me on some of the equipment. I only do a few pieces. The ones I know."

"I have to admit, I'm surprised you're talking to me. I figured I'd get a cold reception."

"Why?" She gave her mother's patented eye batting routine. "Just because you broke up with me and accused me of things that shattered my heart? One of the things the coach drills into you, playing basketball is not to hold a grudge, but to keep on going." She shrugged as she ran. "An elbow in the eye or a knockdown on your ass and, once the game's over, you forget it."

She pointed to one of the machines. "I've never used that piece of equipment over there. What part of the body does it work out?"

He glanced around and so did her pinky, increasing the rate of incline on his machine. His legs pounded away. He looked back. "Which one?"

"See the guy in the red t-shirt and blond hair?" Boyd nodded; her pinky tapped the speed button again a few times. "It's the machine he's on. See how it lifts him off the ground?"

"Yeah?"

She increased her own speed and incline so there wasn't such a noticeable disparity between his and hers. "I see how he pulls his weight down, using his arms, but how does he get up there in the first place? I mean, I wouldn't know how to get on the darn thing."

Boyd studied it for a moment while his legs pumped away and her pinky inched over to tap his incline and speed buttons a few more times. Sweat began to pour off him, kind of like her tears did last night.

"I've got five more minutes to run and then I'm stopping. I did twenty on the bike. If I can do twenty on this, then that will be enough for my first day back." She touched her speed button another time running hard before she began slowing the machine down in increments.

Once the treadmill stopped, she grabbed some paper towels and a bottle of spray disinfectant. "Enjoy your time here." She began spraying and wiping down the surfaces she'd touched. "Oh, a word of warning. I'll be at the station tomorrow night to finish up my pictures. The guys won't enjoy the process as much without Flash, but since I'm not allowed to see him anymore, I'll photograph alone. I will need you for a boat shot with the rest of the marine rescue crew, but it'll be a back shot. No one will see your face. And I'll choose someone else for the cover of the calendar. I won't put you in a difficult position with your trial coming up." She tossed her paper towels in the trashcan below where the spray bottles were stored and stormed away.

Thank God she'd gotten through that final speech without breaking down. To be honest, she didn't know whether to jack his jaw for the way he'd acted yesterday or throw herself on him and beg for mercy. And what really ticked her off was she didn't know why she wanted to beg for mercy. Just what the hell had she done wrong?

Nothing.

Except fall in love.

Tears blurred her vision as she headed for the women's dressing room doors. She blotted them away with her towel. *How much longer am I going to cry over this big jerk? I hate being an emotional weakling. Hate. It.*

She grabbed her bag of work clothes and purse from the locker and jogged out to her car. She'd shower at home tonight. Do a load of laundry. Have tomato soup and grilled cheese and go to bed. She only hoped she could get through the night without thinking of Boyd or Matt.

Something was slipped between the crack of the door and its frame. Just her first name was scrawled on the envelope. She ripped it open and tugged out the card. On the front was a picture of a woebegone jackass with the words, "I'm a sorry ass." It didn't take a rocket scientist to figure out who this was from. She walked into her condo, locked the door behind her and set her security alarm.

After dropping her bag and purse on one end of the sofa, she plopped on the other end before reading what he'd printed inside. "Graci-Ella, I was wrong for the way I acted and the things I said. You are a wonderful woman who would never do what I accused you of. I thought I was happy with Matt in my life. Now I know I need you both. Please think about giving me another chance, about starting over. I love you. Boyd."

The card and a smidgen of her anger dropped onto the sofa next to her. "You big jerk. You had no right to talk to me like that over the phone. So what do I do now? Make it easy on you and accept the first or second apology you give…or be a bitch and demand more?"

She stood and hung her purse over her bedroom doorknob, removed her cell to plug into the charger and returned to the card, shaking her finger. "If I forgive you too easily, it sets a pattern, a precedent." She wiggled her fingers in the air next to her head. "Oh sure, walk on Graci-Ella all you want, call her anything you want and accuse her of whatever. It'll be okay. The first time you say "sorry," she'll forgive you. Well, I won't be any man's doormat!" She threw her arms up. "And would someone please tell me why I'm yelling at a freaking jackass card?"

She stepped in the bathroom and peeled off her workout clothes. After a hot shower she hoped would soothe her nerves, she put on pajamas and braided her hair. She started loading the washer and remembered her bag of clothes she'd worn to the office still out on the sofa. Picking it up, she glanced at the card. "You drive me freaking nuts! Men. You all ought to be castrated...with a fork."

She stormed back to her bedroom and pulled out items from the bag she wanted to throw in this load of laundry. The rest she folded for the dry-cleaners and put away her heels and jewelry. She stood in her closet trying to decide what to wear tomorrow since she'd be going to the station after work. Her doorbell rang.

When she peeked through the peephole, Boyd was staring right back at her. Oh God, hadn't she had enough of him today. Still, like an idiot, she opened the door. "Yes?"

"May I come in to talk to you about Matt and his helping you tomorrow evening?"

The jerk had looking contrite down to a science. She'd give him that. "Okay, for a couple minutes." He opened the screen door and she stepped back to allow him inside. He limped in. "What's wrong with you?"

He stared at her. "Let me see that pinky finger of yours. That damn thing ought to have callouses on it, the way you were sneaking in pushes to my control panel." He faked a high falsetto. "Oh look, two mice dancing the cha-cha!" Then he pretended to press buttons with his pinky. "Hell woman, did you think I wouldn't notice you had my incline to equal that of Mount Everest?"

She laughed before she could stop herself. "I'm sure I don't know what you're talking about."

He cupped her face and stepped closer. "It's okay. I deserved it." His lips rubbed gently over hers and her nipples peaked in recognition. "Did you like your card?"

"You wanted to talk about Matt." She stepped back and he looked at the effect he'd had on her nipples. Dammit, he could see he still turned her on so easily. She crossed her arms over her braless breasts, although it was a little late now. At least she was grownup enough not to glance down to see if she'd had an effect on him. Because she would not give it a single look. *Oh my, he's sporting a woody under those jeans.* Her gaze snapped back to his. The smile he wore told her he knew she'd peeked. *Damn traitorous eyes.*

"I have no problem with his being your assistant again. He had an absolute ball helping you before. His helper t-shirt is clean."

"I'm surprised you didn't cut it to shreds."

He grabbed her upper arms. "Stop this! You make it sound like I hate you."

She jerked away. "It's how you made it sound the other night."

"Maybe it's how you perceived what I was saying. Haven't you any mercy in your soul for a man who'd just pulled two dead children from a fire?"

"Yes, even though I'm a lawyer, I have a lot of mercy in my heart—for you, for the parents of those children and for the little ones who died. I worry if they knew what was happening to them. To lose a child is a horrendous thing."

She glanced at Eli's picture on her mantle. Near it was a professional photograph of their little family used in their last Christmas card before his death. Her parents would never get over their loss and she would never get over the closeness she and Eli shared and the instantaneous forfeiture of it. Yes, she had mercy and compassion for others.

"Why don't you ask Flash if he'd like to help me tomorrow

night? Do you by chance have the number of one of either Milt or Sam and also Wolf? I'd like to call them about tomorrow. I hope Wolf's wife can bring her German shepherd in for the photo shoot."

"Yes, I have their numbers." He followed her to the pad she kept next to her landline phone on the bar between the kitchen and dining area. She copied the numbers as he read them from his cell.

"Thanks, I'll call them after you leave. I'm glad you'll allow Matt to work with me again." She was hesitant to turn around. He was right behind her, shifting to put his cell away. His warm hands slid down her arms and covered her hands. It was as if it all happened in slow motion and she was powerless to move away from him. She was nearly trapped between the bar and the front of his warm body.

"I'm sorry for the way I talked to you the other night, Sweetness." He kissed the back of her neck, first on one side of her braid and then on the other. Tremors of need rippled through her body. "I know you can't forgive me right away. Just so you know I can't give up on you. I love you too much."

He stepped away from her and walked out her front door, leaving her a mass of feminine need. She hurried over and locked her door to keep herself from running out after him like some needy woman. Which she was. One look from his steel grey eyes, one sound of his deep voice, one touch of his powerful strength and she was so damn horny for this man, she didn't know what to do.

She was about to start making her supper when her cell rang. It was Matt. "Hi, Flash."

"Guess what! You'll never guess in a million years. I overheard my dad and Aunt Jinny talking. My mom's gonna have another baby. She can't take care of me and the new kid too. So she's dropping the custody case. Dad went to his 'lawler' this morning to have papers drawn up for her to give up rights, whatever that means. I'm hoping it means I won't have to stay at her house overnight again."

"That would be great, Matt. If you're sure that's what you want."

So, when Boyd came to her office this morning it was after meeting with his lawyer, yet not one word to her about Chantel's dropping the case. Nor did he mention a thing when Graci-Ella pointed out his ex-wife's file and talked about how she realized she'd been assigned the case. He just stood there and listened to her explain—hell, she damn near groveled. Just when was he going to tell her the freaking truth?

"Dad told me you need my help tomorrow night. I can't wait. What time will you be by to pick me up?"

She'd knock off work an hour early which would be fine since this was a project for the corporation. "I'll be there around four-thirty. Make sure you tell Aunt Jinny."

"Can I stay overnight?"

"No, my love. You have school and I have to go to work. I'll try my best to have you home by eight-thirty or nine."

How could a secretive man have such an adorable son? Why wouldn't Boyd tell her he'd heard from Chantel, that the custody case he'd obsessed over for months was dismissed? Did he enjoy holding something over her head to make her feel bad about herself?

Tomato soup and a grilled cheese no longer held any appeal, but a pint of chocolate chip pecan ice cream did. She was halfway into it when her cell rang. Boyd. She left it go to voice mail. A minute later, he called again. This time she got a text. "Answer your phone."

She sent him a text back. "You are not the boss of me."

Another text dinged in. "Stop being so damn childish."

"Childish?" The word echoed off the walls of her condo as she threw her phone into a basket of blankets. After retrieving it, she replied. "Stop being so damn secretive. At least Matt was honest enough to tell me about the custody hearing. Do you enjoy making me feel miserable?"

She paced from her living room to her kitchen. Her arms waved as she pitched a bitch of a fit. Men! First her dad had tried to control her. She had bosses at work pushing her this way and that.

And now the man, who she thought loved her, was lording over her head she might have represented his ex-wife in their custody hearing. He'd accused her of gaining information to use against him in court. She didn't operate that way and he ought to know it.

The hell with him, if he didn't.

CHAPTER TWENTY-FIVE

Thank goodness Aunt Jinny could come sit with Matt while he drove over to Graci-Ella's to try to straighten out another mess he was in. Right this moment, he was mad as hell. Yes, he was probably wrong not to tell her about the call but, damn, she could get under his skin in a hurry. Right now, his temperature meter was in the red zone.

He rang her doorbell twice and pounded on her door. Finally, it was yanked open by a storm cloud in pink pajamas. Her eyes so dark green, they resembled the sky during a stage four hurricane. "What the hell do you want?"

He stepped in, took a deep breath and prepared to do battle. "I want you to take that braid out of your hair." Keep the woman off kilter, Sam had told him.

Her beautiful eyes widened and hands fisted at her waist, drawing the material of the thin pajama top tighter over her lush breasts. "What? What the hell makes you think I'd follow one of your orders?"

"I want to fist my hands in your hair while I kiss some sense into you. Yes, I was wrong to say what I did the other night. Hell, baby, I didn't mean a word of it. Don't ask me why it all came tumbling out, it just did. And I was wrong to keep Chantel's phone call a secret from you. That's why I didn't come out to talk to you when you brought Fella back, I was on the phone with her getting all the surprising information. I had no clue Matt would hear me talk to Aunt Jinny about the call and tell you. I've just been getting deeper and deeper in shit with every breath I take." He pointed to the floor. "It stops now. It stops here."

Graci-Ella's jaw dropped, her eyes narrowed and her hands curled into fists. Hell, he'd be lucky to get out of here unscathed. She was as angry as he'd ever seen her.

"You know I mean you no harm."

"No, you just want another chance to break my heart. I can't take another chance with you." Tears pooled in her eyes.

He reached around her shoulders, so her fists couldn't make contact with his face, and he began to undo her braid. "I love you like I've never loved anyone. This custody business has nearly driven me out of my mind. Hell, maybe it has. But you've brought me back to sanity, slowly, but you've brought me back."

"Well, you have a hell of a way of showing your gratitude." Her chin jutted like she was madder than a cat in a tub of soapy water.

Once he had the braid undone, he sifted her long, dark hair through his fingers. "We have so much to get straight between us." His fingers tightened around her tresses and he backed her against the wall. "First, you have to believe how much I love you. That I couldn't live without you. That I adore your mind, your spirit and your body." He ran his tongue over a nipple, making her pajama top wet. Then he drew the nipple into his mouth and sucked while he pulled her head back.

She moaned his name and clamped his biceps. His hands slid down her back and under her pajama bottoms.

He placed his forehead against hers. "I was so upset when I left the house, it never occurred to me to bring a condom. All I wanted was to make you understand how much I love you, that all the things I've said to you in the past were true—except for that gawd awful night on the phone, when all the stresses of my life came rolling out at you, of all people."

213

"I won't be spoken to like that again. You take me apart verbally once more and I am gone from your life, from this state for good. You want me to respect you. Well, it goes both ways."

"Fair enough. I agree." He snuggled against her neck, inhaling the fragrance he loved so much. He nipped and kissed the sensitive area where her neck met her shoulder. Meanwhile, his hand slipped to the front of her pajamas. "I know you can't forgive me for everything at once. I'm willing to earn it in steps. If I can just leave here tonight with you believing I truly love you, then that will be step number one." He kissed her softly intermittently with his words, while first one and then two fingers entered her wet channel. He pumped them slowly while his thumb circled her clit.

He repeated over and over that he loved her while she moaned over what he was doing to her. She began to writhe and her muscles cramped. "Tell me, love, tell me you love me too." He pressed the pad of his thumb on her clit and she flew apart.

"Yes, Boyd. I love you. It scares me how much I love you."

He scooped her off her trembling legs as the aftershocks of the climax rolled through her and carried her to bed. Scooping away her decorative pillows, he pulled back the covers and gently placed her between the sheets. He kissed her forehead, her neck and her lips. "Sleep well. Dream of how much a certain fireman loves you. I'll see you tomorrow afternoon. Oh…" he bit her bottom lip, "the front of the calendar is my spot. No one gets it, but me. Just like no one touches you, but me." He covered her, told her again he loved her and strode out of her house.

Part way home, the irony hit him. He'd taken romantic advice from a man in the early stages of dementia, and it had worked. Did Sam even recall what he'd told him?

Boyd was gulping his first cup of coffee at the station while he made two more pots for the guys leaving their shifts and his co-workers coming on. He was still emotionally battered from his near break-up with the love of his life. He'd texted her once he reached the station. "I love you. I hope you believe that."

She responded with "Who are you? The man who put me to bed all wet and sated?"

"Damn straight, baby. Have a good day."

Captain Steele strode in and poured a cup of brew. "Graci-Ella called me last night to make sure it would be okay for her to finish up her calendar photographs today. She said she'd be shooting Gas Ass and Hell's Bells. If she can make them look sexy, she needs to quit the law business and go into glamour photography. I'm telling you, *this* I gotta see." He took a gulp. "Is the Flash coming with her?"

Boyd nodded and grinned. "He's so excited about tonight, I expect to get a note from his teacher concerning his behavior today. There'll be no sitting still for him, I can guarantee you that."

"Hell, fuck the teacher." Captain topped off his cup and headed for his office. "When he yelled 'Quiet on the set,' I thought I'd piss myself from laughing. And when he worried about your 'peepee' popping out. Oh, God, that was classic!"

Even though the firefighters were trained to be prepared at a second's notice, it was always a jolt to hear the siren and the dispatcher's directions. This morning, it was Tucker's Crabs, an older seafood restaurant; one that was almost an institution in Clearwater.

Quinn was in his driver's seat, revving the diesel motor and his team was hauling ass to climb aboard so he wouldn't get pissy about someone being late. He blew the horn and they were off to their destination near Gulf Boulevard. Tucker's was a wooden structure, sun bleached and wind battered by seasons of hurricanes. The old man who owned it should have retired years ago, but running his crab hut kept him alive.

Jace hooked up the water hoses to the fire hydrant, while Boyd got the hoses ready for dousing the fire. Ivy Jo used a tool to turn off the electric box. Emily unhooked the tanks of propane gas. Wolf and Barclay climbed the ladders, the hoses slung over their shoulders.

Boyd used his hatchet to break through the door. To reduce the flames, so he could see what lie ahead of him, he hosed his way in. He found old man Tucker dead in front of the large deep fryers, either trying to put out the fire or overcome by the smoke. Using the fireman's carry, he removed him from the building and yelled for Jace. After all, Boyd could have been mistaken by the man's condition. Maybe all he needed was some oxygen.

But they'd been too late. George Tucker was gone. The captain called the police and the fire investigator to report the death. This meant the fire would be meticulously investigated. And Clearwater would be minus a longtime eatery of fresh seafood—and one ornery old cuss.

Once they rolled their smoky apparatuses into the station, the clean-up began of fire-trucks, hoses, equipment and fireproof uniforms.

Not quite an hour later, EMT's Ivy Jo and Jace took off in an ambulance for a potential heart attack at a residence. Before they made it back, reports that a knife fight had broken out at Clearwater Senior High School came in. Two students were injured—both girls. So the other ambulance with Emily and Barclay zoomed out of the station headed for the school.

Another typical day at Station Thirty-two.

Graci-Ella had a productive day at work after a night of deep slumber once Boyd put her to bed. He had a way of making her feel loved and sexually satisfied. They still had issues to work through. She hoped their base of combined love was enough to build on, because they both had low irritation levels. Not abusive, but extremely touchy in numerous spots.

She eased her SUV in front of Boyd's townhouse and Flash exploded out of the door, wearing his shirt and ball cap backwards. He leapt into her arms and kissed both her cheeks. "I'm ready to go to work!"

216

She laughed and waved at Aunt Jinny who stood in the doorway. "I hope to have him home between eight-thirty and nine." Aunt Jinny nodded and waved. Graci-Ella opened her back door and Matt slid into the booster seat. He clicked the seat belts and she made sure they were tight enough.

"Who are we taking pictures of today?"

She started the vehicle and backed out of the spot. "Well, we have Lil' Wolf, his older brother, Wolf and the German shepherd, the marine rescue unit..."

"Dad's in that. Right?"

She glanced both ways before pulling out on Sunray Street. "Yes. Then there are two senior citizens the squad has kind of adopted. Their names are Gas Ass and Hell's Bells."

"Can I use those bad words? Dad doesn't usually let me say ass and hell and stuff like that."

"I'll ask him just to make sure you don't get in trouble."

"Okay. Dad's been really sad the last couple days. I'm worried about him."

Their breakup was something she did not want to get into with Matt, even though she and Boyd were slowly working things out. So, she took the chicken way out and asked him about school. When she pulled onto the fire station's parking lot, the garage doors were open and everyone was waiting. The captain motioned her into a closer parking space.

Boyd jogged over, opened her door, leaned in and kissed her as he unbuckled her seat belt. "Don't you look pretty in your navy and purple plaid dress and purple heels? If you've dressed to impress, it's worked on me." He kissed her again.

"Dad, people are watching."

"Then I better kiss her again, only longer." He winked at Graci-Ella.

"I think you've kissed me enough. Step back so I can get out." He groaned and she laughed. Matt unbuckled himself and jumped to the ground. He tugged her skirt and glanced at her, jerking his head toward his dad. "Oh, we have a little dilemma. I told Matt who all we were going to photograph today. When I mentioned the two older gentlemen's nicknames, he got concerned because you don't allow him to use the ass and hell words. So I told him I'd ask you what he was to do."

Boyd stooped in front of Matt. "Son, I'm proud of you for asking instead of saying what you know I don't approve of. Out of respect for their age, when you talk to them, call them Mr. Milt and Mr. Sam. Mr. Milt farts a lot, so you'll always know which one he is. Mr. Sam has a disease that's taking away his memory. He has good days and bad days. Sometimes, you have to repeat things twice."

"But he can't help it just like I can't help it on days I can't get enough air?"

"That's right, son. Now, when you call them up to get their pictures taken, I'll allow you to call them Gas Ass and Hell's Bells." He held up his index finger. "But only then. Got it?" Matt nodded.

"I was thinking while I took their pictures, you could walk Matt out to the Cutlass and stay with him while he takes some pictures of it."

Matt's face beamed and he did a fist pump.

She placed her hand on his little shoulder. "What I want is for you to take pictures that show the whole car—front, back and sides. Like twelve or more shots. You did an awesome job with Black Thumb's dead plant. I know you'll do great with Mr. Milt's car. He's very proud of it."

Graci-Ella handed Matt his hyper-focal distance tape measure, which he slipped in his pocket and her older camera that he hung around his neck. She dangled her good camera from hers and carried her accessory kit.

"I see you braided your hair again today." Boyd leaned in and kissed her sensitive spot.

"Dad! We're working here!"

She couldn't help herself; she laughed the whole way into the apparatus garage where everyone was waiting. Laying her hand on

Flash's shoulder, she instructed, "I'd like a few shots of the marine rescue team in just their swimming trunks."

Flash reared back like a rooster and crowed, "Marine rescue team in swimming trunks, front and center."

A car roared into the parking lot, zipped into a spot and back-fired twice. Poor Flash jumped and peered around the corner at the duct-tape-mobile, then narrowed his eyes at Graci-Ella. "Is *that* the car I'm supposed to take pictures of? First a dead plant and, now, a taped together car? Don't I get any respect as a photographer?"

Captain Steele bent over at the waist laughing. The two elderly men pumped their way to the open doors. Gas Ass, who carried a plastic bag, tooted all the way. Flash, his eyes wide, spun to the captain. "If he was a balloon, he'd be over Tampa by now!" The captain slid down the wall in hysterics.

"Are we late? Oh, I hope we aren't too late." Milt passed more gas. "Sam had to stop to take a crap on the way."

Graci-Ella placed her hand on Flash's shoulder to keep him quiet, but the kid shot a look at the captain and muttered something about Milt needing a crap break too. The captain gulped a breath of air only to erupt into another fit of laughter. "You're my assistant. Go greet them politely."

She had no idea he could groan like his dad, but he stepped forward. "No, Mr. Milt and Mr. Sam, you ain't late. We're just getting started. I'm the photographer's assistant and my nickname is Flash. You probably know my dad, Boyd or Tiny."

Milt elbowed Sam. "Look, it's Tiny's boy. Isn't he the most polite kid? Now what would you like us to do?"

"Well, you can stand with the others. We're going to take pictures of the marine rescue team first. They're changing clothes now. Here they come." Flash turned to Graci-Ella. "Raccoon boss lady, how do you want them positioned?"

"Let's try side-by-side with Wolf and Tiny in the middle, Lil' Wolf beside Tiny and Comic beside Wolf. Do your measurement from Tiny's foot. Oh, and tell them to take their shoes off." Gosh, they all looked fabulous in their grey swimming trunks. Pure muscular sex, especially her man.

She did a couple shots that way and then had them stand less formally. "Guys, can we move to the inflatable boat or whatever it's called? I want a back shot of the four of you holding it up on its end." Once several photos were shot that way, she asked if it were possible to take their boat out far enough to turn it around so she could get photos of them coming back to the dock.

Once the team got back, she leaned down to her assistant and asked him to have Lil' Wolf get ready for his shot. "Tell him to wear his firefighting pants and put up the suspenders. Oh, and have him put on his hat at a rakish angle."

Flash reared back and the chuckles started. "Up on deck, Lil' Wolf. Wear your firefighting pants with the suspenders up and your fire hat as if you're going to rake the yard."

Everyone broke out laughing and Lil' Wolf stopped in front of Graci-Ella. "What did he just say?"

"Wear your hat at a rakish angle. He didn't quite catch my drift." After Lil' Wolf walked away, she explained to Flash what the word rakish meant.

The child's eyes got big. "I'm not wearing my hat like that. I don't want the girls looking at me." He glanced at the Cutlass. "What I'm worried about is taking pictures of that car."

What had Graci-Ella a little more than concerned was taking pictures of the two old men. It seemed like a good idea at the time, but how was she going to make them look sexy?

CHAPTER TWENTY-SIX

A baby blue Beetle convertible zoomed into a parking spot. A middle-aged woman in grey sweat capris and a pink t-shirt jumped out of the car, her angry gaze zeroed in on the captain. "Hold on folks," the captain warned, "you're about to witness a happy explosion."

She marched to her potential target, waving a pregnancy test stick in front of his face. Sensing a special moment, Graci-Ella started snapping pictures. The woman she presumed to be his wife started to cry. "See this, Noah Steele?" She waved the stick at him. "I'm pregnant! I'm forty-two and pregnant!"

He enveloped his arms around her, kissed her neck and then her lips. "Why are you crying? I'm thrilled." He picked her up and swung her around. "You're beautiful all the time, but twice as pretty when you're pregnant." He rubbed his cheek against hers. "Maybe we'll get that little girl we always wanted. I wasn't looking forward to an empty nest. Were you?"

"No. You know I wasn't. We talked about having a child and maybe I did forget a couple pills, but I never thought that would be enough. But then you've been dragging me to the bed every chance you got."

The captain glanced around at his crew. "This is Susan, my doll baby since our senior year in high school. And we're pregnant.

Happily so, right?" He looked at her with such tenderness and she nodded before laying her head on his shoulder.

Everyone cheered just as Lil' Wolf came out, dressed as ordered. The captain held her in front of him, his arms around her abdomen and whispered in her ear, no doubt telling her what was going on. She nodded.

Graci-Ella told her assistant to have Lil' Wolf stand in front of the hook and ladder apparatus with one foot braced against the bumper.

Firecracker reared back and crowed, "Lil' Wolf report to the hook 'em ladder and brace one foot against the front bumper. Boss lady, is his hat rakish enough for you?"

"No, tilt it more to the right, Lil' Wolf. The first few shots I want your arms crossed below your pecs." Her camera clicked and whirled. "Now hands in your pockets and turn to your right a couple inches for me." After she was through with that pose, she asked if he could jump up on the hood to sit with his hands on his thighs.

"Okay, Flash, tell him he's done and call Gas Ass and Hell's Bells up on deck."

He leaned against her. "I know dad said it was okay, but he can be strict about using bad words. I got soap in my mouth once."

She told Lil' Wolf he was done. "Flash, your dad gave you permission to use Gas Ass and Hell's Bells this once. It'll be okay. I promise."

Flash wiped his hands on his pants, reared back and crowed, "Next on deck is Gas Bell's and Hell's Ass." Everyone in the place roared with laughter which evidently unsettled the little boy. Flash ran to his dad. "I did what you said. Am I in trouble?"

Boyd stopped laughing long enough to shake his head and hug him. "No one else could have done any better." He glanced at Graci-Ella who smiled and nodded her approval. "Let's go get pictures of Gas Ass's car. It even has a nickname. The duct-tape-mobile since it has so much duct tape all over it."

Graci-Ella told the two old men there were swimming trunks like the marine rescue team wore and tank tops lying on the washer outside the changing room. They should wear them only. No shoes. Off they bustled, leaving a trail of blue gas behind them.

Several of the firefighters came over to ask practically the same question. She'd been taking pictures to make them all look buffed and ripped and sexy. How was she going to do the same with a hollow chested, skinny bald man with a grey fringe of hair and a pot-bellied, bald codger?

She told them she wasn't sure herself and that they should wish her luck. "Believe me, any ideas would be appreciated. But I think it's important they're included."

The two men swaggered out wearing their yellow tank tops and grey swim trunks, amid a chorus of *Jesus*. They both had cucumbers stuffed in their swim trunks. Hell's Bells had his positioned along the inside of his leg while Gas Ass had his sticking straight out, as if he had a hard-on. He was snapping his fingers as he danced a few steps toward her.

Her mouth opened and closed twice. She didn't know what to say without insulting them. Well, what the hell. "Gentlemen, stand beside the largest fire truck and both of you place one foot on the step." She turned to Quinn. "Could you bring them each a fireman's hat?" When Quinn returned, she stopped him. "Think you could get Milt to lay his cucumber down like Sam's?"

"Sure, I know how to handle him."

Once Gas Ass adjusted his cucumber, she walked over and praised how they looked. Both men's chests puffed out. "Now, I want you to wear your hats low over your faces like a cowboy hat from those old movies. I think that'll give you a sexy air of mystery." Milt elbowed Sam and nodded. "I might have you hold your arms a variety of ways to showcase your muscles. It's what I've done with everyone."

"You've got it doll face. Are you and Boyd making up yet? He was in pitiful shape when we saw him the other day. He was sure sorry for all the things he'd done wrong."

"We're working on it, day by day."

Cucumber men both hugged her. Sam was nearly sobbing. "He loves you so much."

"Let's get our pictures taken shall we? I'm using everyone's nickname. Would you mind if I used The Cucumber Coots instead of both of yours? You know, to save space?" Both men looked at each other and nodded. "Next I have Wolf and his German shepherd."

Milt farted. "You'll love Einstein. He's a well-behaved dog. I've got a Chihuahua named Killer. He's a pip."

By the time she had their photos taken, Wolf's wife had arrived with Einstein, who made instant friends with Flash. Wolf kissed his wife and wrapped his arm around her waist before escorting her to Graci-Ella. He motioned the captain and Susan over, too, as he did the introductions and shared the news of Susan's pregnancy. Both women squealed and hugged each other.

For the first time in Graci-Ella's life, she felt deprived of the feminine experience of bearing a child. Granted, she'd thought about becoming a mother—years from now. She also knew whose child she wanted to have. Her gaze deliberately collided with Boyd's. He sauntered toward her, determination on his face. She was too fragile right now, too needy, too confused. She pivoted her back toward him and walked between the ambulances.

"Sweetness." The voice was low and sexy. Of course her body responded. Didn't it always? "I saw an expression of pain cross your face when the two pregnant women shared their joy. It upsets me to see you sad. I want to take you in my arms and hold you, but deep feelings between us are so fragile right now."

"Unbraid my hair. I want to feel your fingers in it."

Very few things could relax her as much as his hands in her hair. He spun her to face him while one hand fingered her hair and his other cupped her cheek. His lips covered hers in short nips and then more demanding kisses.

"I love you, Sweetness. I have from the first moment I saw you."

"Yes, but is it lust or love?"

"Oh, baby, this is far better than lust." He kissed her once more.

"Again? I turn my back to play with a dog and you two sneak off to kiss *again*? I'm telling you right now, I better get a new mom out of this."

Boyd chased Flash off amid giggles and squeals, and Graci-Ella went out to talk to Becca about Einstein. "I understand your dog used to steal your thongs and carry them over to Wolf."

"Einstein figured how to open my underwear drawer with his teeth. Wore the finish right off the wood." She gave a wave of her open hand. "He's snatch a pair and, first chance he'd get, he was out the door on the run to find Wolf. It was comical, yet embarrassing as hell."

"What do you want me to wear for the pictures Raccoon boss lady?" Wolf's eyes twinkled with humor.

"There's no need to imitate Flash. One six-year old like him is enough. God, I love him to pieces. Ah…jeans and boots will be fine. No shirt. I'd like to have Einstein sitting or standing next to Wolf with a pair of your thongs in his jaws. Do you think Einstein will cooperate?"

"It might take a couple of tries."

Graci-Ella lowered her voice. "Look, I just had two old men prance out of the dressing room with cucumbers jammed down their swimming trunks."

Becca gasped before she started giggling. "Wolf is always telling me the most comical stories about those two."

"Well, believe everything he tells you. I'm positive it's a sight I'll never forget. Sam had his lying down the side of his leg and Milt had his sticking straight out like the mother of all hard-ons." She smacked her hand over her eyes. "I wanted to run for the eye rinse. So, doing a dozen reshoots with Einstein is no big deal. We won't worry about it."

She motioned Flash over. "My camera makes a whirring noise between shots, not loud, but enough Einstein should hear it. I'm concerned it'll draw his attention and make him come to me to see what the noise it. How about you also take some pictures from the front of that palm? Between the two of us, we ought to get what we want. Okay?"

He smiled and nodded. "I told Einstein a secret. I told him who I wanted for my new mom. He licked my face so I'm thinking he thought it was a good idea too."

Graci-Ella bent down. "I'm afraid to ask. Minnie Mouse? Miley Cyrus? Selena Gomez?"

Flash grabbed her around the neck and kissed her cheek. "You've got some weird taste." She couldn't tell him she wanted the same thing and get his hopes up. What if she and Boyd couldn't work out all their issues?

Getting Einstein to pose next to Wolf was no problem and both got some good shots. But as soon as Becca gave the canine her thongs, he thought it was play time and ran and jumped with them in his mouth. "Maybe if you have Wolf hand them to him. Men are the boss of the family. Right?" Flash glanced from Graci-Ella to Becca. "How come you women are groaning?"

Wolf ordered the German shepherd to sit beside him. Ordered him to stay. Ordered him to hold. He did—for all of fifteen seconds. Both photographers got as many shots in as they could before Einstein ran through the firehouse with Becca's thong.

"I think we got what we need. Flash, thank everyone and call it a wrap."

He reared back and hollered, "Thanks, folks. It's a wrap!"

Einstein started barking and jumping. Wolf clipped on the dog's leash and walked him to the car. Both he and Becca leaned against it to talk.

"Matt, go ask your dad if he wants to walk us to the car and say goodnight. A bath and it'll be time for Aunt Jinny to put you to bed."

Boyd must have heard her. He came running and picked them each up with one arm.

"See how strong my daddy is?"

"Your daddy's got strong love. For his boy." He kissed Matt. "And for a special lady he adores." He kissed her cheek. "Safe travels home. Both of you call me."

She'd kept her phone turned off since she picked up Matt. She didn't want phone calls to interrupt her photography session. It had been her aim to wrap it up and she was thankful she and her helper were able to do it. The kid had a real talent for helping. She was eager to see the pictures he took today to see how they'd turned out with next to zero training.

A couple of blocks from Boyd and Matt's townhouse, she glanced in her rearview mirror. His eyes were closed and drool trickled out of the side of his mouth. She pulled in Boyd's parking spot and carried Matt up the sidewalk. Aunt Jinny opened the door. "Boyd just called. He said to expect a sleepy boy."

"I'm afraid he's out for the night. He did a really good job."

Aunt Jinny snorted. "Did he really call one of the old men Hell's Ass?"

Graci-Ella nodded. "It was the funniest thing. Thank goodness I'd thought to have Boyd take him to the old man's car to take pictures of it, because they can say and do some really inappropriate things." She told her about the cucumbers. "Honest to Pete, I'll never be able to eat another one again." Both women laughed as she passed Matt over to his great aunt.

"Boyd, get out here to the big screen, quick! Important news!" Wolf's voice sounded damn urgent over the intercom. He ran out in time to see Darryl Weir's face on the screen as the police chief walked to a podium to give an update.

Boyd sat on the sofa. "What the hell?"

"Darryl Weir, charged with attempted vehicular homicide of a local woman, malicious harassment of the same woman and breaking a restraining order against her, as well, escaped from jail today around noon by strangulating a guard and hiding in a canvas laundry bin of a local washing company used for several years by the jail system here in Clearwater. While there, he beat a male employee to death and bludgeoned a female employee, who is in intensive care at one of the local hospitals. He stole clothes to help disguise his appearance. We had suspected he fled the area in the car of the employee he critically injured. But the 2005 black Honda Civic has been found torched in an alley near Johnston Street. Please consider him armed and dangerous. Should you see someone…"

By now, Boyd's mind blocked out the police chief and focused on his Graci-Ella.

The captain stood behind him, his hands on his shoulders. "Is Matt home?"

Boyd nodded. "Yeah, Aunt Jinny called about half an hour ago. I haven't heard from Graci-Ella." He removed his phone and dialed her number. It went to voicemail. "Hey Sweetness, call me when you get home. It's important."

He glanced over his shoulder at the captain. "You know Darryl's not left the area. He's gone for her. He's got some kind of fixation on my woman. I think he'd kill her in a minute because she put him down."

"Yeah, before he got fired. Before you and him had come to blows here in this room, he kept bragging how she wanted him and he was going to fuck her over and over." The Virgin spoke up. "I thought he was just blowing off like he always did. Frankly, I was glad to see him loose his job."

Boyd jumped off the sofa. "Captain, I need a personal night, sick night, emergency leave. Whatever. I'm going to her condo for the night."

"Not by yourself, you're not. Need some volunteers, people." Everyone stood up. The captain shook his head. "What if there's a fire? Or I need an ambulance? I want one ambulance crew remaining here. If there's a fire, I'll drive another truck and contact Quinn on the way. Gas Ass and Hell's Bells, you'll stay and be my help. The rest of you can go in Quinn's fire truck. No sirens or lights. Does she have a balcony in the front of the building?"

Boyd nodded. She's on the third floor.

"All of you use the ladder to charge through her balcony doors one after another. God help the poor woman if we're way off base and she's in no harm. She'll piss her pants."

CHAPTER TWENTY-SEVEN

Graci-Ella stepped off the elevator and almost ran into Mrs. Howard. "Hello Graci-Ella, I'm on my way to a late night Bingo party. Want to come along?"

"No, thank you. A bowl of soup, a shower and I'll be in bed. Good luck to you. Hope you win big."

"Thanks, darlin'." She patted her silver curls.

Graci-Ella unlocked her door and stepped inside, entered her security code before hanging her purse on her bedroom's doorknob. After removing the data cards from both of her cameras, she put all her photography equipment on the top shelf of her coat closet. She laid the data cards beside her computer before sliding out of her stilettoes and rubbing her toes.

Something creaked. Was it in her condo or upstairs? Maybe the Richfield's cat had jumped onto something. Like her balcony railing? Every so often, Marcus got out and came down for a visit. And *every* time, the Richfields acted as if Graci-Ella had enticed the cat down to her condo for some despicable reason.

An unexpected item caught her eye.

On her kitchen bar.

A black rose.

Oh, dear God.

Darryl was here!

How? Her heart pounded a fear-filled beat. He was locked in jail! How could he be here in her home? Sand must have packed her mouth absorbing all the moisture, for she could barely swallow. Chills of deathly terror coiled around her body and squeezed like a boa constrictor. She backed against the wall and snatched the receiver for her house line; it was dead. Thank God for her cell, she swung to her bedroom door.

The doorknob was empty.

Her purse was gone.

Her gaze swept the room. The lights were out in her security system. He must have cut the lines to it when he cut her phone line.

Darryl also must have grabbed her purse, which meant he was where he could watch her. How else would he know where she'd hung her bag? That was probably the creak she heard. From where she stood on trembling legs, she noted several black roses scattered across her bed's decorative pillows. The implication made her sick.

"Fight for the offensive," her basketball coach had preached. "Someone on the defensive was already weak."

She went to the refrigerator and pulled out a few beers. She carried them into her living room and sat them on the coffee table before she plopped down. "Hey, Darryl. Want a beer? I've got two Coors, one Old Leg Humper and a Blithering Idiot." She laughed. "My God, they've even named a beer after you. Come on out and have a brew with me. This hiding business is kind of juvenile. If you want to kill me, have a beer and do it."

How ironic was this? She was offering herself up for a sacrifice. "Hey, it's kinda funny when you think about it. Suds and sacrifice. How many killers get this opportunity? Come on out and wet your whistle before you silence mine." If he got close enough, could she belt him a few times? A hard elbow in the eye? Hey, she was going to die anyhow. She had nothing to lose. Why not make him fight for it? Her insides trembled and her hands shook. Who knew what he'd planned on doing to her. She picked up her high heels and silently strode toward her front door. One flick of her deadbolt and she'd make a mad dash for the elevator.

The floor creaked and a knife was thrown into her door next to her hand and lock. She whirled around in terror. Darryl appeared—as maniacal looking as ever. "You are one ballsy bitch if you think you can get away from me."

She returned to her sofa, snapped off a top on a Coors and saluted him. "Come join me, then." Her hand shook so badly, she spilled some beer on her dress. She took a long drag, allowing the cool liquid to wash away some of the sand in her dry mouth.

He snatched a beer and twisted off the top. "You have no idea how I'm going to enjoy choking you until that smart mouth of yours finally shuts up forever."

"I've had a lot of women basketball players threaten to do the same thing. It never really scared me." Darryl grabbed her forearms and threw her across the room.

Okay, maybe I went too far with that remark.

"I'm tired of your superiority." He bore down on her, jerked her onto her feet and hit her jaw. She crumpled to the floor.

Yeah, wrong battle tactic. My big mouth got my ass in trouble.

"What's wrong, bitch?" He kicked her in the ribs a couple times. "Not as tough as you thought you were?" He slipped a long knife from his pocket. "Imagine how this will feel slowly sliding into you."

Glass shattered and boots hit the floor. She rolled away from her attacker. A gang of firemen charged Darryl. Ivy Jo made a call on her cell, then rushed to see to Graci-Ella's injuries.

Boyd pummeled Darryl. Her man had a feral look in his eyes as he choked the criminal, who'd threatened to kill her. Darrel stabbed Boyd's shoulder and arm. Wolf broke Darryl's arm and kicked away the knife. And still, Boyd kept pounding Darryl. There was so much violence and blood. How badly was Boyd hurt?

His fellow firefighters pulled him off and, one by one, punched the criminal.

"What are they doing?" Graci-Ella grabbed Ivy Jo's hand.

"Protecting Boyd. He did some severe damage. Now when the

cops ask who hit the intruder, they can all show bruised knuckles and claim they did it. He shouldn't have to pay for protecting the woman he loves. Besides, he's hurt." Both women crawled over to check on him.

The police swept in, guns drawn as a circle of firemen stood around a dead murderer.

"How badly are you hurt?" Boyd cradled her in his arms and gently held her, his blood soaking her clothes. He pressed his lips to her ear. "It's over, baby. I made sure it's over. He'll never hurt you again."

"I know, Love. No woman could ask for a better hero. Thank God you came when you did."

"I love you more than my own life. I'd die before I'd let some bastard take you from me."

They rode in the ambulance together, their gazes locked on each other, whispering words of love and promises for the future. Boyd mentioned marriage several times.

Once they were wheeled into the ER, Graci-Ella insisted her man be treated first. He was losing a lot of blood. Boyd needed both internal and external stitches and bitched the whole time about the doctor using a knitting needle to sew up his arm. Graci-Ella held his other hand. "Now, sweetheart, you have to be a big strong boy like Matt." That earned her a scowl, and she did her best not to laugh. Her ribs hurt like hell.

Because Graci-Ella's was less than three months out from brain surgery, she was thoroughly examined and given an MRI. Her surgeon proclaimed her well in that department, although her face was badly bruised and two ribs cracked. Both were kept in the hospital overnight for observation.

Boyd asked Aunt Jinny to bring Matt to the medical center, so he could tell his son what all had happened before he heard it on the news or from other kids in school. He also wanted his son to see he was okay, just stitched up like an old baseball.

The medicine for pain made Graci-Ella sleepy. At first, she

thought she was dreaming when Matt crawled in bed with her. "I came to kiss your boo-boos." Gentle kisses feathered across her face. "I also think you and Dad need to be married. The two of you belong together. You're both a little klutzy."

She hugged him close. "Yeah, sometimes we are. How about you? Do you get klutzy?"

"Nah, I just trip over stuff." He wiggled his hand in his pants pocket. "I brought this along, because I knew Dad wouldn't have a ring on him. I know how it's done. I saw it in the movies." He produced a plastic Superman ring and took her hand. "Graci-Ella, will you marry Dad and me?" He pushed it on her pinky finger.

Well, really, who could refuse a proposal like that?

The first Saturday of November was an ideal day to get married. The sun shone brightly. The waves rolled gently. And the staff of Bayshore Club had arranged the small wedding to perfection. A tent with a floor was set up in which the bride and her attendant, Ivy Jo, were to get dressed. Her mother, too, of course. She had chosen the bridal gown and attendant's garb. Grace was thrilled to see to every fashion and make-up detail of her only daughter's wedding.

All the members of Station Thirty-two and their significant others were there. So were a couple lawyers from Baker, Brannock and Hughes. Graci-Ella's grandparents also flew to Florida for the nuptials. The white chairs were decorated with mint bows and a copy of the calendar that had brought the bride and groom together.

Ivy Jo wore a mint green sheath with darker green lace at the bust line and shoulders. She carried a bouquet of gold flowers and ivy. For her daughter to wear at her wedding, Grace chose a white satin sheath with a short train. The top was off-the-shoulder lace with pearls and crystals. The bride had gotten three inches cut off her hair; white ribbons and flowers were woven through her tresses. Boyd had sent Graci-Ella a round bouquet of white roses trimmed in crimson, just as he'd given her in the hospital so many months ago.

Boyd and the captain both wore black tuxedoes. So did Matt.

Grace beamed at her husband. "Look at her, Ellis. She's glowing with happiness. Boyd and little Matt need her and she needs them."

What her mother said was true. The three of them needed each other. Graci-Ella and Boyd had talked their differences through. With Boyd's encouragement, she sold her condo and used the money to open a photography studio. The change in her profession was like a permanent sunrise in her soul. Her man helped her decorate it and built props, with Matt's help, of course. He was completely theirs now. Chantal had signed away her rights.

Graci-Ella's love for Boyd had deepened. They cherished each other more every day. Matt was determined he'd get her for a mother. Deep in her heart, she knew she couldn't imagine being with any other man than her pin-up hero.